"G.M. Ford is must reading."

—Harlan Coben

"Ford is a witty and spunky writer who not only knows his terrain but how to bring it vividly to the printed page."

—*West Coast Review of Books*

"G.M. Ford is a born storyteller."

—J.A. Jance

"He's well on his way to becoming the Raymond Chandler of Seattle."

—*Kirkus Reviews*

"G.M. Ford is, hands down, one of my favorite contemporary crime writers. Hilarious, provocative, and cool as a March night in Seattle, he may be the best-kept secret in mystery novels."

—Dennis Lehane

"G.M. Ford has a supercharged V-12 under the hood."

—Lee Child

"G.M. Ford writes the pants off most of his contemporaries."

—*Independent on Sunday*

SOUL SURVIVOR

OTHER TITLES BY G.M. FORD

Nameless Night

Threshold

Leo Waterman Series

Who in Hell Is Wanda Fuca?

Cast in Stone

The Bum's Rush

Slow Burn

Last Ditch

The Deader the Better

Thicker Than Water

Chump Change

Salvation Lake

Family Values

Frank Corso Series

Fury

Black River

A Blind Eye

Red Tide

No Man's Land

Blown Away

SOUL SURVIVOR

A LEO WATERMAN MYSTERY

G.M. FORD

This is a work of fiction. Names, characters, organizations, places, events, and incidents are either products of the author's imagination or are used fictitiously. Any resemblance to actual persons, living or dead, or actual events is purely coincidental.

Published by Thomas & Mercer, Seattle

www.apub.com

ISBN-13: 9781503903999
ISBN-10: 1503903990

Cover design by Ray Lundgren

Printed in the United States of America

To my friend John Walsdorf
A man to match the mountains and the sea. You will, now and forever, walk this path with me.

Chapter 1

Art Fowler came to me on the last day of January while I was sitting in my front parlor drinking coffee and watching a blizzard blow in from the south.

Out in the orchard, the drifting snow had harlequined the trees black and white. Looked like every apple and pear had one stubborn leaf, a sole survivor, waving like a drowning sailor as the skeletal branches were slapped to and fro by the wind.

Those were the profundities I was dwelling upon when the gate buzzer went off and turned everything to nofundities. I took my sweet-ass time getting to the front door, hoping whoever it was would either freeze solid or get lost. When the buzzer sounded again, I winced, leaned my ear to the speaker, and pushed the button. Like most everybody, I'm sick of peddlers and religious fanatics showing up unbidden on my doorstep, so the most polite response I could muster at eight thirty in the morning was, "Yeah."

"Leo . . . that you?" Long pause. "It's Art Fowler."

Took me a minute to put a face to the name. Hadn't seen Art since my father's funeral . . . fifteen, sixteen years anyway. Guy had to be at least eightysomething by now. One of those city functionaries who'd hung around my old man during the last years of his life. I'd never been clear what it was he did for the city, but he'd occupied one of the imaginary uncle positions of my adolescence. In those days, anybody who was always around the house and older than I was got designated an aunt or an uncle. We all knew it was horseshit, but it was *our* horseshit.

"Yeah, Art . . . here . . ." I pushed the gate button. "Come on in . . ."

I opened the front door and watched the gate plow snow as it slid open. Art was wearing an old-fashioned fedora, with a thick, red-and-white-striped scarf wound around his neck like a Seussian python. I watched as he hunched his shoulders and began shuffling up the drive. There was enough snow that most people would lift their feet to avoid tromping in it, but it didn't seem like he could manage that much effort. Looked to me like a big wind gust might have sent him to his knees. I closed the gate behind him and hoped like hell he made it to the front door, 'cause I surely didn't want to have to go out there and fetch him from the storm.

When he stumbled to the stoop, I took him by the elbow and helped him up the fieldstone stairs. Took his hat and coat from him, stashed them in the hall closet, and then led him into the parlor.

"Cup of coffee?" I asked as I got him seated on the gold brocade couch.

"If you got some ready," he said.

"How do you take it?"

"Just milk."

I told him to hang in there and headed for the kitchen, as much to give myself a chance to think about why Art Fowler would be showing up at my door in a blizzard, as for the sake of my world-famous suburban hospitality.

When I got back with the coffee, Art was wiping his face with a pocket handkerchief and looking around the room. "Your mother used to serve me tea in here once in a while," he said as he stuffed the hankie into the side pocket of his houndstooth sport coat. "Real formal lady she was."

"Room's just like she left it," I said. "Mostly I walk past it on my way to the front door." I shrugged. "Except when it snows."

"Yeah . . . don't look much like you or your dad," he allowed.

One of the unfortunate side effects of coming into money is that it changes the way you look at the world. After enough people you haven't seen in decades show up looking to separate you from some folding money, you start to question nearly everyone's motives. Sadly, the only reason I could imagine that would explain Art Fowler's presence on my mother's brocaded couch was that he needed cash so bad he was going to try to trade on his long-ago relationship with my old man.

He buried his face in the coffee mug. I sat back in the wing chair and waited for him to get around to whatever he had come for.

Took a while. Finally he looked up over the rim of the mug and said, "I suppose you heard about Matthew."

"Matthew?"

"Martha's boy, Matthew. Matthew Hardaway."

I remembered his daughter Martha. A few years behind me in school. Always part of a big gang of girls. Dark hair. Always wore a headband. Different color every day. And then, years later, after she'd grown up and moved away, her son . . . Matthew. Him . . . him I really remembered.

Way back when, I had a friend who worked at a car dealership in Renton. On nights when none of the dealership brass was in the mood for baseball, he could get us Mariners tickets directly behind home plate. I mean like row one. Which, I suppose, was why my old man asked me if maybe I couldn't get the tickets and take Martha's husband (I couldn't for the life of me remember his name) and their son, Matthew, to a game. In those days, I was always good for a ball game and generally owed my old man more than one favor.

Matthew was seven or eight at the time. The twitchiest kid I'd ever seen. Seemed to be uncomfortable with just about everything in the universe. Stairs. Escalators. Crowds. Being alone. Being so close to Felix's fastball. The sound it made when it hit the catcher's mitt. The guy in the seat next to him. You name it—it bothered Matthew. A true stranger in a strange land, that boy.

We made it through the game, Matthew ordering things he didn't eat and flinching at every pitch. When it was over, the family went back to wherever it was they'd come from; I filed it under T for *takes all kinds*, and that was the last time I'd seen or heard from any of the Fowler clan, until this morning.

"No," I said, "I . . ."

"The shooting up in Everett. Last week. The politician guy."

I felt like I'd been flash frozen. My brain couldn't come up with anything more articulate than *Holy shit. Holy shit.*

"Matthew killed the guy," Art said. He looked as if he were begging me to tell him he was delusional, that he'd made it all up, and this was all a bad dream. "Walked into a city council meeting and shot the poor fella in the head."

"And Matthew?"

He hung his head. "The cops shot him in the hall outside . . . on the floor."

A swirling gust of wind and snow rattled the leaded windows. As I turned my head and watched the storm, shame rose up in me like an overflowing toilet. I felt my cheeks getting red. I'd made it a point not to know. Made it a point to ignore a front-page killing that had occurred less than a week ago, barely forty miles north. I'd hurriedly scrolled by it at least a dozen times on the Internet and changed the channel whenever it had come up on the boob tube. I felt saddened about how I was able to shrug it off and go on with my life, secretly thankful that, once again, I wasn't one of those poor bastards whose only sin was being in the wrong place at the wrong time.

"Jesus," escaped my throat.

"I gotta know, Leo."

"I'm sorry, Art. Man . . . such a thing. Is Martha . . ."

"She's all right . . . you know . . . considering and all. Phil too." He sighed and looked out the window. "I went up there . . ." He let it trail off.

I clamped my jaw and waited for him to go on.

"She—my daughter—she told me I was just making things worse. Told me to go back home." He threw an exasperated hand into the air. "I stuck around anyway, got a hotel room downtown. I tried to . . . she wouldn't see me . . . the police . . . they're getting death threats. People are blaming Martha and Phil for what happened."

He looked at me like one of those abused dogs in those harrowing TV spots. I knew better. Knew this was the point where I ought to keep my mouth shut . . . but I couldn't do it. Story of my life.

"How can I help you?" I asked.

Yeah . . . I knew better. This was the point where they tell you they need a hundred thirty-five Gs to pay a lawyer, and you have to tell them how you'd like to help but how that just ain't gonna happen. I knew the drill, but if there was something else I could have said at that point, I sure as hell didn't know what it was.

The situation was made worse by the fact that I had the better part of three hundred Gs sitting in the office safe. The proceeds of a sketchy land sale I'd made down in Arizona several months back. As the parcels officially belonged to one of my old man's dummy corporations, and the buyer, for his own reasons, had insisted on paying cash, I was still trying to decide whether to claim it on my taxes and open my father's long-ago finances to even further official scrutiny or to just leave it in the safe.

"I gotta know, Leo," he said again.

"Know what?"

"How . . . how that little boy . . . how he could have turned out . . . how he could have done something like . . ."

"I'm lost here, Art. Wadda you need from me?"

"Well . . . you know . . . you being a detective and all . . . I thought maybe you could . . ."

I held up a stiff hand. Waggled it back and forth. "First off, Art, I don't do that kind of work anymore." Before he could open his mouth, I went on. "Secondly, even if I did, this isn't the kind of thing I was ever, in my best day, competent to handle."

He was giving me that hangdog look again, so I kept talking. "The world's gonna be all over this one, Art. Everything about this is going to be put under the microscope. People are going to write shitty books about it. Whatever there is to learn is going to be dissected ad nauseam. I'm guessing that before this is over you're gonna know more about it than you want to."

"I got to know, Leo," he said again. "Somebody musta . . ."

"Musta what, Art?"

"Musta . . . you know . . . musta done something that changed him . . . somebody . . ."

I'd like to tell you I cut to the chase to spare his feelings, which was part of it of course, but mostly it was to spare mine. "I can't help you here, Art. I'm not a private detective anymore, and even if I was, this kind of thing is way, way out of my league."

Art set his coffee mug on the table and pushed himself to his feet.

"Your father . . . he could fix things, you know. I thought maybe . . ."

"Different times," was the best I could come up with. "These days, about the only thing I can fix is coffee."

"How do you go from being a sweet little kid to somebody who shoots somebody? I don't understand."

Part of me wanted to tell him that the boy I'd spent a single evening with had quite obviously needed professional mental health services, but somehow, this didn't seem to be an auspicious occasion for a reality check.

"Wish there was something I could do," I hedged.

He nodded, as if to say *Me too*.

I followed him out into the hall, retrieved his coat and hat from the closet, helped him into everything, and then pulled open the front door.

The storm had gotten worse. The wind raked the freshly fallen snow, filling the air with a glittering curtain of ice. I stood in the doorway and watched Art short step it back up the drive until the swirling snow made him fade to white.

I closed the door, stifled a sigh, and ran a hand through my hair a couple of times. I don't recall how long I stood there leaning against the door, with those big, wrought-iron hinges digging into my back, wishing I was somebody else, doing something else, somewhere else.

Next thing I remember, I found myself sitting at my desk asking Google to tell me everything it knew about young Matthew Hardaway. Surprise, surprise. Musta been a thousand pages of it.

When you waded through it and eliminated the opinionated assholery for which the Internet was both the cause and the repository, and then compared it to the fragments of film that various bystanders had taken on their phones, the facts, as nearly as I could ascertain, were these:

Last Thursday, at 8:34 in the evening, seventeen-year-old Matthew Hardaway had walked into Everett City Hall, strolled through the metal detector without so much as a chirp, and lucked into a vacated seat at the rear of a contentious Everett City Council meeting.

At 8:59, Matthew rose from his seat, walked toward the front of the room, shouted something that included the words "communist bastards," and then proceeded to shoot Ricardo Valenzuela, a city councilman whom the article described as Everett's only City Council socialist. Hit him more or less between the eyes.

In the American spirit of fixing the blame rather than the problem, early media speculation obsessed on the question of how Matthew had managed to smuggle the weapon through the building's metal detector, with the general consensus being that he must have stashed it in the building on some earlier occasion. When and how was a matter of fevered conjecture.

By Saturday morning, however, a check of the building's security records showed conclusively that Matthew Hardaway had never been in city hall prior to the night of the shooting, and that it had apparently taken him twelve minutes to get from the security station to the council meeting room, a journey that, in the worst of times, took no more than three, leaving open the question of how he'd spent the missing nine minutes. A conspiracy theorist's dreamscape.

After shooting Valenzuela, Matthew had sprinted back down the aisle and backed out the double doors, red faced and screaming, waving the gun like a conductor's baton, and then disappeared into the corridor, where, according to bystanders, he was confronted and then shot dead by an unnamed city security officer. Witnesses in the hallway also agreed that the security officer had demanded that Matthew drop his gun, and had been equally clear that the young man had instead begun to raise the weapon. There'd sure as hell be an official inquiry, but from what I could see, it was a righteous shooting if ever there was one.

The rest of it was the kind of non-news that passes for information these days. Unconfirmed bits and pieces of Matthew's life story, most of which, due to his age, consisted of school and medical records to which the media were not privy, which of course didn't stop them from speculating their little hearts out. Whispers of emotional problems, problems in school, it was all grist for the rumor mill. Attempts to interview Matthew's parents had yielded nothing more definitive than a stiff "No comment" from their respective attorneys.

I kept my nose buried for most of the day. The only thing I found out for sure was that the gun was a Sig Sauer P320 and had belonged to Matthew's father, Phil Hardaway, who was both the proud owner of twenty-seven registered firearms and the newly crowned poster boy for irresponsible gun ownership. The final news photograph was of a throng of antigun protestors waving picket signs and trudging back and forth in front of Phil Hardaway's Everett townhouse.

By the time I gave up, I could barely push myself to my feet. I stood, leaning on the chair, stretching, groaning, and thinking about how a person's life—how the millions of individual events that make up a life—could, in an instant, not matter anymore.

■ ■ ■

Two days later, Art Fowler shot himself in the head. According to the police report, his wife, Sandy, found him in the bathtub when she got home from church at a little after one on Sunday afternoon. Supposedly he'd left a note, but so far nobody was revealing the contents.

The first ten seconds of the news report were about his death and how he used to be an official in the Seattle water department; the next fifteen minutes were about his grandson, Matthew Hardaway, and the shooting in Everett. Gore Vidal once suggested that the only things people were actually interested in were sex, death, and money. I'd like to imagine our range of interests is a bit wider than that, but were I forced to place a bet, I'd wager ol' Gore was right in the ballpark. Gotta keep those ratings up, and murder sells.

Guilt's a funny thing. Sort of a phantom feeling, because you don't have to be guilty of anything in order to experience it. You can even feel guilty about not feeling guilty, about stuff you had not one damn thing to do with in the first place. It's like guilt's an equal opportunity abuser. Another funny thing: people who have the most to feel guilty about generally don't. Makes my head hurt.

Truth be told, I'd been a little off my feed ever since I'd turned Art Fowler down. Normally, I like to joke that I gave up guilt for Lent, but ever since Art had darkened my door, I'd been giving myself pep talks about how there was nothing I could have done for him. That it was okay that his long-gone association with my father created in me little sense of obligation. And especially about how some kid I'd taken to a ball game once, no matter what he'd done later in his life, wasn't my responsibility.

It was a good story, but deep down inside, I didn't believe a word of it. When the news story of Art's suicide flashed across my TV, I felt as if I'd taken the gun and blown his brains out myself. In that instant, I had no doubt that I was diminished and less than the man I'd always imagined myself to be.

■ ■ ■

I didn't have to wonder who it was when the gate bell tinkled on Wednesday afternoon. Since the bell announced somebody was using the remote from the street, and there were only two remotes, the tinkle meant Rebecca was showing up unannounced—which, while not her usual MO, wasn't all that surprising either, since I hadn't answered my phone for a couple of days. By now, it was a safe bet that Art Fowler's deflated corpse had arrived on one of her autopsy tables and had been sliced and diced for the good of humanity.

We'd had dinner Sunday afternoon and spent the night together. I'd told her the story about Art showing up on my doorstep. She'd done her best to help me rationalize my innocence, but we both knew this was something I was going to have to work out for myself.

She let herself in. Found me standing next to the kitchen sink, leaning against the counter. "You still beating yourself up, or did you just lose your phone?" she asked as she unwound a bright-purple scarf from around her neck.

"Full-scale pity party in progress," I said.

She threw her coat and scarf over the back of one of the kitchen chairs.

"That's what I figured," she said. She walked over and threw her arms around me and gave me a big hug. We stayed that way for about as long as standing upright permitted. She whispered in my ear, "I know this is going to come as quite a shock, but you're not a superhero, Leo." She gave it a moment to sink in. "Contrary to rumor, you can't cure all the world's ills, so there's no sense in making things up." She hugged me harder. I hugged her back.

"I've got an idea," she said, without letting me go.

"I could use one about now," I said, without letting her go.

"We released Mr. Fowler's body to the family yesterday. The funeral's tomorrow. I've got a ton of comp time coming. I'll take the day off. Let's go to the funeral, and maybe we can put some closure on this thing."

I thought it over. As far as I was concerned, *maybe* was the key concept, and closure was for windows. "When all else fails, nothing like a little symbolism," I said finally.

"Can't hurt, can it?"

"Okay. Where is it?"

"Up on the Hill. Saint Mark's Episcopal. They're giving him the whole retired-city-official send-off."

"And burying him where?"

She chortled. "Lakeside. Four o'clock," she said. "Over on the back side of the Hill."

My entire family was buried in the Lakeside Cemetery. On the good side of the Hill, with the sweeping views of Portage Bay, the stone angels, and the outsize marble mausoleums. The back side of the Hill was reserved for the less well-heeled and was thus considerably less Baroque. It was location, location, location, even in death.

"I'll count it as my annual family graveside visit," I said.

"Two birds with one stone . . . an all-around expiation of guilt."

■ ■ ■

Been quite a while since I'd been inside a church, but no spontaneous claps of thunder split the sky as we walked across the parking lot. No basso profundo admonitions from the heavens or accusatory fingers from the great beyond, so we just moseyed over the speed bumps and found a seat about halfway down the aisle.

First and only time I'd ever been in Saint Mark's had been to attend the funeral of one of my mother's friends. I was about ten at the time and could still recall my first glimpse of the inside of the church. Looked like somebody had gotten partway through the construction, given up, and turned the project over to somebody with a completely different vision of how it was supposed to look. Or maybe like the roof had started to collapse, and they'd shored it up with four enormous concrete pillars that didn't look a bit like they went with the rest of it. Somebody once said that a camel was a horse designed by a committee. That's what Saint Mark's looked like to me, then and now.

My mother had explained that, in a sense at least, I was right. The church construction had begun immediately prior to the Great Depression. When the money ran out, the project defaulted on its loans, and the building was taken over by the bank, who rented the unfinished cathedral to, of all people, the U.S. Army.

After the Depression ended, the Episcopalians scraped together enough cash to finish the project, but on a considerably less grand scale than the original plan had called for, which, my mother explained, was why the building had a rather fortresslike quality and was thus known locally as "the holy box."

If pressed, I generally told people I was a Frisbeeitaranist and that we believed that, when you died, your soul went up on the roof and nobody could get it down. Any number of people I knew didn't find that in the least bit funny, but I did, and that was all that mattered. For the record, the rest of my family was Catholic. My mother and several of my father's sisters were big-time donors and fundraisers for the Archdiocese of Seattle. My father? He just wasn't the type. The only omnipotent being he'd believed in was himself, and the only rewards that held any appeal for him were as far from celestial as you could get. Strictly a here-and-now guy he was.

Rebecca? She liked to say she was "spiritual" but not religious and never failed to get pissed off when I suggested that notions such as "spiritual" were not only terminally vague but maybe even vapid. We'd been arguing the subject for the better part of thirty years, with no end in sight.

On the right side of the church, the first five rows were full of bowed heads. On the left side, not so much. We forced ourselves up the aisle, as if leaning into a stiff wind. Wasn't till we got settled in the pew that I noticed the half mile between us and the rest of the assembled multitude.

"*Lord, we come into your presence to remember and to seek your comfort, for we know that nothing can separate us from your love and that you support us in our sorrow.*"

Rebecca leaned close to my ear. "We should move up," she whispered.

She was right. We looked like we'd been expelled from the garden, so we slid out of the pew and tiptoed up front, maybe ten rows back from the altar.

On the right I could see Martha Fowler and an old lady I figured to be Art's widow folded together in the front pew. The other side of the aisle, where I figured we'd find Matthew's father, just a few gray female heads . . . no Phil.

The whole thing took maybe a half an hour. By the time the motorcade had wound its way to Lakeside Cemetery, a steady west wind had pushed the cloud cover into Idaho, leaving sunshine and bright-blue skies for the graveside service.

Rather than following the funeral procession into the cemetery, I parked the car down by the cemetery office, and we walked up the hill. I'd always thought it funny that my father's family had all found it necessary to mark their time on earth with ostentatious graveside architecture, while he lay under a simple stone that offered nothing more than his name and the years of his birth and death.

The ground was squishy from the last snow, welling up around our shoes as we marched along. We slid and slipped our way up the hill. Right before we got to my dad's final resting place, a weeping marble angel marked my aunt Gene's. Forty feet north, my uncle Pat's mausoleum looked big enough to house a Pakistani village. I smiled, took hold of Rebecca's hand, and lengthened my stride.

Dad's gravestone was clean and white. Recently tended. William Waterman. 1945–2001. My entire family was buried within a hundred feet of where I was standing, and suddenly I could see all their faces. All the white dresses, new suits, communion celebrations, the graduation parties, the family Christmas Eves, and most of all the Thanksgiving dinners, at a table so long that, by the time the pie rolled around, the cigarette smoke completely obscured the far end of the festivities. Rebecca rubbed my shoulder. I took the hint, wrapped my arm around her waist, and pulled us up over the crest of the hill.

Art's grave was nearly at the bottom of the west side, peeping through the winter branches at the urbanscape of Capitol Hill. Rebecca and I tiptoed down to the assembled multitude and wedged ourselves in, nodding solemnly at those who met our gazes, until we could see the preacher and grave site.

"*And now to him who is able to keep us from falling, and lift us from the dark valley of despair, to the bright mountain of hope, from the midnight of desperation to the daybreak of joy.*"

Over the years, I'd come to regard funerals as the theater of mass denial, wherein the permanent is made to seem temporary so that the gnawing rat fear in our guts can be kicked back into its cage once again.

The preacher was winding his way toward eternity, and I was ruminating on a veritable vortex of variables when the first shout found its way to my ears. Not a discernible word, more like an angry current floating on the breeze.

I sneaked a peek over my shoulder. A TV cameraman was backing over the top of the hill, shooting something on the other side of the rise. Instinctively, I started to turn. Rebecca's fingers squeezed my upper arm. The *don't you dare stick your nose in* squeeze. I squared my shoulders and turned back toward the grave.

I did pretty good too. Lasted right up to when the preacher stopped talking and just stood there, scripture in hand, looking out over the crowd. I swiveled my head. Protest signs popped up over the brow of the hill. **Stop Gun Violence Now. Protect Children, Not Guns.**

No More! That was as far as I got before the main body of protestors came into view.

Maybe a dozen of them. Three or four standard-issue Seattle hipsters. Big, bushy beards and the permanent scowl of underemployment. Several of them filming the scene on their phones as they stomped along. A middle-aged couple with two kids in tow was leading the parade. A prematurely purple Goth girl with a red, white, and blue **What Is It You Don't Understand?** sign was the one doing most of the yelling. "Stop now! Stop now!" she bellowed.

It wasn't like I made a conscious decision to intervene. Just sorta happened. Next thing I knew, I was circling around the cameraman and bellying up to the family with the **Protect Children, Not Guns** sign.

"Maybe this isn't the best time," I suggested, in my reasonable voice.

"Stop the madness," the wife screeched at me.

I stayed calm. "They're just putting the guy in the ground. Maybe you could . . . you know, for the sake of his family," I said.

The little girl hopped forward and kicked me in the shin.

"Maybe if you guys . . . ," I began again.

I didn't see the wife step behind me as I approached her husband. Up close, he was about forty, sporting a serious comb-over and about fifty extra pounds.

"Listen, man," I said. "Don't get me wrong . . . I don't necessarily disagree with your message . . . but, you know, maybe this isn't the right time to . . ."

That's when father-guy's feet lost their purchase on the slope. His eyes went wide. He waved the picket sign, trying to regain his balance. I fired out a helping hand but caught nothing but air. He was still windmilling his arms as his feet came out from under him. I winced as he smacked into the muck. I leaned forward, extended my hand, ready to haul him back to his feet, when somebody jumped onto my back and began flailing at me with a picket sign.

"No . . . no . . . I was—" I growled.

"Don't you dare," my assailant shrieked, pounding on my back like a tom-tom. "Don't you—"

The third time the wooden placard handle scraped across my face, I lost my sense of humor, reached back, and muscled my attacker up and over my shoulder. The wife face-planted directly in front of my feet and began to groan piteously. I watched openmouthed as she rolled over onto her side and looked my way. She looked like a divot, her howling face covered with mud and half a bale of grass.

I was still trying to decide which of them to help first when my feet began to move. I swivel hipped myself sideways and dug in like I was skiing, trying to edge with the soles of my shoes. No go. It was like I was on a conveyer belt. I waved my arms, trying desperately to keep myself upright. And then *bang*. I slid into someone and came to a stop. Someone who rested a video camera on my shoulder and kept whirring away. I groaned.

Took Mom and Dad a couple of minutes to get themselves upright, scrape off some of the mud, and check one another for damage. By that time, half a dozen guys from the funeral service had cramponed their way up to where I was standing and had begun to cajole the remaining protestors back over the rise.

The preacher wasted no time. Five minutes later, the service was over and the assembled multitude was slip sliding their way back to their cars. Rebecca had an arm looped around my shoulder.

"Well . . . that went nicely, didn't it?" she said.

I clamped my mouth shut, took Rebecca's hand in mine, and started sloshing toward the car.

■ ■ ■

I felt lousy but was putting on my brave face. Rebecca, as usual, read me like a book. By the time we were halfway back to the car, she'd twice tried to get me off the hook.

"Hey," she said, bopping me in the arm. "Maybe we ought to just call it a day."

"I made us a reservation at Lark."

"We can call. Tell them we won't be making it."

"Nah" passed my lips before it ever visited my brain. "I could use a drink."

"Let's go back to my place," she pressed. "I've got a bottle of Highland Park. We'll do takeout."

I'm not sure listening to reason would have made much of a difference at that point, but we'll never know for sure, because I was having none of it.

We spent the next hour and a half eating excellent food and pretending we were having a good time. I'd stuffed the last of the pineapple tarte tatin with ginger-caramel and matcha-almond-crunch ice cream into my tarte hole, any pretense of gaiety had long since hit the bricks, and I felt like a prisoner having his last meal. Rebecca was trying to keep things breezy, but even in romantic restaurant light she looked like she'd rather be having a Pap smear.

Silence settled over us like a mantle as I drove Rebecca back to her place, walked her to the door, and kiss kissed my goodbyes. By the time I made it back to the top of Capitol Hill, both my attitude and the onshore flow were thick enough to qualify as rain.

Rolling along Elliott Avenue, I felt like I was made of lead. As if something vital had been removed from my body, leaving only the shell behind. I shook my head in the darkness and heaved a sigh big enough to show up on the Weather Channel.

My phone began to ring just as I started up Dravus. I ignored it and kept driving. It stopped and then started again. I reached down to pop my seat belt so I could reach the bottom of my pocket, but it stopped ringing again, so I pulled my hand back to the steering wheel and gunned it up the hill, my knuckles white.

Ring. Ring.

Fuck. Fuck.

Whoever wanted to talk to me was big-time serious about it. The phone kept ringing, and I kept silently telling it to piss off. By the time I rounded the corner in front of the Morrisons' house, I'd made up my mind to never call whoever was buzzing my balls. Not if I lived to be a thousand would I call that motherfucker back. Oh, how they'd suffer. I'd . . . I'd . . .

The KING 5 TV remote truck parked on the far side of my driveway pulled me back to the here and now. I grabbed the gate remote from the visor and thumbed the "Open" button. As the gate began to roll across the asphalt, I put the pedal to the metal, screeching a ninety-degree fishtail into my driveway with one hand while pushing the "Close" button with the other. No go. They was too quick for me.

When I checked the mirror, I could see a shadow flowing down the driveway as the gate closed behind. I stomped on the emergency brake and got out of the car.

In the purple glow of the streetlight, I saw another guy with a camera fanning out to the left, quickstepping it along the edge of the shrubbery, red light winking, filming me as he hustled over the grass.

I walked quickly toward the guy with the microphone. He smiled and brought the microphone to his mouth. I matched his grin tooth for tooth, grabbed him by the elbow, and spun him like a top.

"But—" he blurted as I took hold of his belt with one hand and his collar with the other and began to frog-march him toward the gate.

"This is private property," I said to his back. "I'm ordering you to leave. If you don't, I'm going to call the police, and then I'm going to call your employer and lodge a complaint."

"We want to give you a chance to tell your side of the story," he sputtered as I propelled him over the pavement. "Can you tell us—"

I had no clue what he was flapping his lips about, and at that point, I didn't much give a fig. I was reminding myself to hold my temper when parka boy went all macho and decided to extricate himself from my grasp with a single violent twist of his health club–honed body. A bad idea if ever there was one.

I felt him tense up, knew what was coming, and tightened my grip. He began to throw himself around like a marionette having a seizure. Didn't matter. I kept surfing him forward, his feet chattering for traction as we slid toward the street. On about his third convulsive escape try, he inadvertently raked the microphone across my face. That was all it took. It had been a tough few days. I could feel blood rushing up my neck as I slammed him face-first into the gate.

He huffed out a great gust of air and whimpered. I reached up and pushed "Open." The gate began to move. I pushed him harder. The steel rails played bongos on his face as, one by one, they slid by. I was enjoying the catchy rhythm when a movement in my peripheral vision pulled my eyes to the right.

The camera guy was tiptoeing my way. Red light winking. The gate clanged open. I grabbed talking head's collar and propelled him out into the street like a lawn dart. I watched as he took a couple of off-center steps and then sprawled facedown on the pavement.

I pushed "Close." The gate's metal wheels hissed like a gas leak. I pointed at the cameraman. "You've got five seconds before you're gonna be locked in here with me, and if that happens, you're gonna need a proctologist to get that fucking camera back."

He took me at my word, scampering out the opening like a scalded rat. I watched as he set the camera down on the street and then began to help microphone man to his feet. The guy came up in sections. When he was finally standing on both feet, waving back and forth like a willow in the wind, I turned and walked away.

As I hopped up onto the driver's seat, I heard car doors slamming and an engine ratcheting to life. I nearly smiled for the first time in a week.

I locked the Tahoe in the garage and, just to be sure, walked around the house to check the front gate again. Mercifully, the news van was gone. I stifled a sigh and let myself in the front door.

I lived in the downstairs of the house. I'd renovated it a few years back, right after my old man's pile had finally found its way into my pocket. Took out a few walls, went from eight rooms to five, and updated everything in sight, except the big front parlor. As Art Fowler had noticed, it was pretty much just like my mother had left it thirty years ago. My old man never saw any reason to mess with it, and neither had I. The two upper floors looked like the Addams Family was away on vacation. The only people who ever went up there anymore were the Merry Maids, who shuffled the dust around a couple of times a year and then sent me a bill.

The mind is a strange thing. It was like my brain had had enough stress for one day and switched on the cruise control. I wandered into the TV room and made myself a Manhattan. Two sips in, I knew I was too depressed to enjoy it but that I sure as hell was gonna drink it anyway. And a couple more too.

And then I was moving, walking around the house like I was taking a tour of Graceland or something. Walking up the central stairway. Second floor. Rooms I hadn't entered in years greeted me with empty faces and ghostly furniture, but for some reason, I kept moving forward, traipsing through doorways and sipping at my drink, trying to remember the last time I'd stood in that spot.

Wasn't till I ran out of booze on the third floor, after I'd eaten the cherries and sucked up the last few drops of rye, that I found my way back downstairs to the bar. That's when I noticed the message light on the landline blinking. The mystery line. The one where my old man must have known somebody in the phone company and had it installed on the sly. Never even got robocalls. The line I never got a bill for, and once, when after my father's death I'd tried to have it removed, I was told by the phone company that no such line existed. Who was I to argue?

Only four people had the number. Rebecca, of course. George Paris, who along with a few other chronic degenerates constituted the last mortal remnants of my dad's political machine. Carl Cradduck, who handled my IT work when I had any, which wasn't often lately, and Tim Eagen, a lieutenant in the Seattle Police Department, whose acute fondness for Rebecca had more or less forced us into an uneasy alliance over the past few years.

I turned my back on the message light and made myself another drink. Used up the last of the vermouth making it too. Shit. Checked the ceiling for falling anvils and wondered where my Acme jet-powered roller skates could possibly have gotten to.

I lasted maybe ten minutes, thinking about anything and everything except that friggin' landline, before I set my drink on the bar, angrily crossed the room, and picked up the receiver. First message was from Carl. "Nice," he growled. "Leo Waterman, the scourge of suburbia. In case you missed your newest fifteen minutes of fame, I emailed you a link. Nice work, jerk." Wild laughter. Click.

I shuffled over to my desk and hit the space bar. The iMac glowed to life. I checked the mail program. Half a dozen sales pitches and a message from Carl. Sure enough. *Nice!* was all it said, with a link to the King 5 website.

I waited a long moment and then double-clicked the link. Big red letters at the bottom of the screen. Breaking News. The talking head's lips were moving, but I had the volume turned all the way down. As I reached for the volume control, the screen changed from the studio to . . . to . . . Oh Jesus . . . Art's funeral . . . just as the first of the picket signs bobbed up over the top of the hill. Then the screaming Goth girl came into view as I shouldered my way past the cameraman, filling up the screen with my back as I fought for traction on the hill.

Then the camera backed up, and I was standing in front of the father, trying to get him to let the funeral service finish, when his wife stepped between me and the cameraman just at the moment when hubby began to lose his footing and I reached out a steadying hand.

I groaned out loud at the sight of the husband hitting the ground like a sack of feed. I stopped it. Rewound. Started it again. Same thing. Holy shit. With the wife between the cameraman and me, it looked as if I'd hauled off and coldcocked the guy. I rewound again and watched it twice more. Looked exactly the same both times.

The part where the wife bravely came to her husband's rescue only to be hurled down into the muck by the beefy bad guy was particularly cinematic. They ran that footage twice. You know . . . in case anybody missed it the first time. They finished with a still shot of the wife caked with mud, blinking into the camera like a breaded veal cutlet.

I leaned back in the chair and closed my eyes. The landline started to ring. "Fuck," I bellowed, into the empty room. My first inclination was to tear the phone from the wall and fling it across the room. Instead, I took a couple of deep breaths and snatched the receiver.

"What?"

Long pause.

"I guess you've seen it," Rebecca said.

"In living color."

"Really looks a lot like you hit him."

"Watched it three or four times, and it looked like that every friggin' time," I said. "I especially liked the slow-motion shot of me body slamming the wife."

"You want me to come over?" she asked.

I thought about it and couldn't see any sense in spreading the misery around. "Nah," I said. "I'm not very good company right now."

"You sure? It's still early."

"Thanks for the offer, but . . ." At which point I ran out of words.

Another silence.

"The best-laid plans . . . ," she said finally.

A short, bitter laugh escaped from my chest. "Yeah," I said. "If today was closure, I think I'd opt for a lifetime of regret."

"Look on the bright side," she offered. "The news cycle is very short these days. Won't be long before some celebrity does something stupid, and everyone will move on and forget about you."

"Boy . . . don't I feel better now," I snapped and immediately regretted it. "Sorry," I said. "I shouldn't be taking it out on you."

Pin-drop moment.

"I'll call you tomorrow," she said finally.

"Yeah," was the best I could do.

▪ ▪ ▪

I did what I always do when my life starts circling the bowl. I got busy. Crazy, batshit, OCD busy. Taking care of six months' worth of things I'd either ignored or postponed. No matter what anybody tells you, money changes everything, and despite a lifetime of power-to-the-people, egalitarian babbling, I'd turned out to be no exception to the rule. These days, I hire out anything I don't feel like doing, or, more likely, simply ignore it, telling myself that even if it gets worse, which it unquestionably will, I can afford to have it fixed. Yes sir . . . a real man of the people I am.

The TV assholes made a nuisance of themselves for a day or so, parking out in the street and wearing out the gate buzzer, which I'd long since turned off, but as Rebecca had predicted, they lost interest sometime on the second day and disappeared into the ozone.

On days three and four, I excavated an old pair of coveralls from the basement and personally cleaned out the garage. A trip down memory lane it was too. Shit that had been stowed in there since my father's time. Piles and piles of rusty chains. Tools so old I had no clue what they were intended to accomplish. Took two full days and produced enough trash so's I had to call two guys and a truck to haul it all away.

Rebecca stopped by a couple of times in the evenings, soothing my soul with her silky enchantments, but mostly I was just killing time, waiting for Art Fowler's carcass to get far enough behind me on the sidewalk of life.

Day five. The security system's floodlights had about eight bulbs out, so I called Home Sentry and had them send out a crew and a cherry picker. By that time, I wasn't even local news anymore, which might be why I was so spaced out, watching the two guys in the basket bobbing about like kites in the wind, when the unmistakable rasp of a skateboard pulled my head out of my hindquarters.

Now a skateboard isn't something you hear a lot up where I live. This is Old Moneyville up here. Way more likely to hear the hum of pacemakers than the grind of a skateboard. Besides which, this was the top of Magnolia Bluff. Anyone attempting to skateboard down the hill to Interbay either had a death wish or real good health insurance. I stepped out into the street for a better view, kinda like people go to NASCAR races to suck down corn dogs and wait for a wreck.

He was half a block up the street. Long hair fanned out behind him. Red headband and a pair of cargo shorts big enough for a water buffalo, blasting down the middle of the street like an Olympic downhiller, cutting back and forth. I watched admiringly as he caught sight of the orange traffic cones that the Home Sentry guys had put out in the street, grinned, and veered my way.

He was flying now, arms out for balance as he rocketed around the first cone, shifted his weight, and danced, wheels screaming, around the next and the next like a speed-crazed hootchy-kootchy dancer. I was certain he was going way too fast to make it around the next cone, when he suddenly dug in, ground a wide arc way out into the middle of the street, and then came rolling at me like a bullet train.

The cherry picker was in the entrance to the driveway. The gate was open. Nowhere to run. Nowhere to hide, so I stepped quickly to one side, putting one of the stone gate pillars partially between the skater and me.

When I peeked around the corner, he had the front wheels off the ground and was grinding to a halt. Two seconds later, he was standing in front of me with the skateboard tucked under his arm.

I couldn't help myself; I gave him a standing ovation. I was still putting my hands together when he stuck his hand out. I stopped clapping and took it. "Tommy," he said as he used his free hand to transfer his backpack from his back to his front.

"Leo," I said.

The crocodile smile should have alerted me right there, but I guess I was pretty much brain-dead at that point. I watched as he pulled an envelope from his backpack and then looked over at me.

"Leo Waterman," he said.

Brought me up short. "Who wants to know?" I asked.

He slapped the envelope against my chest. Instinctively, I reached for his wrist, but he was too quick for me. All my hand ended up with was the envelope.

"King County wants to know," he said. "And of course, inquiring minds," he added. "You've been served, sir."

When I looked up, he was filming me as I stood there open-mouthed with the court paperwork in one hand and my dick in the other. Figuratively.

"You know, kid . . . I used to do this," I said.

He backed up a little, ready to hotfoot it up the road.

"Do what, sir?"

"Back in the day it was called serving process," I said. "My old man knew some fleabag ambulance chaser downtown. Had me serving divorce papers, repos, evictions, all the stuff people really, really didn't want to see."

The kid looked me over like a menu. The crooked grin that bent his lips told me he had his doubts.

"I was a bit more lithe in those days," I felt compelled to add.

"How long did you last?"

I thought about it. "Couple of years . . . on and off, whenever I wasn't pretending I was going to college." I shrugged. "It was quite an education, in its own right."

"Why'd you quit?"

"I got slower."

"The ravages of time," he allowed as he turned and walked away.

■ ■ ■

"I'm being sued."

"For what? By whom?" Rebecca wanted to know.

"That couple from Art's funeral. They're suing me for three million and change, saying I not only assaulted them but that I interfered with their constitutional right to peacefully demonstrate, which they're claiming is a hate crime and therefore worth an extra million or so."

"Call Nancy."

She was referring to Nancy Pometta, the attorney she'd used when she'd been wrongfully suspended for dereliction of duty. Nancy was a junior partner in my friend Jed James's law firm. Ever since Jed had been appointed to the Court of Appeals bench, he could no longer personally bail me out of whatever mess I'd gotten into, so he had somebody else in the firm do it. Nancy being one of those.

"You still have her number?"

She gave it to me. I stored it in my phone.

"Seems like you're in a bit of a trough," she said.

"An abyss," I corrected.

"Well . . . ," she began.

"Let's not," I said quickly. "I'm gonna call Nancy."

Another pin-drop moment.

"I'll call you later," she said.

"Hey . . . ," I said as we were about to break the connection.

"Uh-huh."

"Thanks for putting up with me," I said. I thought maybe I heard a derisive snort. "Say hi to Nancy for me," was how we left it.

So that's what I did. Nancy was in a meeting and had to call me back. Half an hour later we were exchanging pleasantries. I started to tell her the story. She interrupted to say she'd seen the TV footage. More than once. Said she'd get somebody on it right away and would call me whenever she had any further info.

So it was a real brow creaser when, two seconds after I hung up with Nancy, my phone started chirping again and Rebecca's mug showed up on the screen. Seemed like we'd already said what we had to say.

"Hey . . ."

"I need you to come to my office."

Gotta admit . . . I was instantly relegated to mouth breathing. We'd long since established that seeing my lady love elbow-deep in rotting cadavers was not to be counted among my preferred entertainment options. I'd seen her at work, of course. You can't make whoopee with the King County medical examiner for twenty plus years and not witness autopsies; but you know, given my druthers, I can do without watching somebody get parted out like a Buick station wagon. Color me with a squeamish crayon if you want, but that's the way it is.

"How come?" I asked.

Somebody said something to her. I heard a door opening and closing. Sounded as if she'd stepped into another room.

"Martha Fowler is sitting in my office," she hissed.

"Why would Martha Fowler come to see you?" I asked.

"Because she couldn't get in touch with *you*. *You're* not answering your phone. She says she spent a whole day sitting outside *your* gate. So she figured . . . you know . . . everybody knows about the two of us . . . so she came to the office."

"What's she want?" I asked.

"She wants to talk to you."

I considered the matter. "Listen . . . ," I began. "Tell her—"

"No." Like a gunshot. "You tell her. I've got work to do."

Like I said, you spend a couple of decades with another person, if you've got any brains at all, you get to know the lay of the land. I recognized this tone of voice. We were in nonnegotiable territory here. The place where you couldn't change Rebecca's mind if you put a gun to her head, so you may as well save your breath.

Then, of course, there was the fact that she was right. My life had slopped over onto hers, which was not part of the general armistice agreement. I grabbed my leather jacket from the hook and headed for the back door, with the phone jammed against my ear.

"I'm on the way," I said. "Probably take me half an hour."

"I can't just leave her sitting there in my office," she snapped.

"Call the parking lot. Have 'em let me in. That'll save some time," I said and let the kitchen door slam behind me.

■ ■ ■

Twenty-four minutes flat. When I walked into Rebecca's corner office, Monica, the receptionist, was sitting behind Rebecca's desk. Monica wore pink. Everything pink. All the time. Nice enough girl, but looking at her always made me feel like I was trapped inside a bottle of Pepto-Bismol.

She jumped to her feet. "Leo," she blurted. "Whenever Ms. Fowler is ready to leave, I'll show her out."

Orders from the boss, no doubt. Here in the land of the dead, they frowned upon the living wandering about the building.

"Thanks, Monica," I said.

She scurried for the door with the rustling swoosh of a flock of flamingos.

I walked around the desk and plopped down in Rebecca's chair. Seeing Martha up close, my first thought was, "Wow . . . she's gotten older"—a realization that somehow never includes me, as if I am for some reason immune to aging. It isn't until I pass by a mirror and catch sight of my own composting carcass that I'm forced to fess up to reality. Hate when that happens.

Her face was the color of old putty. Looked like if you pressed it with your finger it would stay dented forever. We like to tell people, "I know how you feel" when disaster strikes. But we don't. I mean how do you imagine what it's like to have your son murder someone on camera and then lose your father to a self-inflicted gunshot wound a week later? Anybody who can conjure up how it feels to have that happen to them needs a shrink worse than I do.

I was trying to come up with a suitable lead-in but found the repartee cupboard bare. Something like "sorry to hear about you losing your son, your father, and your peace of mind" didn't seem to have quite the proper cachet, so I buttoned my lip and left it that way.

We just sat there, the sounds of traffic punctuating the silence.

"You were looking for me?" I said after an uncomfortable decade or so.

She nodded but didn't say anything, so I tried again.

"Goes without saying . . ." I cleared my throat and kept talking. "Sorry about all of it."

She folded her hands in her lap and closed her eyes. The air in the room was thick enough to swim in.

I watched as she dry swallowed several times and then choked out, "My mother says my father came to see you right before he . . . before . . ."

I didn't want her to have to say it out loud, so I jumped in.

"Yes he did."

Her face suggested she'd expected me to deny it. "What did he want?"

Not sure I ever wanted to weasel out of a conversation that bad in my life, but I sucked it up and then spit it out. "He wanted to know why Matthew did what he did," I said. "He figured . . . you know . . . I used to be a private eye, so he thought maybe I could find out what . . . what pushed your son over the edge. He seemed to feel that . . . that there must have been other . . . outside . . . forces involved."

She cut me off. "He loved Matthew," she said.

"I'm sure he did."

Out in the street somebody's car alarm was bleating to the sky. Usually not something you want to hear, but not surprisingly, right at that juncture, both of us were silently grateful for the interruption.

"I think he came to me because of my father," came rolling out of my mouth, unbidden. She turned in the seat and looked at me. Felt like I was being skewered.

"Why would he do that?" she asked.

"In his time," I began, "my father could fix just about anything you needed fixed. He knew who to talk to and what it was going to take to get it done. You needed a traffic ticket fixed, you called Big Bill. Your kid got a DUI you needed to go away, he could make that happen." I shrugged. "Provided either he owed you or he wanted you to owe him."

I took a deep breath and went on. "I think your father . . . I think maybe . . . somewhere in his desperation . . . he thought maybe Big Bill could somehow make it all go away for him . . . you know . . . even from the grave."

My words seem to revive her. I watched as an underlying redness crept up her neck and then to her cheeks. She unfolded her hands. Rubbed them back and forth on her skirt and squared her shoulders.

"That's what I thought," she said bitterly. "Phil couldn't face it," she said. "Neither of them could. No matter how many times I told him or other people told him . . . doctors, teachers, counselors . . . Everybody told them . . . He just couldn't admit it. It was like it so offended his maleness that Matthew might be sick . . . He kept making excuses for it. It was just a stage he was going through. He'd grow out of it. It was the school's fault. With the proper medication, he'd be fine." She waved an angry hand in the air and looked away. I watched her stifle a sob.

I put an awkward hand on her shoulder.

"Mr. Macho man gun nut," she went on. "It was like there was no possible way the fruit of *his* loins could possibly be defective. Oh no! There had to be some other explanation. Somebody or something other than *his son* had to be to blame." Her anger settled over the room like cannon smoke.

"I wish I could have helped."

Her voice rose. "What's to help? It's done. The media's turned my son into some kind of urban terrorist. My father shot himself. Phil and I are both under siege. I had to sneak out of my house in the middle of the night to drive up here and attend my own father's funeral last week and again today. I've got cars following me around." She got to her feet. "What's to help," she said again. "We've become the pariah." She gathered her purse under her arm. "Sorry to have bothered you, Leo." She shrugged. "I was just . . . I don't know what I was thinking."

I did. Knew all too well. People go to private eyes when they've already tried everything remotely sensible and have made a substantial dent in their crazy list too. Something inside them knows, without being told, that unless they do everything and anything they can think of, they're never gonna get a decent night's sleep for as long as they live.

"It's cool," I assured her. "Where'd you park?"

"Over by the Sorrento, on Madison."

"I'll walk you to your car," I said.

She didn't bother to argue. I guided her down the hall to the elevators, stopped at Monica's desk to make sure she knew we were leaving, and then we stepped out onto Jefferson Street, or almost, anyway. The driving rain appeared to be in danger of turning to sleet. Just looking at it gave me the shivers.

I took her arm and walked her back through the building, the short way, out to my car in the swell-folks parking lot. We hunched across the asphalt, the rain hissing around us like silver wasps. I started her up, buckled myself in, and dropped it into reverse. “The receptionist . . . ?” Martha said out of nowhere.

“Monica?”

“Does she always dress like that . . . I mean . . .”

“Yeah. Pink on pink.” I leaned a little closer and tried to lighten things up a bit. “Underwear too.”

Her eyes narrowed. “And how would you know that, Leo?”

“I’ve inadvertently seen her bra straps on several occasions. Pink. So I’m assuming . . . you know . . . you gotta figure . . . a coordinated ensemble . . .”

“Good bet.”

We drove the rest of the way in silence, the rain hitting the car like gravel. I let her out across the street from her ride. She got out and stood in the open door. She was so wet, I couldn’t tell if she was crying or not. “Thanks for the good humor, Leo. I didn’t mean to be a burden. I’m just sort of at my wit’s end, I guess. I don’t even remember driving over here, to tell you the truth.” She lifted an arm and then let it drop to her side with a slap. “I didn’t even know where I was until you came into the room.”

“No problem,” I assured her. “I don’t know if things in your life are going to get better . . . because . . . you know I really hate it when people say that shit to me, but I feel pretty confident saying they couldn’t get a hell of a lot worse.”

The rain had made her mascara come unglued. She looked like a drowning raccoon as she gave me a wan smile. “Take care of yourself,” was the last thing I got out of my mouth before she closed the door and hurried across the street to a red Toyota and let herself in.

I nosed into the Sorrento Hotel's circular driveway only to find it was no longer circular. Been a while, I guessed. They'd converted it into kind of an outdoor patio where guests could enjoy the fresh air and sunshine on any of the eleven days a year when it wasn't raining its nuts off. If I ran this place, somebody'd be looking for work.

I used the little turnaround they'd left for the valets and nosed back out onto Boren Avenue just in time to watch Martha pull away from the curb, heading north. I was about to turn the other way and put all of this behind me, literally and figuratively, when a dark-blue Range Rover nearly ripped off the front of my car as it came off the curb like a pool ball, squealed a tight half circle, and began rolling up the street in Martha's wake.

It was the old wait-and-then-hurry-up maneuver that got my attention. The moment Martha disappeared around the corner, the driver of the Range Rover stomped the accelerator and roared after her.

I knew that one all too well. Trying to follow somebody in city traffic. That's how ya did it. Didn't work worth a shit, but that's what it looked like when you gave it the old college try.

If any competent law enforcement agency wanted to tail you around a city like Seattle, it wouldn't be two guys in a Range Rover. They'd have anywhere from eight to twelve nondescript vehicles and maybe a helicopter involved, depending on how congested a particular part of town was at a particular time of day. They'd trade off following you. Trying to keep both behind and ahead of your computer-projected route. And even then, even with an eye in the sky helping out, there was a decent chance the subject would slip the net. Cities were like that. Too much of everything.

I bounced out onto Boren and fed the Tahoe nine dollars' worth of unleaded.

Our little motorcade wound its way down to Broadway and turned north. That's when the whole Jim-Rockford-tails-people-all-over-L.A. scenario shit its pants.

This was Capitol Hill. Between the cars, delivery trucks, streetcars, buses, and the hordes of pedestrians—and I don't mean regular pedestrians, no no no—I mean *entitled* pedestrians. These were people with *the goddamn right of way*, people who'd step right in front of your car wearing skinny jeans and earbuds, reading a book on their Kindle, and then throw you a withering PC sneer when you were forced to skid to a stop in order to keep from turning them into meatballs.

By the time we got up to Seattle Central College, Martha's Toyota had disappeared like a cool breeze. Three cars up, waiting for the light to change, the guys in the Rover didn't seem to mind a bit, so I chided myself for misreading the situation and started thinking about where I was going to have lunch.

The light went green, and as Seattle geography would have it, we were already pointing in the direction I was going, so I just kept tootling along behind the Range Rover until we got all the way up to Roy, at which point they turned left and started down the ski-jump hill, past Annie Cornish, down through the nasty little curve where Roy drops straight down the face of the hill and all of a sudden you're driving on Belmont, heading right at Lake Union.

The wind had turned the surface of the lake into a green-and-white washboard. Out in the distance, through an iron curtain of rain, the Aurora Bridge arched like a questioning brow as a yellow-and-white floatplane waggled down over Gas Works Park.

Belmont was narrow as hell. A steady stream of traffic labored up the hill in the oncoming lane. I was planning to turn right at the bottom of the hill, run over into Eastlake, maybe grab a sandwich at Mammoth on my way home, but as I pulled up to the stop sign, a quick glance to my left changed all that.

Martha's car was rolling down the big airborne ramp they'd built from the base of Capitol Hill to the newly crowned center of the known world—South Lake Union. Amazonville Central.

Either the guys in the Rover had just gotten real lucky and stumbled onto Martha again—a coincidence my brain rejected before I was through thinking it—or perhaps they already knew where she was going because they'd been following her. Or—you know—if I wanted to get all James Bondy about it, maybe they'd put a transponder on her car. I was trying to keep an open mind, but hard as I worked at it, I couldn't come up with another reasonable alternative.

I pumped the brakes harder, letting the Rover put some distance between us. When the Rover put on its left-turn signal and followed Martha down the ramp, any doubts I had about whether or not they were shadowing her hit the bricks.

The car behind me tooted its horn, getting impatient with my *I brake for gravel* approach to driving. I turned left and checked the mirror as soon as I rolled onto the ramp. Nobody behind me. I fed the Tahoe some gas.

After ten minutes of seeping along at the speed of lava, I was so intent on watching Martha pull into the Sheraton Seattle Hotel valet area, I nearly failed to notice the Rover slipping into a deliveries-only zone across the street from the hotel. I feathered the brakes. Slowed to a snail crawl. A herd of horns brayed their displeasure. I cursed, kept the Tahoe moving as I tried to find a spot to stash the car. Nada. Screwed and blued. No place to stop, so I goosed it up to the next light, turned left, and repeated the process a few times, until five minutes later I was parked half a block up from the Sheraton on Sixth Avenue. There'd been major changes in my absence.

Martha was gone. The valet was nosing her Toyota down the ramp into the underground garage. The Rover was gone too, and all of a sudden I was being tossed on the horns of a dilemma. Should I go inside and tell Martha there actually *were* two guys following her? It seemed a bit excessive, since she's the one who'd told *me* she had a tail. At the time, I'd assumed it hadda be more of the antigun crowd. I mean anybody nutsy enough to picket a guy's funeral because he was a killer's grandfather was certainly bonkers enough to follow the killer's mother all over the Pacific Northwest.

So I decided to break all precedent and mind my own damn business. Not necessarily the most ethical decision I'd ever made, but as long as it got the Fowler family out of my life once and for all, I figured I could live with it long term.

I dropped the Tahoe into gear, waited a year and a half for a hole to open up in the traffic, and started downhill, hoping to get all the way to Western before I became eligible for social security.

It was the pulsing red-and-blue lights up ahead that got my attention, and not in any former-detective sort of way. More like in a road rage kind of way. Two blocks up, a cop had pulled somebody over, but since there was no *over* in the downtown core, they'd stopped him in the right-hand lane, forcing everyone to move to the left through a stream of cars whose drivers would rather get rabies than let anybody in front of them. The way I saw it, that $150 traffic ticket was going to add an extra fifteen or twenty minutes to several thousand people's commutes. To protect and serve. Yeah. I was all atwitter at the thought.

Wasn't till I got to Second Avenue that I changed my tune. Right there on the corner of Second and Union, an enormous SPD motorcycle cop had stopped the Range Rover and was standing in the right-hand lane scribbling in his citation book. I read the Rover's license plate number into my phone and smiled for the first time in a week or so.

Must be true what they say about a smile too, because for the first time all day, I got lucky with the traffic and ended up first in line at the light. I threw a quick glance toward the Rover. The cop was in the way, but I could see the driver was a curly-haired white guy. Fortysomething. Thick neck. Greasy face and mean little eyes.

I leaned forward, trying to see around Officer Humongous. The passenger was a white woman. Big gal. Nest of blonde hair of a shade that doesn't appear in nature, wearing big, red hoop earrings and a red satin jacket with something embroidered on the back. A dragon maybe.

A black number nine adorned her left shoulder. Some kind of team jacket, for sure.

The light changed. The steady rain was taking its toll. Every cross street was a nightmare of scurrying, rain-soaked pedestrians looking for shelter and wherever the hell it was where they threw the fish around.

Down by the Labor Temple I parallel parked in front of a Costco delivery truck and called Tim Eagen. Straight to voicemail. I read the Rover's plate number into his machine and then asked nice if maybe he wouldn't run the plate number for me. Carl could do it too, but first off he'd charge me up the yak, and second off he'd bust my balls for a half an hour before he came up with the info. Yeah . . . Tim Eagen was a way better choice, even if he was in love with my girlfriend.

CJ's Eatery was two blocks behind me on the other side of First Avenue. One of my favorite downtown no-frills joints. Breakfast and lunch. No dinner. Just good food and no pretense. I began perusing CJ's menu in my mind, wondering if a guy could still get Swedish pancakes at this time of day. I'd made up my mind to beg if necessary, grabbed the door handle, glanced at the mirror so's not to get my big ass run over, when, what to my wondering eyes should appear but the Range Rover, zipping past me up toward Denny. Except that the blonde woman was now driving, and the greasy guy had a black leather elbow sticking out the passenger window.

Like a moth to the flame, I slid the key back in the ignition, pulled my door shut, and bounced out into traffic. They took First Avenue all the way to the end, where it runs into Denny, hooked a left in front of Tini Bigs martini bar, and then a quick right, and then another, up the alley behind Tini's into the construction zone for the new building next door.

I pulled to the curb, got out of the car, and walked up to the corner. Peeked around. The rain hissed like a locomotive. The alley opened onto city streets at both ends. No Rover. I hustled back to my car, fired her up, and wheeled into the alley.

The portable construction office was forty yards ahead on the left, wedged between a fenced enclosure piled high with debris and the yellow construction crane looming in the sky like a steel mantis.

I was guessing the high wind had sent the crew home for the day. Halfway down I could see the church parking lot at the far end. That's when she stepped out in front of me.

Unlike Martha's coif, Blondie's mane seemed to be completely impervious to the wind and water. I braked to a stop. She stood there looking at me like I was a creature from another planet.

I slid out of my seat, closed the car door, and took a couple of tentative steps in her direction. I thought about yelling something but couldn't figure out what to yell. I shoulda known better. The question wasn't, What in hell was Blondie doing standing in the middle of a rain-washed alley? The question that should have been bouncing through my circuits was, Where the hell was her partner?

The scrape of a shoe provided the answer. I got halfway turned around when the back of my head exploded, sending me staggering forward, my vision nothing more than a flickering collection of silver spheres. I reached for the back of my head and fought for balance in the flicker before the second blow dropped me to my knees. Last thing I remember seeing was Blondie running up the alley in my direction, right before another blow from behind put my lights out altogether, and I found myself French-kissing the concrete.

■ ■ ■

I'd like to tell you about my dreams—you know, falling forever into the obsidian abyss, huge gothic houses with no doors, Dracula eating my liver for lunch with some nice fava beans, that sort of thing—but truth is, I didn't have any dreams. Next thing I remember was something cold trickling down my throat. I remember gagging on it. And then becoming aware that I was sucking cold water through a straw, and how I could barely work up enough suction to pull it down my throat. The top of my head nearly blew off when I dropped my eyes toward my chest to see what was wrong. Somebody moaned out loud. Me, I think. I forced my eyes to focus. Took three tries. A hand holding the cup up by my mouth. Straw. Red-and-white stripes. Little wrinkles. One of those bendable straws that either meant I'd been demoted back to grammar school or I was in the hospital. My body was leaving no doubt the answer was door number two. Felt as if I were lying on a bed of nails. As if every square inch of me had a separate pain. Worst part was my chest. Felt like you could char a steak on it. Another moan. And then it was back to the bottom of the ocean.

Little face. Big glasses. Saying my name. Over and over. Holding a blue plastic cup up by my lips. "Mr. Waterman. Mr. Waterman." I tried to lift my arm, guide the straw into my mouth. No go. Couldn't get my hand up off the sheet.

Tried to move my legs. The pain tore a howl from my throat. Also, no go. My legs felt as if they were encased in concrete. For about ten seconds, I was sure I was a paraplegic. The thought of being paralyzed flooded me with a level of grief I'd never experienced before. When I began to sob, the unknown hand pulled the cup away from my face. As I moved my eyes toward the side of the bed, it felt like somebody was pounding nails into my skull.

My hand was tied to the bed rail with a thick piece of surgical gauze. A jungle of tubes and wires sprouted from the back of my hand like plastic swamp grass. I wiggled my index finger. I nearly smiled but thought better of it. Very slowly, I shifted my eyes in the opposite direction. Same thing over there. Except there was a silver tree. Took me a while to figure out that the low-hanging fruit were IV bags. I watched the mystery hand take a syringe and inject something into a valve in one of the bags. My vision began shrinking to a pinpoint, like the end of an old black-and-white movie. Roll the credits. Goodnight, Irene.

■ ■ ■

"Leo. Leo." I knew the voice.

I tried to bench-press my eyelids open. Hurt like holy hell, so I backed off and went for the incremental approach to lid lifting. A couple of minutes and I managed to get my left eye open far enough make out Rebecca standing at the foot of the bed.

I tried to force a greeting but couldn't push the razor blades out of my throat.

"No . . . no . . . don't," she whispered, putting her hand on my forearm.

A nod in her direction nearly knocked me unconscious. I waited for my vision to stop doing that strobe-light thing and tried to say something again, with the same blindingly painful result.

When I opened my eyes again, Rebecca had moved up to my side, and tears were running down her face. I tried to reach out to her, but my medical manacles wouldn't let me. "Stay still, Leo," she sniffled. "Please stay still."

I groaned in frustration. She put her hand on my forehead. I asked her with my eyes if I was going to die. She shook her head.

"It's bad this time, Leo. You've got two semicompressed skull fractures. Six broken ribs. A lacerated kidney. A substantial chunk of your fifth lumbar vertebra is broken off completely. You're having spine surgery tomorrow to fix that . . ." She shrugged. "As best as they're able. They're not promising anything." She paused as if gathering herself and took a couple of breaths. I didn't like that at all. When somebody who looks at dead bodies every day pauses before she gets to the bad part, you know it's pretty much guaranteed to be the shits.

She looked over at the window. I followed her gaze and waited for her to spit it out. It was dark. I was in Swedish Hospital, looking out over the First Hill. I wasn't sure I'd ever seen her this upset before. I must have made some sort of sound. She looked over at me. Her lower lip was quivering. She looked away again. "They ran over your legs," she blurted.

I heard her suck in some air. "And, Leo . . . those sons of bitches . . . they carved something into your chest." She sounded as if she were welded inside a fifty-five-gallon drum somewhere in central Illinois, all tinny and far away. My pulse pounded my skull like artillery fire as I looked down the length of myself. I was a friggin' pup tent. I looked up at her. She read the question in my eyes.

"I haven't seen it, but I'm told it looks like arrows."

That was the last thing I recall before I started pushing the blue button.

▪ ▪ ▪

Turned out, that wasn't the worst news either. That came a few days later in the form of a middle-aged ER surgeon named Dr. Hyman Morse, who stopped by my room right after the day nurses had finished getting me spiffed up, a routine that consisted of cleaning up any unauthorized leaks I may have sprung since their last visit and making sure my IV bags were working. The little blue button they'd hooked me up with to push whenever my pain got too intense didn't do a heck of a lot for my IQ. I kept thinking of things I wanted to ask, but before I could put a sentence together, whoever I wanted to ask had left the room. But it kept the fire at bay, so I was good with it.

Dr. Morse gave me a quick wave as he slipped into the room and introduced himself. He was a medium-size guy with a fluorescent-light pallor, wearing a fresh pair of the green scrubs, hat and all. If his wooly caterpillar eyebrows and forearms were any indication, Dr. Hyman Morse was, quite possibly, completely haired over in the manner of a gibbon. He walked to my side.

"I hear you're making noises," he said.

"A few," I croaked.

"Consider yourself lucky."

I took his word for it.

"How long?" I asked.

He seemed astonished by the question. "How long what?"

"Here," I coughed up.

"How long are you going to be here? In the hospital?"

"Yeah."

He thought about it. "Six . . . seven weeks, I'd guess."

"Noooooo."

He grabbed my chart from the foot of the bed. Put on a pair of half glasses and gave it a full AMA gander.

"Looks like you've got three more surgeries scheduled." He offered a palm to the ceiling. "Just the pre- and post-op will keep you here that long," he said. "Presuming there's no complications of course." Neither his tone nor his facial expression suggested he held out much hope for perfection.

"My legs," I rasped.

He whistled and made a face. "Whoever did this to you was trying to cripple you, Mr. Waterman. Permanently. No doubt about it," he added. "If you weren't such a big galoot, with bones the size of a triceratops, they'd have managed it too."

"But?"

"But . . . miraculously, they didn't break anything when they ran over your legs. Partly because of your unusual bone mass and partly because I think they were going fairly fast when they ran you over."

I swallowed a couple of times. Got my throat loosened up. I managed to dredge up enough spit to say, "On my feet again?"

Okay . . . it wasn't really a question, but he got the idea. I could tell from his frown that, like most doctors, he wasn't anxious to speculate.

"How long?" I asked again.

He decided to humor me. "Six months maybe. Something like that. Maybe a little longer. Assuming everything conforms to protocol and the creeks don't rise."

He rubbed his hands together. "So . . . I'm glad to see how you're coming along," he segued. "I had my doubts there for a while."

"Me too."

"There's a cast of thousands waiting to see you," he said. "Dr. Duvall. A guy I've seen a bunch of times before, so he's probably a cop. Another fellow in a wheelchair . . . and a"—he made a motion with his hand—"you know, the dreadlocks."

I couldn't work up sufficient moisture to spit out *Rastafarian*, so I settled for, "Charity . . . wheelchair's caregiver."

He gave me a two-fingered salute and a wink. "I was you . . . I'd stay out of alleys for a while."

He pulled open the door and disappeared into the hall.

▪ ▪ ▪

Turned out Dr. Hyman Morse was an optimist. Ten weeks after they'd brought me in, I was still on the premises. And the bottom half of me was still totally immobile. My legs looked like giant purple eggplants, but the swelling had abated considerably. My torso was Velcroed into some sort of plastic body cast, so I still hadn't seen what my chest looked like, and where they'd fixed my back felt as if somebody'd driven a railroad spike into my spine. But I could sit up as long as somebody put me there, and I could use my arms and hands—which, all things considered, was progress, or so everybody told me anyway. As for me, I'll admit I had my doubts about coming all the way back from this one. Two and a half months of being manhandled by nurses and orderlies had made a serious dent in my rugged Northwest individualism.

Hospitals thrive on routine. Mostly, the same things happen at the same times every day, so when three nurses showed up an hour and a half early and changed my dressings, unhooked me from all the electronic monitors, and then got two orderlies to help strap me to a gurney, I knew for sure something was up.

Five minutes later, Rebecca came into my room, trailed by Joey Ortega and a pair of his urban gorillas. They had scrubs on, but I knew the smaller one from when I occasionally went to Joey's place. He was always holding down the elevator that went directly up to Joey's office. His name was Marty something. The other guy needed a bigger pair of scrubs. He looked like a sausage packed into a giant blue casing.

Joey and I were childhood friends. His father, Frankie, had been my father's chief leg breaker and bagman for twenty years. Joey and I had spent endless hours playing together in the backyard while Frankie and my old man were inside working out new ways to feather their nests at the taxpayers' expense. We'd double-dated as teenagers. Played on the same Legion baseball team. All that kind of stuff. Unlike me, however, Joey had followed his father into the business. Chip off the ol' block and all of that rot.

In the years since his father had passed away, Joey had parlayed three strip joints and a couple of sleazy massage parlors into a quasi-legal entertainment empire stretching from Tacoma in the south to Bellingham in the north. You wanted a rub and a tug, some of the forty bucks ended up in Joey's pocket. Feeling frisky, lookin' for a little poke in the whiskers . . . more money in Joey's pocket. Wanna gamble? He was a silent partner in a dozen card rooms. Yeah . . . if you were lookin' for a little something you couldn't get at home, Joey was your man. All of it under the banner of Entertainment Associates. Truth in advertising at its finest.

Rebecca gave me a quick kiss on the forehead and then used her toe to unlock the wheels of my IV tree. Joey had always made Rebecca nervous. Whenever he was around, she generally made it a point not to be, which I could understand. She was a county employee and an officer of the court, and Joey wasn't exactly somebody you'd want found on your speed dial in the event of your demise. Seeing them together was a bit like seeing Nancy Reagan and Charles Manson having tea together in the Rose Garden. I wondered why the sudden spate of détente.

"What's up?" I asked.

"Takin' a little trip," Joey said from behind me.

"Where to?" I tried.

"You ready?" Rebecca asked.

Marty and his buddy each took one end of the gurney. Joey took charge of the IV stand. Rebecca got the door. They wheeled me down the hall to the elevators, all the way down to the parking garage, where an unmarked ambulance was waiting. The Bruise Brothers opened the back of the van, hoisted me up, rolled me inside feetfirst, and tied me down. The minute I saw the back of the driver's head, I was sure of two things: First, I knew who it was. Second, it meant, somehow or other, things had gotten serious. I opened my mouth right as Joey climbed into the ambulance with me. He folded one of the jump seats down and took a load off.

He'd gained a little weight since the last time I'd seen him but still had a full head of slicked-back hair so thick you couldn't have pulled a hay rake through it.

"How ya doin', big fella?" he asked.

"Middlin'," I said.

"So I hear." He leaned in close. "You got any idea who the assholes were?"

"Never seen either of them before."

"You musta really got under somebody's skin . . . which as we both know—"

"Yeah . . . I do have a knack for it," I interrupted. "But I'm telling you, not this time . . . Okay, I'm following somebody, and they make me. So what? That's grounds for beating the shit out of me and leaving me for dead in an alley?"

"Not unless they got something else entirely goin' on."

He made a face that looked like I'd run a turd under his nose. "I broke all precedent and had a word with your cop friend Eagen," he said. "The plates from the Rover came off a half-ton pickup from

Yakima. A car that according to DMV records was scrapped late last year."

"Yeah," I said. "I figured if Eagen had come up with anything useful, he'd have let me know by now."

"Cops found the Range Rover. Up by Paine Field someplace. Stolen from down in Burien. Wiped clean."

"I got sloppy," I said. "Early onset arrogance," I joked.

"Happens. But that don't give anybody call to be running over a guy's legs."

I told him everything I knew, about Matthew and Art and Martha, and her telling me that people were following her, and how I'd assumed it was the antigun crowd and nothing to worry about. About the funeral. About all of it.

Joey frowned. "You talkin' about the kid who aced that commie city councilman up north?"

"That's the one," I said.

Behind him, the ambulance rocked. A second later Gabe Funicello walked around the back bumper. I craned my neck.

"Can't leave your big ass alone for a minute, can I?" Gabe said with a grin.

Gabe and I had managed to keep one another from being killed back when Rebecca got suspended from her job. In the process, we'd formed a bond I'm not sure I have the words to describe. Gabe was what the medical community calls *genetically ambiguous*, meaning that no matter how one parsed the X and Y chromosomes, there was no definitive answer as to Gabe's gender. But, you know, when somebody saves your ass a couple of times, exactly what they've got for plumbing parts ceases to matter much. What I was sure of was that if I had to face the hordes from hell, there's nobody I'd rather have at my back than Gabriella Funicello. Nobody.

Joey patted my arm and climbed out of the ambulance. Gabe climbed back in the driver's seat.

I twisted Joey's way. "So what's all the cloak-and-dagger stuff?" I asked.

Joey shrugged. "Your house," he said. "People came over the wall. Couple of days after they found you. Set off the security system both times."

"Slow learners," Gabe said from the front seat.

Joey leaned toward me. "Your girlfriend was the security company's emergency number. They couldn't get hold of you, so they called her. She called Gabe." Joey made his dubious face. "You climb over an eight-foot stone wall, with all those signs and the gate and lights and the fucking motion sensors, you either got a real good reason, or you ain't the brightest bulb in the box."

"Burglars?" I tried.

Joey shook his head and made his *don't be stupid* face. "Girlie's got the pictures on her computer. See what you think. Second-story men don't generally show up with assault rifles."

"No shit."

"Only thing I can figure is they were looking for you and got scared off when the security lights lit the place up." He shook his mane in disbelief. "Fucking twice," he said. "Don't make no sense."

Gabe piped up again. "And the second time it don't look like the same two bozos neither. Only thing the same are the heaters. Full autos."

"You know . . . if you was up and around," Joey began, "I'd figure you could take care of yourself, but what with you being down for a bit, and since we're more or less running blind here . . . might be best if you got back on your feet someplace else."

I was still pushing that one around my circuits when Rebecca climbed up and strapped herself into the jump seat on my right. Her face was tight. The muscles along her jawline rippled like snakes.

"You're officially signed out," she announced.

"You're my doctor now?"

"One of the perks of a medical degree," she said with a thin smile.

"Does that mean I'm dead?"

"Probably soon," she answered, without a hint of levity.

"And nobody's gonna tell me where we're going?"

"You know what the Hells Angels say?" Joey said from behind me.

I didn't figure he needed a prompt, so I kept my mouth shut.

"Three people can keep a secret, as long as two of 'em are dead," he finished.

■ ■ ■

We were on the freeway heading south. Rebecca had rolled the top half of the gurney up and stuffed a couple of pillows behind me so I could see between the two front seats, and was sitting next to me monkeying around with her laptop. I had my hand resting on her knee. She was pretending it wasn't there.

About the time we started up the Southcenter hill, she turned the laptop in my direction. "This is from your home security cameras. Their first attempt," she said.

Northwest corner of my yard. The darkest corner of the property. First one guy climbs on top of the wall. Looks like he's getting a push from below. Outside guy hands him something. Twice. First guy helps second up onto the top of the wall. Guy two climbs down into the yard. First guy hands something down to him and then something else. First guy climbs down too. They get three steps across the grass, when they trip one of the motion sensors and the place lights up like Safeco Field.

Rebecca stopped the tape. Camo coveralls visible in the stark black and white. Ski masks. Each with an assault rifle hanging around his neck, like SWAT team macho men. The lights paralyze them for a few seconds; then one of them says something to the other, and they sprint back to the wall, where one boosts the other up to the top. They pass the weapons up, pull the second guy to the top of the wall, and disappear back out into the neighborhood.

"Go back to the beginning, when the first guy climbs over," I said. "Can you make it slo-mo?"

First one hand appeared on top of the wall. Then another. "Stop," I said.

I pointed at the screen. "Look at the other hand."

She leaned in close. "He's got a glove on one hand," she said.

"Why would somebody wear a glove on one hand?" I asked.

"Michael Jackson impression," Gabe threw in.

"Maybe he was trying not to leave prints," Rebecca suggested. "Or maybe he had some reason to take the other glove off."

"Maybe," I said.

Gabe was right about the second pair too. Different guys. They'd tried to climb over the gate instead of the wall and set the system off in about two seconds. Both of them were noticeably shorter and stouter than the first pair, which probably explains why they chose the gate. Same guns, though. Got a real good look at them during the gate incursion, when one of them laid the weapons on the driveway as he helped his buddy over.

"Joey called your security company. They're going to be checking your place twice a day . . . armed security . . . on foot."

"Thanks," I said to Rebecca. "For everything."

If I was hoping for a tender moment, I was ripe for disappointment.

"Nancy called," she said.

Took me a bit to process. "Oh yeah . . . the lawsuit." Amazing how your brain automatically prioritizes things when the shit hits the fan. I had a pair of lying skunks suing me for three million bucks, and I hadn't thought about it once.

"What's up with that?"

She almost smiled. "We should have known," she said, shaking her head. "The world is a selfie. Five different demonstrators filmed the scene on their phones from five different angles, all of which, according to Nancy, show that you never laid a glove on either of them . . .

with the possible exception of when you spiked the wife over your shoulder . . ." She waggled a hand. "But to make a long story short, Nancy has everybody's footage in hand. She had a powwow with the complainants' lawyers, and they've withdrawn their suit."

"See? The righteous shall prevail."

"She wants to know if you want to countersue for damages. She says it's a slam dunk. You can get them to pay your end of the costs." She held up a finger. "But I gotta tell you, they had a sixteen-year-old son shot and killed on his way home from the junior prom in Chehalis last spring. That's what got them into the movement. So . . . if I were you . . ."

"Yeah," I said. "I've had about all I can stand of being the big bad wolf. I'm thinkin' I just wanna let this one go."

She didn't say anything. Went back to fiddling with her laptop instead. I kept picking up Gabe's eyes flicking back and forth between the road ahead and the rearview mirror. Wondered what was so damned interesting back there but couldn't twist around far enough to see for myself.

"We got company?" I asked.

"Just Marty and Ken," Gabe said. "They're driving two cars down so's they can leave us one to use and they can bring the ambulance back to the city."

"Down where?" I tried again.

"Hoquiam."

"Jeanette's place."

Jeanette had been Joey's half sister. Different mothers, same father. Ten years older than Joey and a drama queen of monumental proportions. I'm a kind of an under-the-radar guy, so suffice it to say, we never got along very well. Or at all, maybe. Ten years ago, just to get her crabby ass out of town, Joey had bought her an oceanfront home over on a desolate stretch of the Washington coast. I'd heard she'd died a while back. Some sort of cancer.

"Joey just had it all fixed up so he could sell it," Gabe said. "Had people come in and stage it too. And then this shit storm came up. Seemed like a natural."

Somewhere between Olympia and Elma I fell asleep.

■ ■ ■

As promised, Marty and his buddy arrived in time to lift me out of the ambulance and roll me inside. They did a quick sweep of the house and grounds, and then Marty jumped into one of the white GMC Yukons they'd driven down, the other guy took over the ambulance, and, within about twenty minutes, they were gone.

We moved into the big bedroom on the ground floor. Gabe and I both would have preferred for Rebecca and me to be upstairs, but there wasn't any feasible way to get me up there short of a block and tackle, so we set things up the other way.

They'd leased a hospital bed from some medical supply place in Aberdeen. I was fiddling with the controls, sitting myself up so I could see, when Gabe came back into the room with a shotgun and a small black semiautomatic.

Gabe put the handgun and a box of ammo on the sheet next to me, leaned the shotgun between the bed and the wall, then looked over at me and grinned. "Mossberg 500 Home Defense Pump Action Shotgun, 12-gauge, eighteen-and-a-half-inch barrel. Five rounds. Synthetic short stock. Matte black finish. Bead sight."

"I've got one just like that," I said.

"Then you know it's big, serious water buffalo shot. Got five in it. Safety's on. All you gotta do is get close. Whatever you hit ain't coming back."

I looked down at the handgun lying next to me.

"Looks a lot like my little Smith & Wesson too."

"Amazing how these things work out."

I didn't bother to ask how they'd gotten into my gun safe. Didn't imagine I'd like the answer a bit.

The first two weeks, Rebecca was there full-time. Whatever it was we weren't saying to one another hung over us like a shroud. This wasn't her kind of thing at all. She was strictly a straight-ahead, by-the-book kind of person. Things like hiding out in the hinterlands were foreign to her sense of propriety and order.

Since Gabe had no intention of leaving me at the house alone, Rebecca had to do the legwork. Locating a drugstore. Finding the nearest hospital—just in case. She was that way. Finding a supermarket in town. Doing serious shopping. Enough stuff to keep us going until she could get back down here again. Filled up the Yukon from floor to ceiling. Maybe thirty or forty bags of food and drink.

Next night, she changed the dressing on my chest, and I got my first look at the artwork. She got all the tape loose and looked me hard in the eye. Her serious face.

"I want you to understand something, Leo." She sucked in some air. "Whoever did this . . . they didn't just cut you . . . They carved something in you the way you'd carve something in the bark of a tree."

She paused, making sure I got what she was telling me. "They took out some of the flesh."

"Feels like they skinned me," I said, trying to lighten things up.

"I had Harry Townes look at it while you were still out of it." Harry was a plastic surgeon friend of hers from med school. "He said your surgeons did a good job but that you're more or less going to have to live with the scar. It's going to fade over time, but short of a couple of years of skin grafts, that scar is going to be with you"—she hesitated—"mostly forever."

The curtain went up. I was peering down at my chest in disbelief. Four arrows of scab. One pointing up. One pointing down. One left, one right. Sonovabitch had carved Vs in me. I nearly burst into tears.

Then I felt like maybe I was gonna puke. I've been shot. Beaten up more times than I can count. Left for dead. But this . . . this affected me in a way I'd never experienced before. I felt like a defiled synagogue or something. Like somebody had violated me in a way I'd never even imagined possible, and I was never going to be the same, no matter what I did. Not ever. I lay back in the bed and closed my eyes while she buttoned me back up. That was the moment. Right there. The back-breaking straw. I didn't know it at the time, but a great deal of what was to follow was a direct result of that moment, when I realized what it was going to take for me to get past this. I yearned for that wonderful blue morphine button.

Lying around in bed all day didn't suit me much, so about a week later, Rebecca drove into Aberdeen and came back with a walker and a wheelchair so's I could roll myself around the house and out onto the front porch.

Things went like that until the second Saturday night. Marty was coming down the next day to pick up Rebecca and bring her back to the city. Gabe had retired upstairs to another rollicking night in the middle of nowhere. We were lying down, but not together, as our beds were at opposite ends of the room. Felt like I was living in a convent or something. I was ruminating on the infamy of the situation when Rebecca finally managed to spit out the pit she'd been rolling around her mouth for the past couple of weeks.

"This is the last time, Leo."

My first instinct was to stall, ask for a clarification, do the old *Whatever do you mean?* routine, but I managed to regain my senses and stifle it.

"I didn't go looking for this one," I said.

"You have a knack for finding trouble whether you're looking for it or not."

Couldn't argue with that, so I didn't bother. Good thing too. Even from the other side of the room I could feel her anger, crackling like unseen lightning on a muggy summer evening.

"This isn't how I want to live my life," she said. "I assumed—silly me—that when you came into your dad's money . . . I just assumed that would be the end of this sort of thing. Now . . ."

She stopped herself. All I could think of was more excuses, so I clammed up.

"Didn't mean to put you through this," I said finally.

"I know," she said, and then rolled over and faced the wall.

■ ■ ■

I was sitting on the front porch in my wheelchair, watching Marty and Rebecca drive off into the sunrise, and feeling about as conflicted as I ever have. Much as I loved and admired the woman, it was a relief to be out from under a constant cloud of recrimination. On one hand I felt bad about feeling that way, on the other I felt like an upright freezer had been lifted from my shoulders. I'm not good with ambiguity.

Fortunately, Gabe didn't give me much time to think about it. About the time Marty and Rebecca drove out of sight and the dust settled back onto the swamp grass, Gabe walked out onto the porch, set the brakes on my chair, kicked up the footrests, and extended a big, rough-looking pair of hands in my direction.

"I don't know," I said. "Not sure I can stand on them."

"Let's find out."

I took the hands, wrapping my fingers around the thick wrists. Gabe started to pull. I pulled back and began to stand. Hurt like hell. My legs felt like a giant bruise as more of my weight began to press down on them. In the second before I was upright, I thought I was gonna lose it, but Gabe muscled me out of the seat like a handful of popcorn.

"Oooooooooh," escaped from my mouth as I stood there, on my own two feet for the first time in months, wavering in the morning breeze like a dried-out cattail.

Gabe let my hands go and checked the time. "Let's see how long you can stand there."

It was seven minutes before my legs were shaking like a polio victim's. I gritted my teeth and hung in there for another minute or so before plopping back down into the chair, covered with an oily sheen of sweat.

"Not bad," Gabe said. "A little longer every day."

"Nice to have something to look forward to," I huffed out.

▪ ▪ ▪

I was sitting out on the front porch catching some rays and researching signs and symbols, trying to find an exact match for the divots on my chest. I'd found any number of similar arrow-based signs, but I was beginning to wonder if maybe the guy hadn't just carved something at random. Frustrated, I pushed the button and snapped the iPad shut.

Later that afternoon, Rebecca called to say she was buried at work and wasn't going to make it down that week. I sympathized robustly but was secretly grateful. Gabe and I had a good routine going. I was feeling better than I'd felt in a long time. Not only was I now able to stand for long periods of time, but I'd graduated to the walker, which I could shuffle along behind as soon as we rolled up all the throw rugs. Problem wasn't my legs. They were getting livelier by the day. It was my back, where they'd given me a bone graft on my spine. About as sore as sore could be. Every step, even with the walker, felt like I was gonna dissolve into a puddle on the floor.

But we kept at it. Gabe kept me moving every day while I used the downtime to burn up the Internet looking for a match to those arrows. Couple of months went by. I discovered that a walker doesn't work worth a wet damn on the beach. Rebecca came for another couple of romantic weekends of living alone together . . . except, of course, for the genetically ambiguous gun monkey in the upstairs bedroom and the various and sundry firearms stashed here and there around the house. I think it's safe to say that both of us were grateful by the time Sunday afternoon came around and she took the two-hour drive back to Seattle.

They say time heals all wounds. I don't know about the "all" part, but things surely get better. Slowly . . . but better. I could ride into town now, catch a bite with Gabe at the pizza parlor. Go along on the shopping runs. Hell, I could even be left alone.

I remember the day we drove over to Hoquiam High School and took laps around the track at a brisk pace. We'd been heel-n-toeing it for over an hour when Gabe looked over at me and asked, "You notice?"

"Notice what?"

"You ain't limping anymore."

Oddly, my first urge was to protest, but I had a sudden spasm of lucidity and swallowed it. Gabe was right. I was as close to being my former self as I was going to get. But . . . something was missing. I could feel a cold uncertainty hovering at my center that I'd never felt before.

Gabe found a gun range over on the far side of Aberdeen. We went several times a week for several months. Killin' time, you know. Gabe was deadeye Dick. Never missed by more than a couple of inches. I'd always been mediocre at best when it came to marksmanship. Always made it a point to be armed with something where you only had to come close, like a shotgun or something on full auto, where I could spray it like a garden hose. Like anything else, though, practice makes perfect. By the time we'd blown off a thousand bucks' worth of ammo, I was better than I'd ever been in my life.

We hadn't seen Rebecca in nearly a month. She and I talked on the phone a few times a week, but lately it had taken on the air of an obligation rather than a conversation. I could feel both of us waiting for this phase of our lives to be over and neither of us being at all sure what came next.

Gabe went back to Seattle every couple of weeks for a day or two. Marty drove down and took over babysitting until Gabe got back.

Around the middle of May, spring washed over the Hoquiam River valley, and almost before I'd gotten used to the idea, summer showed up. Steam rising from the marshes with the morning sun. Wedges of waterfowl, veering in, veering out of tidal bays. The herd of deer that came down to the estuary every evening at dusk. After a while, seemed like Gabe and me tromping around the Hoquiam's tidal flats blended into the natural rhythm of nature.

Funny thing, though. While my body was telling me that I was ready to rumble, my mind didn't seem to be quite ready for the bell to ring. It felt like I was standing outside a door and couldn't muster up the courage to push the bell. I was telling myself that part of me loved the quiet simplicity of my present life, which had a nice bucolic ring to it . . . except that I knew better. And to make matters worse, Gabe thought I was ready to go too. I could tell. For the past several weeks I'd sensed a bit of impatience where there had been none before, but Gabe wanted me to make the decision on my own, which is how I'd have played it were our roles reversed.

On the sixteenth of July, the universe made the decision for me. Gabe and I were hopping our way through a marsh, jumping from tuft to tuft, trying to keep from falling down into the deep black tidal mud, when Gabe took a misstep and went down hard, with the left leg wedged between a couple of tufts of swamp grass. I heard the ankle go. Sounded like somebody'd snapped a dry stick.

Took me the better part of an hour to get Gabe and myself back to the road. By the time I'd hauled Gabe's big ass up onto the road grade, my back was threatening to go into lockdown, and I was shakin' like a hound dog passing a peach pit. I caught my breath, walked back to the house and got the car, and then drove Gabe over to Grays Harbor

Community Hospital, where my diagnosis was confirmed by prominent medical authorities. Broken ankle. Sure as hell.

I was sitting outside the ER while the folks inside put Gabe back together, when for the second time in a single day, fate reached out and slapped me in the head. Weird thing was, after all the hours I'd put in trying to identify the symbol on my chest, when I found it, I wasn't even looking. I was reading the Google news when I saw a picture of some sort of riot somewhere in the Midwest. Two groups of demonstrators going at it. I clicked the photo twice. It got bigger. And there it was.

On a white paper placard one of them was waving. Four arrows. Just like the ones I was carrying around. The guy next to him carried a sign that said **White Power.** Seemed like all the signs on that side had something to do with race.

The loyal opposition was all peace, love, and inclusion signs. Funny, though, how the hate in their faces looked so similar to one another.

I typed "white power symbols" into the iPad's browser, scanned the headings until I saw one that looked promising, and opened it up.

Halfway down the page, I found what I'd been looking for. I was still sitting there openmouthed and drooling when Gabe came hobbling out of the ER.

"What?" was the first thing Gabe said after getting a look at my face.

I turned the iPad in Gabe's direction.

Gabe leaned on the crutches and squinted down at the screen.

"Well . . . well."

"It's called a Crosstar. White power groups use it in place of a swastika."

Gabe nodded. "Swastika will get you just the kind of attention you ain't lookin' for."

Gabe looked me over again, adjusted the crutches, and said, "Let's gather up the sheep and get the flock out of here."

Fifteen minutes later, we were in a booth at the 8th Street Ale House having lunch. I was about a third of the way through my steak sandwich when Gabe swallowed another section of a club sandwich whole, dusted a pair of greasy lips with a napkin, and looked my way. "So whatcha think?" Gabe asked.

Once again, my first instinct was to make like I didn't know what Gabe was talking about. Except that would have been the old *he knew that they knew, that he knew that they knew that he knew* . . . or something like that.

"We seem to have swapped roles," I said. "Must be time to go."

"Your body's good to go." Gabe waggled a handful of club sandwich. "The head I'm not so sure of."

"Me neither," I admitted.

"Don't bullshit me. You're gonna go lookin' for trouble," Gabe said.

Instinctively, I covered my chest with my free hand. "They took something from me. Something I need to get back."

"And you're gonna either get it back or die trying."

"I can't just let it go."

"I know." Chomp. A shard of tomato fell onto the table. Gabe picked it up and swallowed it. "What about Rebecca? You gonna tell her?"

"I won't have to," I said. "She'll know."

■ ■ ■

Usually I like to be right. Always seemed a lot more fun than being wrong to me, but this was the exception. That evening, I called Joey, told him we were on our way back, got the name of the realty office where we could return the keys and so forth.

Then I spent a useless hour trying to dream up a plausible excuse for not calling Rebecca—for just showing up on her doorstep unannounced. When I couldn't come up with a believable scenario, I took a deep breath and made the call.

I tried to tell her everything was under control, that we'd pack up in the morning and drive back to Seattle, but she wasn't having any of it. No . . . she was on the way. Gonna help us gather anything up and then get me settled back into my house. God knows I tried to tell her we had it handled, that Gabe could still drive, and any other damn thing I could think of, but no . . . she was on the way.

And I got it. Things hadn't been good with us lately. We were more like wary strangers than longtime lovers. Seemed like this might be just the thing we needed to put this episode behind us, and she wanted to milk it for all it was worth. A symbolic reconciliation. I got it.

She pulled up to the house at about quarter to ten. One of those nights when it seemed as if there were way more stars than there used to be. Gabe had already crutched it upstairs for the night. I walked out and met her on the porch. Took her bag from her with one hand and hugged her with the other.

She put her hands on her hips and took me in.

"Look at you," she said.

"The Paul Bunyan of the Pampas," I joked.

"How much weight have you lost?"

"Seventy-three pounds," I said.

She shook her head and smiled. "You don't look even remotely like yourself," she said with amazement. "With the long hair and the bushy beard, I wouldn't know you if I passed you on the street. Honest to God. I'd walk right by."

"The paleo-hipster look."

"Have no fear, there's a Great Cuts in Aberdeen. Not only that, but your maid service went through the house just a couple of days ago, so everything's spiffy and waiting for you." She gave me a big hug. I returned the favor.

We'd reached one of those moments in life when every fiber of your being wants to lie, to postpone, to equivocate—anything except to say what you've got to say, because that seems suicidal. Except I was old enough to know better. I knew that none of that petty shit was going to make the situation better and that coming clean was never going to be less painful than right at that moment.

"Think I'll leave the hair on for a while. I've gotten sort of used to it," I said.

"You'll be the talk of the neighborhood," she said as she let me go and walked into the living room.

"I'm not going home right away," I said to her back, trying to sound like I was talking about the weather. "Got a few things I need to take care of first."

She stopped in her tracks and slowly pirouetted. I didn't have to say more.

"You can't be serious," she said.

"You know what Art Fowler said to me?" I asked.

"No, and I don't give a damn. This isn't about Art Fowler. It's about you. It's about me . . . or us . . . assuming there's still such a thing."

"He said he had to know . . . And you know, at the time, I thought it was a dumb-ass question." I pulled up my Mariners T-shirt. "Look at me. I look like a fucking road sign. There's little strings of my flesh lying around on the ground someplace . . . presuming the rats haven't eaten them by now." I waved an angry hand and tried to keep from raising my voice. "They took something from me, and I'm never gonna be whole again unless I go get it back. And I'm gonna. Come hell or high water."

I had more material, but that was as far as I got. Rebecca snatched her suitcase from my hand and stormed out the door. I stood on the living room floor and listened to her roar off. Sounded like she hit the main road in a full power slide. Out at the end of the driveway, a startled blue heron rose from the tide flats, flapping its massive wings in indignation and splitting the night with its fractured cry.

■ ■ ■

Right away, I had two problems. First, Gabe had heard me making a bunch of phone calls the following morning and had a pretty good idea what I was putting together. True to form, Gabe refused to be left out. Said there was no way, broken ankle or not, I was going to fly solo on this. Gabe made a call to Joey and told him it'd be a while. Joey was good with it. Period. End o' story. Secondly, I couldn't go home. Couldn't let anybody see me in my present configuration. The whole plan depended on my new look, so I couldn't take any chances of my cover being blown. So I went to Carl's.

It was after three in afternoon when I pulled around the back of Carl's house on Crown Hill. Twenty years ago, Carl Cradduck had been America's most heralded battlefield photographer. You could find him in *Time*, *Newsweek*, *Life*, and every other big-time photo rag of the era. He walked through a couple of wars without a scratch and was at the top of the charts when a chunk of Bosnian artillery shrapnel severed his spine in the fall of 1993.

Paralyzed from the waist down and forced to reinvent himself, Carl had taken his photographic expertise and turned it into a highly successful surveillance business. For the better part of two decades he and his hired hands did all of my peeper work for me. Your lawyer needed a glossy of the hubby humping Flossie, Carl was your boy.

That only lasted until no-fault divorce reared its ugly head, a supposed cultural refinement which damn near put us both out of business. Carl refused to work industrial espionage, and so when marriage dissolution lost all commercial luster, he moved into the information business. Cradduck Data Retrieval specialized in skip tracing: finding felons, freeloaders, and deadbeat dads. He was the Duke of the Database. If he couldn't find it, it wasn't there. All pretty much on the up-and-up.

Except when it came to the kind of records that were legally confidential. When that happened, Carl knew people who knew people. His Jamaican caregiver, Charity, always had a cousin who had a cousin who could get you what you needed. For a price, of course. Over the years, I guesstimated I'd probably bought him several new cars.

We were the last to arrive. Charity was stirring a pot on the stove when I opened the kitchen door and then stepped aside to let Gabe crutch by.

I leaned over and sniffed the pot. My nose began to run.

"Curried goat," Charity said with a malicious grin. He looked me up and down. "Don't hardly know you, mon."

Charity and Gabe shared as much of a hug as anybody with one leg could manage. Charity looked at me over Gabe's shoulder. "Who this guy?" he asked Gabe.

"Swamp thing," Gabe joked.

"I'm reinventing myself," I said.

I gave Charity a pat on the back and followed Gabe out into the main room, which most sane human beings would use as a front parlor—you know, where you take guests to sit down—but which Carl had outfitted with wall-to-wall computer monitors and various electronic crap, most of which I couldn't tell you the purpose of. The room smelled like nobody'd opened a window in twelve years.

They'd called out the taxi squad for this one. Carl was rolling around the room at warp speed. Tim Eagen was helping Gabe into an old morris chair. An SPD lieutenant and a professional pistolero. Strange bedfellows indeed.

Across the room from me, sitting on the sagging sofa, Charity's cousin Maxie was drinking a Red Stripe beer and gnawing away at a big blue can of salted nuts. A few years back, a couple of dirtbags had tried to cave Carl's head in. Ever since, at least one of the Jamaicans was with him 24/7. Mostly more than one.

And George was there, and Harold and Ralph. When my old man keeled over on University Street, the stones of his empire almost immediately began to tumble. Within forty-eight hours, the sky had opened, and it had begun to rain grand jury indictments. Of those closest to my father, George Paris, Harold Green, and Ralph Batista were the sole survivors. Many never made it out of prison; others couldn't cope and took the easy way out. All the others had died of old age by now.

George had been in charge of laundering my old man's money. At the time of my old man's untimely demise, George was a prominent member of the local banking community, with a society page wife, a couple of preppy kids, and a four-bedroom condo on Maui.

When the excrement hit the cooling device, George was canned by the bank, divorced by his wife, and then almost immediately convicted of misappropriation of public funds. He served eighteen months in the county lockup before being blown back onto the streets like airborne litter. He'd been at large on the bricks ever since.

Ralph Batista had been my father's Port of Seattle connection. If you believed the cops, Ralph had been in charge of falsifying the paperwork so's hundreds and hundreds of illegal Chinese could be smuggled into Seattle. The cops had kept at him for a week but couldn't put together a case, so they'd let him go. The bad news was that, while they were grilling Ralphie like a cheeseburger, fourteen Chinese nationals were locked in a shipping container on Pier 23, in ninety-five-degree temperatures. Six of them died of dehydration.

Ralph was broken by it. As far as he was concerned, those six lives were on him. And thus began one of the great drinking binges in the history of Western civilization, wherein Ralph had reduced himself to a shambling, bewildered husk of his former self. If George weren't looking out for him, he'd surely have long since been dead.

Harold Green's only sin was being my father's *sign on the dotted line* guy. Unfortunately for Harold, he'd signed on way too many lines, unwittingly making himself de facto CEO of several offshore shell corporations my father had used to hide his dough, a misstep that cost Harold the better part of three years in the lockup and whatever self-respect he may have still been in possession of at the time.

Over the years, I've often wondered where life would have led them if they hadn't been caught up by my old man's machine. Probably wouldn't have included being hammered before ten every morning, which likely explained why, after all these years, I still made it a point to keep an eye on them, to make sure they had at least a little of what they needed. Generational guilt and all that.

By the time I'd reconnected with everybody in the room, Charity had dished out the curried goat into mismatched bowls and found some old silverware, and we'd all made our way to the table.

Over the past several years, I'd gotten used to Charity's cooking. Particularly the curried goat, which was a big favorite around here, so as we settled in to chow down, my focus was on those poor bastards who'd never experienced Charity's brand of Caribbean cuisine. 'Cause I'm tellin' you . . . this shit would light you up.

What was interesting to me was how spicy food brought out the macho moron in people. How nobody wanted to be the wuss who let on that the curried goat was firing up his oral cavity like napalm. Five minutes into the meal, Eagen, George, Harold, Ralph, and Gabe were sweating like draft horses and looking for refills on the iced tea.

I helped Charity load the dishwasher and then walked back to my seat and settled in. Everybody was gawking at me. Ball in my court.

I looked over at Tim Eagen.

"So what'd you think?" I asked. "Can we pull it off?"

He waggled a hand. "Maybe," he said. He ran his eyes over to Carl and Charity. "Assuming the reggae twins here can work up the paperwork, which I'm bettin' they can . . . I don't see why not." He threw a hand in my direction. "You look nothing like you used to, man. I wouldn't know you from friggin' Adam," he said.

"Looks like he's eatin' a muskrat," Ralph threw in.

Eagen almost smiled. "And then there's the fact that you've pulled this kind of asshole stunt before . . . and gotten away with it." He sat back in his chair. "I saw your security tape. Ran it by the SWAT commander. They're amateurs, all four of them. No professional training at all." He raised a finger. "And there was two sets of them, two nights apart, so either they're flying people in from the far reaches, or they're from right around here someplace. The kid shot a city councilman up there. They found the Range Rover up at Paine Field."

"You know anybody on the Everett PD?" I asked.

"Sure," he said. "But your paperwork's gotta be genuine, 'cause he's an OCD little prick and is sure as hell gonna check." He threw a glance Carl's way.

"No problem," Carl assured him. "It'll take about a week, but it'll pass muster."

Charity agreed and added a proviso. "It will work until any of the news organizations conduct an internal audit of some kind. We got no way of knowing what kinds systems dey got in place, so we just gonna hab to take our chances dere."

Eagen wasn't finished. "And . . . I ran those pictures of the assault weapons past the tech boys. They're standard MP5/10s. Most popular weapon for SWAT teams everywhere. According to the manufacturer, supposedly stored in a military warehouse in Salem, Oregon."

"Can we check and see if they're still there?"

"Workin' on it," Eagen said. "They're not cooperating."

I leaned over and tapped George on the shoulder. George and Harold straightened up. Ralph was power napping. "I need to know if anybody's asking around, looking for me. You guys know where I hang out. Press some flesh. You know what I'm talking about. I also need somebody to go up to my house once in a while. Look around. I've got the security guys coming around a couple of times a day, but . . . you know the more eyes the merrier." I reached over and handed George some money. "For expenses," I said. He looked away. "We clear?"

Grudgingly, "Yeah."

"You come up with anything, call Carl. He'll take it from there."

"It's not going to take us long to wear out our welcome in a town that small. Way I figure it, we've got, at the outside, maybe a week."

The consensus was that a week was pushing it, and I agreed.

Eagen looked in Gabe's direction. "Cinderella going along for the ride?"

I nodded. A smirk found its way to his lips. "Some crowd," he snickered.

"The army of righteousness," Gabe said.

Tim laughed and said, "Guy in a wheelchair, a couple of razor-toting Jamaicans, a professional gun monkey, an army of God's own drunks, and a guy bent on revenge." He showed his palms to the ceiling.

"What could go wrong?" he asked.

Chapter 2

Last week in July. Steel wool skies. Wipers scraping back and forth across the glass as we splashed into Everett at one o'clock on a Wednesday afternoon. A sudden wind buffeted the car as I turned onto Pacific Avenue and headed west toward the water. At the top of the hill, a digital thermometer announced a blistering fifty-four degrees in the shade, and believe me, baby, it was all shade. Lots of empty stores, skaters, tweakers, shopping cart squeakers.

Apparently hipster heaven hadn't pranced this far north yet, and neither had the money. In Seattle, as long as you didn't mind living in a neighborhood that looked like it had been designed by Fritz Lang, where everything was concreted and conceited, designer this and artisanal that, then you too could join the great techno paradise.

Not so Everett. I could see it right away. Everett was pickup trucks and cut-rate bail bonds, teriyaki, closed-down paper mills, old people in the streets—and oddest of all, we passed several guys dressed like Uncle Sam waving American flags on street corners.

These were the people for whom the economic system no longer functioned, folks who had voted for "something else," because what they did for a living didn't need to be done anymore. The people whose skills and aspirations were no longer a piece of the continent or a part of the main. People whose bedrock had thinned to mud.

Carl, Maxie, and Charity were in front of us in Carl's tricked-out, handicap-accessible van, and me and Gabe were in a rented Lexus RX as we tooled down Pacific. With Carl along for the party, we either had to be on the ground floor or the joint had to have an elevator, so I'd opted for the new downtown Courtyard Marriott.

We did a full drive around, checking out the terrain on all sides, finally rolling down the alley behind the hotel, past the service garages, where the hotel had everything delivered. Looked like there was a door between the two garages.

I'd reserved four suites up on the ninth floor, including the only adjoining rooms in the joint, so's Charity and Maxie could look in on Carl without going out into the hall. Gabe, who'd by that time graduated to a blue plastic walking boot, had the room down at the far end of the hall, across from the emergency stairs.

By the time I'd managed to shower and change my clothes, Carl and Charity had their own encrypted Internet hotspot up and running so we wouldn't have to go through the hotel's website and were setting up a couple of computer monitors.

"Might as well run my new paperwork by the cops and see what happens," I said.

Carl and Maxie both looked insulted. "Yeah, mon, whatever," Maxie said.

I took the elevator downstairs and then let Mrs. Google direct me to the cop shop, a lovely midcentury cinder block in the North Korean Revival style. I gave my name to the desk sergeant. Told him Detective Shirley was expecting me, which was at least partially true, because I'd been there when Eagen had called him yesterday and assured him I could both walk on and pass water simultaneously and mentioned he'd probably be seeing me the next day.

Shirley had an office of his own, which, in the cop business, spelled big-time. I introduced myself. We shook hands over the desk. He was nearly as tall as I was but real skinny. Big, shiny bald head and an air of mistrust that wafted from him like cheap cologne.

"Tim Eagen says you write true-crime books," he said.

"Depends on which critic you ask," I said.

I pushed my driver's license and Associated Press pass across the desk. Detective Sergeant David Shirley sat down and brought them up close to his face and studied them like there was gonna be food involved.

"You mind if I make a copy of these?" he asked after a while.

I said it was no problem and sat there while he crossed the room and punched up a few copies. "You know I can't go into the details with you," he said. "It's still an ongoing investigation, so there's not much I can share at this point."

"Just trying to be courteous," I said. "You start digging holes in another man's backyard, you probably ought to tell him about it first."

"Where you know Tim Eagen from?" he asked on his way back to his desk.

I gave him a cock-and-bull story about how we'd worked together on a case one time, a story I'd worked out with Eagen a couple of days ago. Detective Shirley was one of those cops who took nothing at face value. It happens to cops after they've been lied to several million times. I was betting Eagen was going to get a phone call about two minutes after I left the building.

"Why Everett, Mr. Marks? What is it about the Matthew Hardaway tragedy that attracted you?"

Yeah . . . that was me. Leon Marks, from Grosse Pointe, Michigan. Must have been true, 'cause I had the paperwork to prove it. Longtime AP stringer and true-crime writer. According to my Amazon author page, Matthew Hardaway and the murder he committed would be my fourth true-crime book. I put a picture of my former neighbor's dog, Pocco, in the author photo window. Left all the personal info blank, like about two-thirds of the bozos on Facebook do.

Like I figured, Shirley was all over it like a cheap suit. "I notice there's no author picture on your Amazon page," he said.

"Being recognized don't make for very good investigative technique," I told him.

"No mystery here, Mr. Marks. No whodunit."

"I'm more interested in whydunit," I said.

I could tell he was choosing his words carefully.

"You know, Mr. Marks . . . took a long time for this to scab over. Feelings were pretty raw around here for a long time. And I think it's safe to say, there's any number of people in this town who'd just as soon this whole thing didn't get dredged up all over again. Matthew Hardaway was a very troubled kid. Maybe you ought to just leave it at that."

"But never anything violent before this incident . . ."

"Until we get a look at his medical records, I really can't speak to any of the specifics."

"What's the holdup?"

"His father hired a big-time lawyer. Taking us to the mat on this one. Won't sign off on anything—medical, school, psychiatric—not giving up a darn thing. He's claiming that since it isn't a matter of evidence—you know, there's not going to be a trial or anything—he claims the state has no right to violate his son's privacy."

"You'd think he'd want to get this thing over with, not draw it out."

"He was under a lot of pressure from the media and the gun control nuts. They were all over him day and night for months. Hounded him. I think he may be looking for a little payback."

"Things must have cooled down by now."

"The Snohomish County DA can't put the Hardaway case to rest."

"If everybody wants this case to go away, why would the DA keep it open?"

"There's a hundred-year-old state law that says a case isn't officially closed until the appeal process is completed."

I started to speak, but he cut me off. "If he'd been convicted of the crime and then killed himself in jail, prior to the end of his appeal process, his conviction would have automatically been vacated. That's the law. The Snohomish County DA is currently suing the state attorney general, trying to close the case, claiming exigent circumstances, but the state AG isn't going for it. And as long as Hardaway's father stonewalls us on anything that might be considered exculpatory evidence, this thing is gonna hang over this community like a shroud."

He had a point. In order for something like this to fade to obscurity, people needed to be able to tell themselves they knew why it had happened and thus had a leg up on how it might be prevented in the future. People have to be able to tell themselves it's a one-off, that it's not going to happen to them next time they walk out the door. That's what lets them go on with their lives. It's what keeps people together as a community.

"You got any ideas why Matthew would suddenly do such a thing?" I asked.

He shook his bald head. "That's way above my pay grade," he said.

"You suppose I could see the CC tape from the night of the shooting?"

I watched him swallow a grin. "Long as you get a Freedom of Information Act ruling. That's what they made the *Sound Sentinel* do, and I'm pretty sure that's what they'll require of you too."

I got to my feet. "Thanks for taking the time to see me," I said.

"Good luck, Mr. Marks. You come up with anything earth shattering, you be sure to give me a jingle."

▪ ▪ ▪

Sometimes people tell you something useful when they're trying not to. The *Sound Sentinel* was down in the south end of town on Forty-Third. Unlike the cops, newspapers were in the business of spreading the news around, so within ten minutes of walking in the *Sentinel*'s front door, I was seated at a desk in the far corner of the newsroom watching the CC tape of the city council meeting.

I was on my second time through the footage when a young man sat down next to me. Young and buttoned down. Thirty at the outside. Nice looking. Even features. Hair getting thin up at the crown of his head. Joe College ten years down the line. I stopped the tape and turned in his direction.

"Ben Forrester," he said.

He didn't offer a hand, so I didn't either.

"Leon Marks," I replied.

"Janice says you're a writer—thinking about writing a book about Matthew Hardaway."

"I'm just in the preliminary research stages," I told him.

"I covered the story for the *Sentinel*," he said. His words carried a hint of a whine. Like what he wasn't saying was that the Hardaway story belonged to him, and I was treading on his turf. Not wishing to debate the point, I tacked.

"What's with the guys in the street dressed like Uncle Sam?"

"Vets. Navy."

"Every place got navy vets," I said. "But mostly they aren't hanging out on street corners in the rain, waving Old Glory at passing pickups."

"Lots of tension around here," he said.

I was pretty sure he was going to explain it to me, so I shut up and waited.

"If it weren't for the navy," he began, "this place might have closed up and floated away by now. The navy's just about the only thing keeping the local economy viable since the wood products industry took a nosedive."

"But why all the flag waving?"

"This is a very divided town. Old money, new money, and no money. The old money around here feels like they're being invaded. They sit there in the north end and up on Rucker Hill, and it looks to them like the Huns have showed up." He sighed. "What happened was folks fleeing the Seattle rents started moving up here and gentrifying parts of the north end, which of course drove real estate prices through the roof. Most of the unemployed mill workers couldn't afford their property taxes anymore, so they sold out and left town, leaving a void that got filled up by immigrants. You know . . . the Southeast Asians, the Mexicans. All kinds of people. Ricardo Valenzuela was the point man for the newcomers. Started something called the Social Justice Project. He was calling for a fifteen-dollar minimum wage, like they have down in Seattle. He opened a free medical clinic. A methadone treatment center. Day care facilities. Food banks. Legal aid services for the poor. To make it worse, he told anybody who'd listen he was a socialist, which just drove the locals and the retired military people apeshit. Far as they're concerned, that's the same thing as a communist. You asked most of those guys, they'd tell ya the city ought to give Matthew Hardaway a medal for services rendered."

"You know, I checked the paper when I first started looking into this . . . Seemed like you guys dropped the story after less than a week."

He made a disgusted face. "The *Sentinel*'s a community newspaper. The paper's mission is to keep the residents up to date on things like the downtown sewer project, not to sensationalize once-in-a-lifetime events that make the city look bad." He checked the area. Then checked it again. "That's what I was told by my editor anyway," he said in a low voice.

I looked the place over. "Not many of these small papers left," I said.

"Swallowed whole by the Internet," he said. "I wanted to be a reporter since I was five, and now . . . now it's just another data entry position."

I kept my trap shut. He went on. "Been thinking about going back home," he said out of the blue.

"Where's home?" I asked.

"Indiana," he said. "Bloomington."

"That where you went to school?"

"Hoosier pride," he joked.

Seemed like we were about to have a nostalgia fest, so I motioned toward the screen. "The voice is fuzzy," I said. "What exactly does he say right before he shoots Mr. Valenzuela?"

"He says, 'fucking communist bastards,'" Forrester told me. "Later, when he backs out the doors after the shooting, he screams, 'Get away from me . . . get away from me'—says it several times."

A heavyset young woman with purple hair walked out from the cubicles. "Ben," she said. "You've got a call from the planning commission on line five."

He got to his feet. "The exciting life of the journalist," he said as he headed off.

He stopped and turned back. "If you need anything . . . you know I'd like to . . ."

"I'll keep it in mind," I assured him.

I waited until he disappeared into the maze of space dividers, then wound the tape back and started from the beginning. One of the few advantages of middle age is that your senses, by necessity, get smarter as time passes. Because they've happened before, things that at one time seemed almost miraculous become recognizable moments of potential insight. A little blinking light from deep space that you have to learn to see.

I got to the part where Matthew Hardaway walks into the SRO City Council meeting room, and the guy in the back corner sees the woman get up from the seat and then gestures to Matthew as if to say, "There's a seat for ya," and then Matthew skitters over and sits down as the woman strolls out. And then the gesturing guy strolls out, and then a few seconds later another guy tiptoes out of the room, and then another. Maybe twenty seconds of the tape. Something about it bothered me. I didn't know what it was, but I knew for sure that something about those ten seconds was blinking my cosmic light, so I ran it again, and then again. Still blinking. Sixth go-round was the charm. That's when I figured out which knob to turn so's I could watch it in slo-mo. That's all it took. Make the tape speed even slower than my brain speed.

When you watched it in slo-mo, it looked like a dance routine. Choreographed.

Matthew Hardaway pulls open the door to the council chamber. The guy leaning against the wall says something—doesn't look like he's talking to anybody in particular, but then the woman immediately gets up from the seat as the guy in the corner gestures to Matthew to take the seat, which he does. The woman leaves. The guy in the corner follows her out. Then the guy who originally said something ambles out next. And finally, another guy standing near the seat heads for the door and disappears.

The unmistakable sound of gunshots booms from the hallway. A guy sticks his head through the doorway, and then, just as suddenly, pulls it back and disappears.

The office chair let out a squeak as I leaned back in the seat. I was trying to decide whether I was just overreaching here, or whether something truly was amiss about the CC footage, when Ben Forrester walked out of cubicle city and sat down next to me again. "You know . . . ," he began. "If you need any help . . . you know . . . if you decide you want to do this . . . I could, you know . . . maybe help you fill in some of the blanks."

I thought about it. He was a nice enough kid, and God knew I could use all the help I could get. Especially the kind of insider knowledge he was likely to possess, so I decided to encourage him a bit, see if maybe he couldn't be of use.

"Watch this and tell me what you think," I said, as I wound the tape back to Matthew's entrance. I pointed at the guy leaning against the wall next to the woman's seat.

"Look at this guy," I said, pointing at the screen. "Don't watch Matthew Hardaway. Watch him." Forrester got up from his seat and leaned down close to the screen. I could smell his breath mints.

I pushed the button and ran it for five seconds.

"Wonder what he said," was his reaction.

"Almost had to be something to her," I said, pointing at how the woman was already half out of the seat and the guy back in the corner had already started his gesture toward the seat, which wasn't quite empty yet. Like a troupe of actors hitting their marks.

"Run it again," the kid said.

I did. Same deal. "What's it look like to you?" he asked.

"Look at the guy standing near the soon-to-be empty seat. He's not looking at the city council meeting; he's watching the damn door. The minute Matthew Hardaway comes in, he tells the woman it's time to vacate the seat; the guy in the corner shows the seat to Matthew, who hustles over and takes it."

Forrester pointed at the last guy to leave. "What's he doing?"

"I think he was there in case they needed a blocker. Somebody to make sure it was Matthew who got the seat. Maybe take the seat himself if it proved necessary."

"I've seen the man in the corner but can't remember where from."

"What about the others?"

"They all seem vaguely familiar to me."

We sat in silence. Somewhere in the maze of cubicles, a phone began to ring. Somebody answered. And then another.

"I could introduce you around," Forrester said. "And I've got a pretty good set of notes."

I pointed at the screen again. "What'd you think?" I asked. "Am I making mountains out of molehills?"

He thought it over. "I'm wondering why nobody else noticed," he said. "Makes me a little nervous that a couple of geniuses like us picked up on something a bunch of other professionals missed. You know what I mean?"

I said I did. He went on. "But when you look at the footage that way, when you don't focus on Matthew Hardaway . . . I gotta admit it looks like the whole thing was planned and worked out ahead of time. It really does."

"I need to know who those people are. The woman, the guy in the corner, the guys against the wall. How are we gonna find out who those people are?"

"Ben." Same purple-haired woman. "Ron wants to see us in his office." She rolled her raccoon eyes. "He's überpissed," she stage-whispered, and then flicked her eyes in my direction. "Come on."

I wound the tape back to the beginning and was about to watch it one last time, when Ben came scooting, white-faced, back into the room. "I'm sorry . . . you gotta go. The boss is really pissed Janet let you see the CC footage."

Muffled shouting found its way to my ears. Ben and I made eye contact.

"You better go," he said. "I think he just called security on you."

I pulled a bright-green index card from my wallet that contained the number of the burner phone I was using. "You come up with anything else . . ."

He grabbed the card, stuffed it in his pocket, and then loped off into the maze. I headed for the fire door in the corner of the room so I wouldn't have to walk back through the office and maybe be forced to deal with security. I pushed it open; an alarm began to sound. The bell hammered my ears as I descended the metal fire escape and eased down to the parking lot into—yeah, you guessed it—a driving rainstorm. Above my head, the sky looked like asphalt. The black trees waved back and forth like ghostly dancers.

Naturally, I was on the opposite side of the building from where I'd parked my car. I heaved a sigh and began to splash my way around to the front. The rain picked at my face. My body felt like I'd been threshed and baled. Everything hurt but my teeth as I shuffled across the asphalt in search of the car.

▪ ▪ ▪

"You look like a fuckin' sheepdog," Carl said with a grin. "Your chest is looking better, though," he added. "You can't really see it anymore."

I looked down at myself. He was right. Four surgeries later, the design on my chest was nearly invisible. Hell, they'd even implanted hair onto my chest, adding further camouflage. Where they got the hair from, I'd made it a point not to ask.

Charity and Maxie had already hacked and then subsequently downloaded the CC footage from the *Sound Sentinel*'s digital files. We'd all watched it half a dozen times, to a mixed bag of opinions. Carl didn't think so. Maxie neither. Charity was keeping an open mind. Gabe, however, jumped on board first time through. "You got half a hundred folks standing up at this meeting, and our guy just happens to get the only available seat. An aisle seat?" Gabe pointed at the screen. "An aisle seat right up in front of where they're letting people stand, so's there's nobody to stop him once he starts up the aisle. No fuckin' way. That was a setup."

I was standing in the middle of Carl's room, amid a dazzling array of computer equipment, drying myself off with a couple of bath towels, when somebody knocked on the door. Gabe pulled out the omnipresent chrome automatic and then wandered over and got behind the door. I threw the towels on the bed, slipped a pullover on, and then padded over and opened the door a crack.

It was my new friend Detective Shirley and a trio of uniformed officers looking all tense and official. "Yes?" I said.

"May we come in?" he said.

I kept it simple. "No."

He didn't seem surprised. I heard Gabe slide in next to me.

"Is there a problem?" I asked.

"You realize, don't you, Mr. Marks, that we don't need a warrant to enter these premises," he said. "Only the innkeeper's permission."

I made a show of checking the hallway. "So . . . where's the innkeeper?" I asked.

"He'll be here in a minute."

"Is there some problem?"

"We had a complaint from Ron West over at the *Sound Sentinel*. Says you fraudulently represented yourself to one of his employees."

I shook my head. "I walked in the front door, showed the girl at the desk the same documentation I showed you, asked to see some research material, which she kindly provided me with. End o' story."

"Allowing you to see that material was not within her purview," Shirley said.

"Giving a shit about the *Sentinel*'s chain of command is not within mine."

The muscles along Shirley's jawline tightened.

"Lemme know when management gets here," I said and started to close the door.

One of the uniforms slid forward and stuck his foot into the doorway. I straight-armed him back onto his heels and slammed the door.

I turned back to the room. Nobody was ever going to mistake this motley crew for an accounting firm from Ohio. No doubt about it. They started checking this group for priors, things were gonna go due south in a hurry. They were gonna be all over us like ants at a picnic. I could smell powdered eggs in my future.

"I'm guessing this is the point where we better get out our gun permits," I said. The assembled multitude heaved a group sigh. People who carry guns on a regular basis learn to keep a copy of their carry permit on their person. Generally speaking, telling a cop you have one, but it's not on you, tends to be wasted effort, and generally means you're going to spend at least half a day downtown in Casa Vomit, while they drag their feet long enough to get paid by the state for your incarceration, because the State of Washington reimburses them only if you are in custody for at least six hours. So, no matter what, whether it be mawkish behavior or murder, your ass was gonna be there for the requisite six hours, unless of course you proved to be a major pain in the ass, in which case things could get *Twilight Zone*, time-travel slow.

We were in the process of disarming ourselves and picturing the inside of the Snohomish County jail when a commotion in the hall stopped everybody in their tracks. Everyone held their collective breath and looked at the door. A tentative knock scraped at the door. I set the Smith & Wesson on the coffee table on top of Leon Marks's carry permit and wandered across the room, thinking they were gonna come in and that the game was probably up. Even when all the paperwork turned out to be on the up-and-up, they were gonna impound everything we owned and then take their sweet-ass time giving it back to us, which of course would put the big-time kibosh on any further investigation. We'd just have to pack up our shit and go home.

I swung the door guard into the locked position and opened the door an inch and a half. Young guy in a blue pin-striped suit. Red power tie matched his cheeks. Nice pocket square. The plastic name tag read: Dylan Rhodes. Night Manager.

The cops were milling around the hall like a lynch mob.

The suit swallowed and said, "Mr. Marks . . . sir . . ." He looked back over his shoulder. "I've been on the phone to my district manager," he said.

I waited.

"Ms. Nevarez wants me to assure you that nothing is more important than the comfort and safety of our guests."

"Nice to hear," I said.

"She also instructed me to tell you that since there are no official charges pending against you and because we have had no internal complaints of any kind . . . she said that whether or not these er . . . gentlemen are allowed to enter your rooms is entirely up to you."

"Well then . . . they're not," I said.

The air hummed with adrenaline. I thought for a second the cops were going to bull-rush the door, but Detective Shirley stuck out his arm. He took a deep breath and addressed himself to the kid in the suit.

"You tell your district supervisor that it might be better corporate policy to cooperate with local authorities."

"Yes sir, I will," the kid said.

Shirley tried to melt me with a withering glare, and then, failing that, addressed me directly. "We don't need to be digging up the Hardaway mess all over again, Mr. Marks. Some things are just better off left alone."

With that, he turned and led his entourage down the hall toward the elevators. The cop I'd pushed kept his eyes riveted on me as he tromped along. I kept hoping he'd trip and fall on his face. No such luck.

Soon as the elevator door closed, the kid in the suit spoke up. "Guys think they're gods. Think they can push anybody they want around."

"I'll tell you what, son," I said. "Those guys carry a gun on one hip and the power of the state on the other. Makes 'em dangerous dudes as far as I'm concerned."

He clearly had something stuck in his throat, so I buttoned my lip and gave him a chance to spit it out.

"That Shirley guy . . . ," he muttered. "He doesn't remember me, but I remember him. Back when I was in grammar school and he was just a street cop, he arrested my dad for growing pot plants in the crawl space under our house. They gave him forty months down in Salem. Ruined his life for something that's legal now. Just doesn't seem right to me."

There was a tragedy here. A suicide maybe. I could feel it. Under most other circumstances, I'd have given him a chance to unload the rest of his story, but not tonight.

"Thank Ms. Nevarez for me," I said.

He grinned. "No such animal," he said.

"Well . . . then thank you."

■ ■ ■

Took an hour of ebbing tension before everybody's blood pressure returned to normal, at which point Charity and Maxie went out in search of food and drink, while the rest of us, how shall we say, freshened up.

Forty minutes later the reggae twins showed up with enough barbecue for a company picnic. No bunting, though. Kinda missed the bunting.

"Had cop company all de way," Maxie said. "Right on our ass."

"Your friend Officer Shirley left some cop friends out front," Charity chimed in.

I walked over to the window and pulled back the curtain. Sure enough. An unmarked cruiser was parked diagonally across the street. Not even trying to be sneaky about it. Low-key intimidation at its finest.

"Can't see how we can have them following us around," Gabe commented.

"We been in this town for half a day, and we've already pissed off the local newspaper and the local heat. Ya gotta call that progress," Carl said.

"We do seem to have a gift for contention," I allowed.

"Engines of conflict," Gabe piped in. "Engines of conflict."

Nobody disagreed. And since nobody'd eaten anything since breakfast, we decided the best course of action would be to consume everything in sight and then worry about the cop problem later.

Didn't take long before the five of us were spread about the room, painting our faces with Q sauce, inhaling brisket, ribs, pulled pork, coleslaw, hot links, beans, and cornbread. Sounded like feeding time at the zoo.

Gabe was right too. There was no way we could get anything done with a pair of cops welded to our back bumper, but the hot links were too damn good to think about that sort of tripe just now, so I set about swallowing the known world. Took me about twenty minutes to induce a major food coma.

Carl belched and asked, "Where you want to start tomorrow?"

"Wadda *you* think?"

"The victim's wife, maybe."

"That's what I was thinking too. Ease into things. Get a sense of the swamp."

"After that?" Carl prodded.

"The one I really want to talk to is the kid's shrink . . . what's her name . . ."

"Bradley," Maxie said. "Suzanne Bradley."

"She got an office down by the marina," Charity added.

"That's gonna be like pulling teeth," I said. "Even when the client's dead, shrinks won't discuss the details of somebody's treatment."

Maxie tapped on one of the computer screens. "She's forty-four, single, and not de worst-lookin' woman I ever seen needer." He spun the monitor in my direction. He was right. Tall brunette. Good-looking woman in a green flowered dress, carrying a half-full champagne glass. Picture looked like it was taken at some sort of gala on a beautiful sunny day, assuming they had such things around here, which I was beginning to doubt.

"You just dazzle her with your world-famous charm," Carl sneered. "Bring her to heel. Have her panting on your shoulder like a terrier."

Gabe snickered and used a handful of paper napkins to swab off the Q sauce.

"You think the father would recognize you?" Gabe asked.

"Not looking like this," I said.

"The mother?"

"Yeah. Probably."

"The father's the one I don't get."

"Phil," I said.

"He's the loose cannon in this thing," Gabe went on. "We need to stay away from him for as long as we can."

I said, "Yeah . . . we save him for last . . . if all else fails kinda thing . . ."

"What are we gonna do about those fucking cops camped out front?" Carl asked.

I got to my feet. "I've got an idea," I said as I reached for the house phone.

▪ ▪ ▪

Dylan Rhodes did what I'd asked. He'd turned off the CCTV in the garage area and then met me in the guest parking garage.

"You're right," he said. "Those jerks are sitting out there in the street plain as day. They don't even care if we see 'em." I watched as he balled his fists. "Is that what we're paying these guys to do?"

I wanted to keep this thing on track, so I walked over to the grated divider that separated the guest parking from the delivery garage. Gave it a little rattle. Sounded like a car wreck.

"Does this open?" I asked.

"Has to," he answered. "Fire regulations. There has to be more than one way out of the garage in case of fire."

"We need a way to get in and out of the parking garage without those cops knowing we're gone."

He thought about it. "You could park in the guest garage, then go through the door here, then out the back and into the alley."

"How's it work?" I asked.

He wandered over to the corner and pointed at a keypad mounted on the wall. Down at the far end of the overhead, a handle curved out from the wall. Dylan followed my gaze. "In case the power's out," he said.

I nodded but kept my mouth shut.

"Code's ninety-two, sixty-four," Dylan said. He punched it in. The door began to shake, rattle, and rise. I followed him through the opening into the delivery garage.

"On this side you just push the button. Green to open and red to close. Same thing on the alley side overhead." He extended his hand. "Here's a remote to get in from the alley."

"Great," I said. "We don't need anybody tracking us. This'll be perfect.

Behind us in the guest garage, the door clanked and began to rise.

"Probably be best if none of the other guests sees you going back and forth," he said. "Might get them to wondering."

"Have no fear," I assured him.

He inclined his head toward the service elevator. "I gotta get back upstairs," he said. "Nobody's on the desk but Jeannie."

"Thanks for the help."

"I work six to six every night except Monday and Thursday. You need anything . . ."

He let it ride and went loping across the concrete toward the elevators.

▪ ▪ ▪

Bright-blue morning skies. One of those Pacific Northwest days when it's warm in the sun but cold in the shade. Carl and the reggae twins were back at the hotel, downloading everything available on everybody we'd decided we wanted to talk to.

Gabe and I sneaked out the service door and drove over on the east side of Broadway to the address we had for the widow Valenzuela. Nobody was home. We got lucky when a little neighbor girl wearing purple fairy wings told us the senora was down at something called the Social Justice Project, which, when we finally found it, looked like it used to be a supermarket or maybe a bowling alley. One story, flat roof, strip mall building. Huge parking lot. They'd put butcher paper over the front windows so's to avoid working in a fishbowl. Somebody'd worn out a whole pack of Sharpies on the handmade sign.

Gabe and I strolled in the front door at a little after ten in the morning. They'd used sheets of unfinished plywood to create a vestibule to the main office area. Sort of a pre-entry security room. Ben Forrester's description of the animosities among the town's groups rang in my ears as I looked around.

Four guys seemed to seep out of the woodwork. Big, thick guy in a yellow tank top stepped forward. Tattooed tears running down one cheek, a wooden cross on the other. He looked from Gabe to me and back.

"I help you?" He looked over at Gabe again.

"I'd like to speak with Annette Valenzuela."

"What for?"

I showed him my empty hand and very slowly inserted it into my pocket and pulled out a Leon Marks business card. He studied it like there was going to be a test, then looked back over his shoulder at his companions. They were going to pat us down.

"We're both heeled," I said.

Everybody stopped moving. The air got thick. The guy nearest the door ducked inside and disappeared.

"Why a writer need to be strapped?" Yellow Shirt asked.

"We ruffle a lot of feathers. Sometimes people take it the wrong way."

He looked at Gabe. "You a writer too?" he asked.

"I'm a shooter," Gabe said. "He pisses them off. I shoot 'em. He writes about it."

He thought it over. "Okay," he said after a minute. "You leave the pieces out here."

Gabe was head shaking before the words were out of the guy's mouth.

"Nope," was all Gabe said.

"I'll be happy to leave mine here, but those two are sorta joined at the hip," I said with a nod toward Gabe. "It's like a fetish thing."

The inside door popped open with a sucking sound. A wave of voices rolled over us, the rustle and scrape of people moving, more than one crying baby. And then the door closed, and the sound receded to a whisper of innuendo.

A sturdy Latina. Five-five or so. Fiftysomething. Looked like she hadn't cut her hair since childhood. Jagged scar running the length of her right cheek. Everybody on the other side of the counter snapped to attention. Hadda be the widow Valenzuela.

"Is there a problem out here?" she wanted to know.

Yellow Shirt leaned in and whispered in her ear. Her deep eyes ran over Gabe and me like ants at a picnic. He handed her my business card. She snapped a quick look at the card and then dropped it on the counter.

"Nestor says you've come here armed."

"Only for our own protection," I said.

"You think you need protection from us?" The short bitter laugh she hacked from her throat had nothing to do with humor. "We've had the windows shot out about five times and had two attempts to burn us out—not to mention the legal obstacles—and you think you need protection from us?"

"No, we don't," I assured her. "But . . . from what we've seen so far, seems like there are a lot of people around here who don't much want me looking into your husband's murder. Kinda makes me wonder why."

"They want to pretend it never happened," she snapped.

"You know . . . on one hand I understand . . . Your husband's murder isn't exactly chamber of commerce promotional material, but it seems to me it's taken on some other aura here . . . I'm not sure what it is . . . It seems to have become symbolic in some way."

"What we have here, Mr."—she looked down at my card on the counter—"Mr. Marks . . . what we have going on here is a class war. The haves against the have-nots. Those that got it against those that don't."

She paused for effect. "When my husband and I moved here nine years ago, everybody in town worked for one of about five wood-products companies down on the waterfront, or they worked for Boeing. There were virtually no public services of any kind. Everybody had health insurance through the company they worked for. Doctors wouldn't take new patients unless they had medical insurance. There was no free lunch program in the schools. No ESL classes. They just let our kids sit there in school listening to a language they didn't understand . . . never did a thing about it . . . not ever."

She crooked a finger at Gabe and me. "Come with me," she said as she pulled open the door and stood aside so we could pass.

When I heard about the various social services Ricardo Valenzuela had started, I'd pictured them spread out all over town. But no. The place was huge. Everything was right there. Other than the methadone clinic, which, according to her, was up on Broadway for security reasons. Big pink building, she said.

She walked us through it. The medical clinic. The day care center, job placement office, ESL classes. Parenting clinics. Housing helpers. So many services I lost track.

Ten minutes later we were back at the door. "Boeing now makes twice as many planes with half the people. Most of the wood-products industries have dried up completely. It's becoming a bedroom community for Seattle, and as such a service-based economy," she said. "And, the way they see it, we're the cause of it. They claim we're taking jobs from the community."

"Jobs they wouldn't take if you put a gun to their collective heads," I said.

"Change is hard for some people," Gabe offered. "Lots of folks would be happier if everything stayed the same forever. The whole retro

Return to Mayberry cracker-barrel crowd. That way their little brains would have less crap to keep track of."

"Racism is at the bottom of it," Annette Valenzuela corrected.

"That's always the elephant in the room, isn't it?" I asked. "We live in a racist society, and our greatest desire is to pretend we don't, or that we're 'making progress'—anything except admitting who we really are and then actually doing something about it."

"People like that see the world as *them* and *us*," Gabe said, "when the truth is that human beings are at the top of the food chain because of their ability to cooperate with one another."

Mrs. Valenzuela wasn't convinced. "Then how come if you look at people, you find hate is right beneath the surface?" She held her fingers about an eighth of an inch apart. "About this far under," she said. She dropped her hands to her sides with a smack. "Why's that?" she wanted to know. "I don't understand."

■ ■ ■

They were building a splashy new waterfront. Or so they said. Only problem was it wasn't actually on the water. I mean like you could see Puget Sound and all, you know, out in the distance, over the parking lots, the boatyards and marinas, on the far side of Jetty Island, where the mouth of the Snohomish River drooled into Possession Bay. In the foreground Whidbey Island sprawled languidly across the near horizon, looking like it was being pinned in place by the majestic Olympic range grinning white toothed out at the far reaches of the sky.

The actual waterfront consisted of a couple of semi-tony restaurants and a single-story office building, all of which were squeezed between the super-tight military security of Naval Station Everett and the upscale Everett Yacht Club. Gabe headed into Anthony's restaurant for a Coke while I toddled over to North Shore Mental Health Services. The sign on the door read: **CLOSED.** Out of habit, I grabbed the knob. The door popped open. Tinkle. Tinkle. I stepped inside.

Standard peaceful waiting room. Couches, chairs, travel posters on the wall, couple of haggard plants strewn here and there. Even had the HANG IN THERE kitty cat over in the corner. Nobody personing what I assumed to be the receptionist's desk.

"Hello," I sang out.

Nothing.

I pulled in a lungful of air and was about to turn up the volume when the door at the far end of the hall opened, and Suzanne Bradley stepped into the corridor. Her hair was shorter than it had been in the picture, and she'd put on a few pounds, but otherwise she looked about the same.

"I'm sorry . . ." she began. "I guess I didn't get the door latched properly. Today's the day we work the clinic." She waved a white phone charger in the air. "I just came back to get this." She pulled the office door closed and walked in my direction. "Who have you come to see?" she asked.

"You," I said.

She cocked her pretty head. "And your name is . . ."

"Leon Marks," I said as I handed her a phony business card.

She scanned the card and frowned. "Are you sure . . ."

"I'm here about Matthew Hardaway."

The name stopped her in her tracks.

"In what capacity?" she asked.

"I'm a crime writer," I said. "Doing a little preliminary research about the Matthew Hardaway murder."

"Not much of a mystery there," she said.

"You'd be the one to know, I'm guessing."

She made it a point not to be amused.

"You know I can't talk about a client."

"The client's dead."

"Doctor-patient privilege, however, lives on."

"I just wanted to—"

She cut me off. "If you had any idea of the degree to which Matthew's father . . ." She paused to collect herself. "If you knew the lengths Mr. Hardaway has gone . . ." She gobbled air. "Mr. Hardaway's attorneys served me with nondisclosure paperwork the morning after the shooting." She waved a frustrated hand in the air. The phone charger flopped around like a wet noodle. "Like he already had the paperwork on hand in case something like this happened."

"I spent a few hours with Matthew some years back," I said. "Nervous, squirrelly, all over the place . . . loony as hell, sure. But seems to me a long way from walking into a city council meeting and shooting somebody in front of half the town. That's quite a stretch there." I kept talking. "Did you think he posed that kind of danger to society?"

She started to snap something back at me but changed her mind and clamped her mouth shut. Took a deep breath. "If I'd thought something like that was even remotely possible, I would have reported it to the proper authorities, which in this case was his parents. Matthew was a referral from another counseling service. They felt as if he'd exhausted their resources."

I watched as she stuffed the charger in the pocket of her jeans.

"I have to get back," she said.

"Seems like nobody in this town much wants me prying into this thing," I said as she pulled open the door and waited for me to walk out.

"Can you blame them?" she asked as she banged the door shut and then tested it. "Nice to have met you, Mr. . . ."

"Marks," I said. "Matthew have any friends?" I asked.

She turned and started across the parking lot. She sneaked a peek over her shoulder and caught me following her ass. She stopped and turned back my way. Even from a distance, I could see the wheels turning in her head.

"You might try a young lady named Wendy Bohannon."

She pointed to the north, toward the side of the hill overlooking the bay. "Her parents live up there," she said. "They won't be hard to find." She wagged a finger in my direction. "Just don't use my name. I'd prefer not to spend the rest of my life in court."

"Thanks," I said. "Be okay if I watched you walk the rest of the way?"

She arched an eyebrow in my direction. No smile.

"Whatever pleases you," she said.

■ ■ ■

Suzanne Bradley was right. They were the only Bohannons in town. Way the hell up on the side of the hill, with the rest of the old money, peering out over Possession Bay like a disapproving dowager aunt. We got lost looking for the house because the streets were designed in such a way as to make it difficult to cruise around the neighborhood gawking at the swells.

If the landscaping was any indication, the house had been built at least fifty years ago. Would have taken that long to grow the boxwood hedge that shielded the house from the street. Gabe waited in the car as I let myself in the wrought-iron gate and gave the big brass knocker three sharp raps.

The sound of running feet leaked under the door. A series of shakes and rattles and then the door popped open. The young woman seemed surprised to see me. "Oh . . . ," she said. "I thought you were . . ."

Looked to be about eighteen or nineteen. Real big-time Goth. Disaffected youth at its finest. Long dark hair. Dark everything except the big twitchy blue eyes that never seemed to come to rest. Over her shoulder I could see a wide hallway running off toward a set of French doors what looked to be a quarter mile away. Overhead a crystal chandelier hung a full story above the parquet floor. Somber oil paintings lined the walls. Place looked like a museum.

"I'm looking for Wendy Bohannon," I said.

She looked back over her shoulder and then did it again, like the hounds of hell were hot on her trail or something.

"I'm Wendy," she said, without ever looking my way.

"I'm a writer," I said. "My name is Leon. If you have the time, Wendy, I'd like to talk with you about Matthew Hardaway."

Her eyes finally landed on my face like a housefly. "Matthew?" she parroted.

"Yes" bounced off the back of her head as she checked the hallway again.

"Wendy . . . Wendy, who's at the door?" a voice called from the far end of the hall.

"You should go," the girl said, swiveling her neck back and forth like she was watching a tennis match. A second later, a silhouetted figure stepped into view and started walking our way.

Wendy stepped in close to me. "There's a little park," she whispered. "Two blocks uphill."

That was as far as she got. The woman who arrived at Wendy's side was maybe thirty. Looked like she took several hours to get ready every morning. Perfectly coiffed auburn hair. Sprayed-on makeup. Seriously put together and fully aware of the impression she made on men. The foo-foo woman at home.

She was wiping her hands with a towel. "Can I help you?" she asked.

I reached into my pocket and pulled out a business card. She made no move to take it from my hand. Just stood there and looked at it like it was a dog turd. "How can we help you?" she asked with all the warmth of a glacier.

"I was hoping to have a few words with Wendy," I said.

She stopped wiping her fingers. "About what?"

"Matthew Hardaway."

Without further preamble, she turned her back on me and went clicking down the hall at warp speed. "Paul," she called. "Paul."

"The park," Wendy silently mouthed.

When I looked up, a big, beefy guy in a bright-blue shirt and a pair of chinos was storming up the hall in my direction. Somewhere between fifty and sixty. Big gut wobbling out in front of him as he walked. I watched Wendy begin to shrink as he drew closer. He threw an annoyed glance in her direction.

All he said was, "Go," and she went skittering off down the hall.

"What's this about?" the guy demanded.

"I wanted to speak with Wendy regarding Matthew Hardaway," I said.

"She had nothing to do with that," he said about twice as loud as necessary. At which point he stepped way inside my personal bubble and got nose to nose with me. "Leave," he growled.

"I'm aware of that," I said. "I was hoping she could—"

"Get off my property, or I'll call the police."

I took a step backward.

"Wendy has problems of her own," he boomed. "She has nothing to do with that nutjob. Now get the hell off my property."

Didn't seem like my famous powers of persuasion were going to win the day here, so I shrugged, stepped down from the stone stairs, and headed back toward the street.

Gabe had slipped over behind the wheel. "No lunch invitation?"

"Supposedly there's a park a couple of blocks up the hill."

Gabe started the car and dropped it into gear.

"I take it they weren't happy to see you."

"Pleased as punch. About like everybody else in this town. Let's go," I grumbled.

The park was right where Wendy Bohannon had said it would be, except it wasn't so much a park as it was a city reservoir and a couple of water tanks surrounded by a few acres of mown grass and dotted with park benches. Gabe and I got out of the car, wandered over to the nearest bench, and sat down.

"We're not exactly kicking ass here," Gabe said. "We're wearing out our welcome in a hurry."

I nodded but didn't say anything. Gabe was right. The way things were going showed scant promise of a happy ending. We needed to either putt or get off the green, before the forces of darkness got hip to what was going on.

Ten minutes later, Wendy came scooting up between houses, using one of those over-this-fence-and-around-that-yard paths that kids always seem to find in their neighborhoods. She crossed the grass and stood in front of Gabe and me, fidgety, shifting her weight from foot to foot and keeping a tense watch over her shoulder.

"Didn't mean to cause any trouble for you with your mom and dad," I said.

"She's not my mom," the girl blurted. The fire in her blue eyes was threatened by a sudden flood.

"Oh," was the best I could come up with.

"Sheila's the trophy wife," Wendy said, wiping her eyes with her sleeve. "She hates me."

"Why would she hate you?" Gabe inquired.

"Because she wishes my father's life started and ended with her. She wishes he didn't have a past . . . particularly not me. She's a mega bitch."

Didn't take Dr. Ruth to see I'd blundered into an ongoing family feud, so I shifted gears. "How do you know Matthew?" I asked.

"From the clinic," she said.

She read my mind. "They send me there because I hate Sheila." She waved an angry hand in the air. "Like I must be crazy if I don't like that bitch or something."

"Don't seem right," Gabe said. "Don't seem to me like hating your stepmother ought to qualify you as nuts. Lots of people hate their stepparents."

"It's bullshit. That's just what they tell people."

"What's true?" Gabe pressed.

She blinked a couple of times. "I'm the one who found Mom," she said in a low voice. The look on her face said she wished she hadn't told us.

"You found your mom?" I said.

"In the garage." She sucked in a big gulp of air. "She killed herself," she said, tossing her head. "They say I'm traumatized."

"Anybody would be traumatized," Gabe allowed. "Nobody walks away from something like that, Wendy. Nobody. You wouldn't be a . . . you wouldn't be human if you weren't damaged by something like that."

I could tell she'd heard it before, and as far as she was concerned, it didn't sound any better coming from us than it had from whoever had preceded us.

"Five months," she said bitterly. "My mom wasn't even in the ground five months when he married that . . . that . . . cow." She swallowed the rest of it.

A shout bounced around the neighborhood. Wendy rolled her eyes.

"My father," she groaned. "You guys better go. He knows everybody who's everybody. He'll get the cops to hassle you."

"Were you surprised by what Matthew did?" I asked.

Another shout. Closer this time.

"Matthew wasn't mean. Not at all. He was confused. He didn't like himself. Didn't think he deserved anything good to happen to him, but he wasn't mean. It was that fucking job. He started to change right after he got that stupid fucking job."

"What job?" Gabe asked.

The job made him different. Before that the only person he ever said anything bad about was himself, and then . . . he just started to change . . . He . . . all of a sudden he hated everybody."

"Wendy!" The name rattled off the nearby houses. More eye rolling.

"Bickford something or other. Up on Evergreen."

Without another word, she turned and sprinted for the street. About the time her father puffed up to the corner and spotted Gabe and me, she'd already ducked back under somebody's shrubbery and disappeared from view. He pulled a cell phone from his pants pocket at started poking at it.

We took our time getting back in the car and driving off. Moving at the speed of lava. Paul Bohannon stood on the corner the whole time, breathing hard, arms locked across his ample torso, trying to set us on fire with his most baleful glare. In the distance a siren began to whine.

▪ ▪ ▪

"We got maybe a half hour," Carl announced as he motored across the room in his wheelchair. Charity and Maxie were working at flank speed. Stuffing all their computer equipment into metal cases, snapping the latches, and then rolling them out into the hall.

"What happened?" I asked.

"They're on to us real hard. They been probing back at us all morning. They know they been hacked big-time. We been misdirecting them for over an hour, but they're linkin' up with one another. I think it was the school records. Way better cybersecurity than the rest of these assholes. That's when things started to go to shit. They're just now trying to triangulate where it's coming from. Won't be long before even these dolts figure it out. We gotta be somewhere else when they get here."

Gabe and I joined in the exodus. Ten minutes later, Carl's van was packed to the rafters, and Charity and Maxie were belted up and ready to go. I walked over to the driver's side. Carl handed me an orange thumb drive. "Everything we got's on there. Better hide it good."

"Thanks for the help," I told him.

"Keep in touch," he said. "We're gonna have to get under the radar for a while here. Real low profile." He jerked a thumb at the rear seat.

"These guys tell me they're feelin' a bit homesick all of a sudden. Thinkin' a little Caribbean vacation might be in order. Like immediately."

"Wish I could go along for the ride," I admitted.

Carl shrugged. "When they don't find anything on you guys, they're gonna be pissed as hell. Means all that taxpayer money they spent on security wasn't worth a shit, but all that's gonna do is slow 'em down. There ain't all that many people with the chops or the equipment to pull this kinda thing off, and we're right up at the top of the most likely list."

"Keep in touch."

"No fear."

We shook hands through the open window. The reggae twins waved goodbye. I walked over and pushed the door buttons, waited for the door to rattle up, and then ducked through and let them out into the alley.

Gabe jogged down to the far end, checked the street. Motioned that the coast was clear. Carl eased the van forward. I followed along in its wake.

Gabe and I stood shoulder to shoulder watching the van motor up Hoyt Avenue, crest the hill, and disappear from view.

That's when I noticed the air vents above the garage door. Three of them, in fact, evenly spaced across the opening. I stepped back into the alley and peered up. Screens on the inside to keep the birds and the bugs out, leaving about a one-foot-by-one-foot ledge on the outside of the building. I pointed upward. Gabe got it right away.

"Gimme a boost," I said.

I pulled the thumb drive from my pocket, and then put one hand on the building to steady myself. Gabe gave me the old laced-fingers lift. I slipped the drive into the center opening and pushed it as far back as it would go. With seemingly no effort at all, Gabe set me back onto the asphalt.

■ ■ ■

The cop with the battering ram looked mighty disappointed. He'd dragged that sucker up nine floors only to find I'd left the hotel room door hanging wide open. Ya hadda love these guys. Open door or no open door, they came in in full combat mode. The black-visored storm troopers of the status quo. Pointing weapons this way and that, shouting at one another as Gabe and I sat side by side on the couch, hands on top of our heads, both of our weapons over on the other side of the room holding down our carry permits.

"On the floor . . . on the floor" rattled off the walls.

The cop I'd pushed the other night dragged me off the couch, knelt in the middle of my aching back, and handcuffed me tight enough to tow a butane truck. About the time they yarded Gabe and me back to our feet, Detective Shirley came ambling into the room like Caesar entering Gaul.

"Some people just won't take a hint." He smirked in my face. "Amazing how I know these things. I'm prescient, I guess."

The day manager was trotting his name tag back and forth out in the hall, handing out passkeys like popcorn. I could hear doors being wrenched open, commanding shouts, lots of jackbooted crab walking, and then . . . all of a sudden, things got quiet. Twenty seconds passed.

Darth Vader with three stripes on his sleeve appeared in the doorway. He lifted his black visor and motioned with his head for Shirley to step out into the hall with him. Shirley sidled over. The SWAT sergeant bent down and whispered something in Shirley's ear. A guy in civilian clothes, cradling a laptop against his chest, joined them. When he turned his back to me, I could see that he was holding a directional antenna in his right hand. He waved it around. Judging from the expression on Detective Shirley's face, the news wasn't good. I watched as his color drained. He slammed the door on his way back in.

"Where's your friends?" he asked, with as much restraint as he could muster.

"What friends?" I asked.

"You rented four suites." He checked a wrinkled piece of hotel stationery in his hand. "The two of you. Leon Marks and Shirley Temple here," he said. "Carl Cosmic. Charity Freedom. And Maximilian Cousins," he read. "None of whom, as it happens, actually exist, as far as I can tell."

"They moved on," I said.

"Moved on where?"

"To a better place," Gabe chimed in.

"Where's the equipment?"

"What equipment?"

Color flooded Shirley's face with a vengeance. He caught me smirking at him and turned away. My favorite cop took a step in my direction and smacked me on the back of the head. Shirley turned at the sound of the crack. He pointed a stiff finger at the cop.

"No," was all he said before stepping out into the hall. I watched him grab his phone and speed dial somebody. I could see his ears getting redder and redder as he tried to make some point with whoever was on the other end.

Officer Unfriendly ambled over by the door, leaned against it, and eased it closed with his hip. He turned back in my direction.

"Now . . . you smart-ass motherfucker," he said.

Outside in the corridor, Shirley's voice took on the urgent cadence of a man who'd called out the SWAT team and the cybercrimes guys, gotten some half-assed judge to sign a search warrant, and then come up stone empty on the other end. Not a good career move, I suspected.

The cop grabbed me by the hair and tried to lift me from the floor. I watched as he drew back a ham-size fist. I could feel it right away. A level of fear and uncertainty I hadn't experienced for as long as I could remember. Hey . . . I've been hit before. Comes with private eye territory, but I'd almost never felt like this. Parts of me contracted like a dying star.

Gabe hopped up from the couch, rushed forward, and drove a shoulder into the guy, sending him staggering backward. In about two seconds, half a dozen weapons were pointed at Gabe and me. Nobody moved. The possibility of dying hung in the air like cannon smoke.

"You fucking freak," the enraged cop bellowed. "I'll kick your homo ass for ya, bitch."

"Fuck you, asshole," Gabe sneered.

Officer Angry launched himself off the wall at the same instant as the door burst open and Shirley stepped back into the room. It was like a Warner Bros. cartoon where a character hangs motionless in the air for a while.

"Unhook 'em," Shirley ordered.

"Whaaa?"

"You heard me, goddamn it. Unhook 'em. And give them their weapons and permits back."

They took their sweet-ass time. Pouting like schoolboys who'd been told there'd be no recess today. Once they had their handcuffs back in their handy-dandy handcuff cases, Shirley motioned them out into the hall, then walked over to where Gabe and I were massaging our wrists back to life and spoke in a low voice.

"I don't know who you guys are or what you're doing here, but you can bet your ass I'm gonna find out."

We stood there on the carpet and watched him leave. Gabe wandered over to the fridge, pulled out a San Pellegrino, and made half of it disappear before offering me the other half. I poured it down my tightly constricted throat. It damn nearly bubbled back out. I stood still and swallowed, a trickle at a time.

"This thing is coming apart big-time," Gabe said. "That cop starts asking the right questions, and he's sure as hell gonna figure out who I am. I'm featured prominently in just about every cop database there is. And after that it ain't but one short step from me to Joey and then to you."

I nodded. "We better get out of here," I said. I checked my watch. 4:25. "The kid . . . Dylan whatever . . . the night manager. Let's wait for him to come on duty at six—that way we can check out without winding up with a police escort. We leave now, and that asshole downstairs behind the desk is gonna drop a dime on us in a heartbeat."

As usual, Gabe caught my drift.

"We're blown here, man. We're right back where we fucking started. If there's some mystery here, we haven't even managed to get a sniff of it. Let's get out of here."

"Not quite yet," I said. "Not quite yet."

■ ■ ■

I leaned on the doorbell. A long minute passed.

"Yes?" she called.

"Martha," I said. "It's Leo. Leo Waterman."

Seemed like a full minute passed before the door opened a crack.

I bent at the waist and got eyeball to eyeball with her.

"It's me, Martha."

The door started to close. I blurted out, "You remember Billy Edlund's party? The night he drove his old man's golf cart into the pool?"

Long pause. The crack reappeared. "You're not . . . ," she whispered. And then she stopped herself. "It is," she breathed. "By God, it's you, Leo." The door opened all the way. She was wearing a black Nike jogging suit. The red headband holding back her hair matched the red stripes on the suit. A coordinated ensemble it was.

"Look at you. I can't believe . . . you're so skinny, and all that hair. What are you doing here?"

"That's what I came to talk to you about." I motioned back over my shoulder, toward Gabe and the car. "Might be better if we could put the rental car in your garage."

Her eyes got wary. "Is someone . . . I mean . . ."

"It's okay," I assured her. She took my word for it.

I followed her inside, while she rummaged through her purse and eventually came out with the garage remote, and then hurried back to the car.

Took Gabe and me maybe two minutes to stash the car, retrieve Carl's thumb drive, and get back inside.

I introduced them. Martha wanted to feed and water us, but we said we were fine. She was still sputtering about my appearance when the three of us sat down in her living room. "I don't understand, Leo . . . What . . . I mean . . ."

I told her. All of it. From the moment I'd spotted somebody tailing her in Seattle, to what happened in that alley, to hiding out and recovering down on the coast, right up to our second confrontation with the cops a couple of hours ago. The longer I talked the more wide eyed and slack jawed she became.

"They cut you?"

"They carved me like a Halloween pumpkin," I said. "Took four separate surgeries to fix it, and I still look like the loser in a machete fight."

Looked to me like she was going to cry. "Oh, Leo," she said when I'd finished. "I'm so sorry. Is there anything I can do?"

"You can sign a consent form allowing Suzanne Bradley to talk to me about Matthew."

"Phil will go nuts," she said.

"Good thing he's your ex, then," Gabe said.

She thought it over at some length. "Maybe . . ." She looked down at the carpet. "You know . . . sleeping dogs and all of that."

"I think your father was right," I said quickly. "I think somebody else had a hand in turning your son into something he otherwise wasn't."

"How can that be?"

"That's what I want to know."

"We got, at the most, one more day before we're gonna have to fold our tents and get the hell out of here," Gabe said.

"You know a girl named Wendy Bohannon?" I asked.

"From the clinic," Martha said.

"Yeah."

"Poor thing. She found her mother hanging—"

"We know," I interrupted. "We met the new mommy. Wendy told us that Matthew got a job. She said the job seemed to change him. Said he was never negative about other people until he started working at this place."

Martha shook her headband. "I don't know anything about any job. Back then . . . back when Matthew . . . you know . . . when it happened . . . he was living with Phil then." She waved an angry hand. "He wouldn't stay here with me anymore because I wouldn't permit guns in the house."

"Bickford something," Gabe threw in.

Martha sat up a little straighter. "Bill Bickford, maybe. He's a friend of Phil's. Has some kind of store up on Evergreen. Up near the top of the hill. They belong to a gun club together. Way the heck out in Conway someplace. Matthew used to go out there with his father for weekends. Run around the woods. Do their little boy gun nut things."

Seemed like we'd taken a left turn someplace, so I steered us back onto the road. "What about Suzanne Bradley?" I pressed.

She sat there, staring into space for a moment, and then got to her feet.

"She was the only one he ever talked to. We'd sent him to other counselors, but he just sat there and didn't say a word. She was the only one he ever shared anything with. I'll call her now," she announced. I sat back on the couch and watched her cross the room, step inside what appeared to be her home office, and close the door.

Three or four minutes later, Martha reappeared. "She'll be over in the morning, before she goes to the clinic," she announced. "She's very nervous about doing this, and I don't blame her one bit. Phil's sued people who even requested Matthew's personal information."

Gabe and I got to our feet.

"Where are you going?" Martha asked.

"Figured we'd sleep in the car if you don't mind," I said.

She shook her headband again. "You can use Matthew's room." I started to demur, but she was having none of it. She motioned toward the stairs with her head. We grabbed our stuff and followed her.

The door to the room was open, and the light was on, as if somewhere inside of her, some small part was hoping against hope he might still come home.

Posters on the walls, little wooden desk with an old iMac sitting on it. A cup full of pens and pencils. College pennants. Bunk bed. Teenage bedroom U.S.A.

Gabe dropped the bag on the bottom bunk.

"In deference to my bad leg, I'll be takin' the bottom," Gabe announced.

I didn't bother to argue the point. When somebody gives up six months of their life to help you get back on your feet and then volunteers to help you on a personal quest for vengeance, a little gratitude is pretty much de rigueur.

I was scoping out the top bunk, thinking it was gonna be like sleeping on a windowsill and trying to imagine the impact when I rolled out in the middle of the night and hit the floor, when Martha began to talk, as much to herself as to us.

"When we bought the bunk bed," she began, "you know, we figured as he grew up . . . like kids do . . . we thought he'd have friends stay the night, you know, sleepovers and such." She stopped talking and swallowed hard. "But he never had a friend . . . not one . . . not ever. He was always the odd number, the one who they bullied and teased."

"It wasn't your fault," came out of me as naturally as if I were making an excuse for myself.

"I keep asking myself what else I could have done," she mused. "How I might have handled things better."

She looked around the room, as if seeing it for the first time. "I wish I could stop wondering."

She straightened her shoulders and walked over to the closet and pulled the door open. The space was filled from floor to ceiling with packages and mail and FedEx envelopes and cookie tins and shoeboxes. Martha looked over at me as if dumbfounded by the sight of it.

"What's all that?" I asked.

"People sent me things," she said. "Bibles, teddy bears, toys, Christian self-help books, handmade wooden crosses. People sent candy too, and brownies, and boxes of chocolate, Bundt cakes. Food from all over the world. I didn't want to throw away anything that people sent, but to tell you the truth, I was too scared to eat any of it. There was no way to be sure it wasn't poisoned."

She took several deep breaths, as if to steady herself. "They don't even count him among the dead," she said. "They say a man was killed. Like Matthew's death doesn't even count."

She walked over and opened the door gently. "I've got some paperwork I need to finish," she said. "If you need anything, just help yourselves. See you guys in the morning."

She worked up a wan smile for me and then left the room, closing the door behind. Neither of us said a word for quite a while.

"How do you not blame yourself for what your son did?" Gabe asked.

"You don't."

"How do you not remember him as the little kid he used to be?"

"I'm guessing that's the hard part."

"Don't see how you could avoid it."

"All you gotta do is remember what he ended up doing."

Gabe crawled into the bottom bunk. The kid's mattress folded around Gabe like a hot dog bun. I pulled the thumb drive out of my pants pocket. "I'm gonna see if maybe I can't use the kid's computer to read whatever Carl and the guys got. That gonna bother you?" I asked.

"Just douse the light, gonna take a little nap." Gabe muttered and turned that broad back my way as I wandered over and pushed the button on the back of Matthew's iMac. The bong serenaded me as I snapped off the overhead.

Sitting in Matthew's chair made it clear that, despite my somewhat emaciated present state, my ass had grown considerably since middle school.

They'd managed to get a little of everything, but not all of anything. Matthew had no criminal record whatsoever. He had a valid library card. Had failed the written test for his driver's license two weeks before his death. What was most revelatory were Matthew's school records. As I had surmised from my brief encounter with him earlier in his life, his difficulties had not come upon him suddenly.

Matthew Hardaway had never been in the same area code as normal. He didn't utter a syllable until he was three and a half years old. By the time he got to school, he was so hypersensitive to touch they had to cut the labels out of his clothes. In kindergarten, he'd been diagnosed with sensory integration disorder and had been put under the care of a school district speech pathologist, who summarily concluded that Matthew should be immediately considered for special education status, which is where Phil Hardaway entered the picture.

From that moment on, Matthew's journey through the public school system was a series of speed bumps, school district attempts to meet his special needs, followed immediately by Phil Hardaway thwarting their efforts. It was like Martha said: Phil was totally unwilling to acknowledge that there was anything wrong with his son and apparently had both the means and wherewithal to put the kibosh on any attempt to label Matthew as being special or different or developmentally disabled in any way.

Now if you want to see a school board melt into a pile of protoplasm, just threaten litigation. And Phil hadn't simply threatened; he'd sued the school district on four separate occasions and won all four cases, turning Matthew's school life into an unfortunate cycle of shifting between special needs classes and being mainstreamed back into the general population at the insistence of his father.

By the time middle school rolled around, it was apparent to everyone but Phil Hardaway that something was seriously amiss about Matthew. His social awkwardness had reached new levels; he had begun to have difficulty sleeping, refused to make eye contact . . . even the way he walked had morphed into an awkward shamble.

The final school district mental health specialist Matthew had seen, prior to seeing Suzanne Bradley, noted in his report that "Young men like Matthew don't have friends. They don't make the football team. In most cases, they have learned to cope with that kind of social rejection on some level. But during puberty, when the specter of sexuality adds itself to the emotional pot, life seems to push them toward more serious behavioral difficulties, as they feel increasingly alienated and alone."

As he'd predicted, things had gotten worse from there. Matthew started having panic attacks in school. On a dozen separate occasions Martha had to rush down to the school to be by her son's side. At which point somebody or other diagnosed him with autism spectrum disorder, thus beginning yet another set of evaluations at the University Hospital Child Centered program, where he was determined to also have obsessive-compulsive disorder, a fairly common symptom among Asperger's and autism sufferers.

That same specialist noted that "Matthew is not open to therapy. He very seldom says anything and will not make eye contact. He does not believe he has Asperger's and does not believe he can be cured by treatment of any kind. He thinks seeing me is a complete waste of time."

And that was it. Three weeks after the report, Matthew began seeing Suzanne Bradley, whose private practice professional evaluations were privileged communication. If what Martha had said earlier was accurate, somehow or other, Suzanne Bradley had connected with Matthew. A miracle in itself, if you asked me.

What struck me was how the possibility of Matthew becoming violent was never raised by anyone. Not his teachers, nor his legion of therapists . . . Nobody ever considered the possibility that Matthew

Hardaway might hurt himself or others. Weird, sure. Crazy, maybe. But not violent.

As a matter of fact, what stuck in my mind was a middle school guidance counselor's observation that "Matthew is far more likely to be the victim than the victimizer in any sort of confrontational situation. The only person Matthew hates is himself."

Which was pretty much in line with what Wendy Bohannon had told us and a notion, if accurate, that left us with the same question dangling in the wind: What had turned an introverted self-hater into the kind of screaming fanatic who calls a man a communist and then shoots him in the head in front of a room full of people?

I sat back in the tiny chair, raised my arms above my head, and stretched for all I was worth. Behind me Gabe was purring like a kitten. I shut down the computer and pocketed the thumb drive. Who knows why I opened the center drawer on Matthew's desk as I waited for the computer to shut down. Habit, perhaps, or maybe I'm just a nosy bastard. What I can tell you, however, is that the sight of that legal pad sent a shiver running down my spine and froze the breath in my lungs.

Hundreds of them. I flipped the pages, all the way to the back. Wall to wall, every page was covered with them, both sides, arrows pointing in all four directions. My hands rose instinctively to my chest. I swallowed a whimper and closed the drawer.

The muted bong of the doorbell pulled me back to earth. And then again . . . four buzzes in a row, real quick, like it was a little kid on the front porch or something.

I got up, sidled over to the bedroom door, and opened it a crack. First thing I heard was Martha's voice. "This is outside our agreement, Phil. You're supposed to . . ."

The front door banged shut.

"Anybody come round here asking about Matthew?" Phil Hardaway asked.

"Why would anyone do that?" Martha hedged.

"There's a couple assholes goin' round town, trying to stir that whole thing up again. Some guy says he's a writer."

"Please leave," Martha said, her voice beginning to break.

"Be real bad stirring that thing up again," Phil said.

"Matthew's gone. He took a life. What could be worse than that?"

"He's better off where he is," Phil said.

"I hate it when people say that," Martha spat. Her voice rose. "Don't you dare touch me," she shrieked.

I opened the bedroom door, tiptoed over to the stairs, and started down. Gabe was about three inches behind me as I crept down to the landing.

"That kid was never long for this world," Phil growled. "You just won't face it. Your old man wouldn't neither. The kid was defective. He was—"

"The kid?" Martha said. "This is our son you're talking about. He's not just some kid."

"Every fish you catch ain't a keeper. You ever think of that? Some of them you just gotta throw back."

"Get out of my house," Martha screamed. "I'm calling the police."

"Those guys come round here, you just tell 'em to take a hike," Phil said. "Don't need that whole shit storm startin' up all over again. You hear me?"

Gabe and I were huddled together on the landing when the boom of the front door slamming shook the whole condo.

Gabe's head inclined back up the stairs. I followed along.

■ ■ ■

Suzanne Bradley checked her case notes. "Matthew never said a word the first two sessions. Just sat there staring at the floor, waiting for the hour to be over. I asked him once if there wasn't anything he could imagine that I could do for him." She paused for effect. "You know what he said?"

I had a feeling she was gonna tell me, so I buttoned my lip.

"He said, 'You could not *be*.'" She looked up. "Those were the first words he ever spoke to me." She shrugged. "After that, I could hardly get him to shut up."

"Any idea what triggered his sudden desire to talk? I mean, by that time, he'd stonewalled any number of counselors. He didn't interact with any of them. Why you?"

She bent an eyebrow in my direction. "If I didn't know that such a thing was both impossible and illegal, I'd swear you've had a look at Matthew's school records," she said. I looked away and broke out my Mount Rushmore face.

"Lucky guesses," I said.

She didn't believe a word of it. "I think it was partly his age. He was growing up. I think perhaps he had a bit of a crush on me."

"Completely understandable." It was out of my mouth without ever coming into contact with my brain. I sorta regretted saying it, but nothing too rueful to be truthful.

She grimaced and went back to her notes. "Did you manage to get in touch with Wendy Bohannon?" she asked.

"Yeah," I said. "She thought he started to change when he got a job a couple of months before the . . . the incident."

"Matthew's opening up to me had more to do with meeting Wendy Bohannon than it did with me. I think she may have been the first girl his age who ever paid any attention to him. I'd never seem him that agitated before."

I could hear Martha moving around the kitchen. She'd signed the consent form and then announced that she didn't want to be present when Suzanne and I talked. "Matthew wouldn't want me to hear any of this," she said simply.

Gabe stayed upstairs on the theory that the fewer people who saw the two of us together, the better off we'd be, so it was just Suzanne Bradley and me facing over the coffee table.

"What do you think was Matthew's problem?" I asked finally.

She shrugged. "At one time or another he was diagnosed with just about every condition anyone could imagine," she said. "I try not to get too involved in putting labels on patients like Matthew. I try to remember that just because I can't put a name on it doesn't mean it isn't real."

We'd been at it for forty minutes before she began checking her watch. I reached down between the seat cushions and pulled out the legal pad I'd found in Matthew's desk. I dropped it on the table between us. "You have any idea what these are?" I asked, fanning the pages so she could see they were completely covered.

She brought her hand to her throat, gulped, and began to rummage in Matthew's case folder. I watched as her manicured fingers picked through the pages until she pulled out what appeared to be a page from a steno pad, perforated across the top, about half the size of a standard sheet of paper. She dropped it on top of the legal pad.

Same diagram doodled all over it, with what appeared to be a purple Sharpie. "He did this during our last session," she said. "He'd never done anything like that before, so I kept it."

Looking at those arrows turned my blood to ice. Felt like I was breathing muddy water. I started to reach for my chest but caught myself and stopped.

I sat back on the couch. Forced my hands to stay at my sides. "It's a Crosstar," I said. "An Aryan Nations symbol. They use it in place of a swastika."

The room went quiet. Somewhere in the back of the house the furnace clicked on with a rush. I heaved a sigh and closed my eyes.

"Are you all right?" she asked, sliding forward on the love seat, leaning over the coffee table, and putting a hand on my shoulder.

I had a sudden vision of those stubborn, solitary leaves out in my orchard on the day Art Fowler had come seeking my help. Sole survivors waving frantically as they fought the onslaught of winter. And then I felt myself come loose from the branch and go veering off into the frozen maelstrom until everything was white and quiet.

And then I started to talk. Like I'd sprung a leak or something. I told her everything. Right from the beginning, from when Art showed up at my door. About the day Martha showed up at Rebecca's office and I'd ended up getting cut to pieces in that alley off Denny. About getting my shit back together down on the coast and then coming up here to see if I couldn't make some sense of the whole damn thing and maybe find some peace with myself.

When I'd just about finished talking, I channeled my inner drama queen and pulled my shirt up to my chin. She frowned and then leaned in closer. Instinctively she reached out and used a red fingernail to trace the path of the faint scars remaining on my chest. She rested her palm flat on my chest and looked up at me.

"Scars heal," she said. "Some of them, anyway."

"I'm going to have to be able to tell myself I did everything that could be done," I said. "Otherwise this is never going to be all right with me."

"Who are you really?" she asked.

"It's best you don't know," I said.

We had one of those phone company pin-drop moments. She reeled her hand back in and slid backward on the cushion.

"Wendy's right," she said out of the blue. "Matthew changed over the last month or so of his life. He'd always blamed himself for his condition. I can't tell you how many times he said things to me like 'I'm broken,' 'I just don't work right,' or 'I'm defective.' It was always Mathew blaming himself."

"And then?" I pushed.

"Then . . ." She took a moment to choose her words. "And then . . . it was like all of a sudden he was more of a victim." She waved a dismissive hand. "That's really the only way I can think to describe his change in attitude. As if suddenly he wasn't completely at fault anymore. He wasn't happening to *it* anymore. *It* was happening to him. Almost as if something had pulled him out from under the pile of self-hatred and guilt he'd lived under all his life."

"Any idea what?"

"No . . . ," she said, "but imagine how good that must have felt to him. What a sense of freedom he must have experienced."

"Did he tell you he'd gotten a job?" I asked.

She shook her head.

"Doesn't that seem a little odd?" I pushed. "I mean . . . the kid's got a job for the first time in his life, right at a time when he's also found somebody he's actually comfortable talking to, and he doesn't say a word about it."

"Everything about Matthew was odd," she said.

Couldn't argue with that, so I didn't bother.

"What are you going to do now?" she asked.

"We've about worn out our welcome around here. Before long they're gonna drum up some reason to arrest us and then lose us in the system for a while, so I'm thinking I'm gonna take a run by the place where Matthew was supposedly working and then get out of town. Regroup . . . After that I really don't know."

"If I can help . . . ," she began.

"I think you want to stay as far away from this as you can get," I said.

"If I can help," she said again as she stashed the case file in her briefcase and got to her feet.

I walked her to the door and treated myself to the sight of her fearful symmetry sashaying to her car.

■ ■ ■

Bickfords Bunker, no apostrophe, sat between a hamburger stand and a car upholstery shop, about a third of the way up the hill on Evergreen Way. **Guns Bought And Sold. Scrap Gold And Silver,** the sign over the door announced. A red neon sign in the window read: **Militaries.** A sticker on the front door proclaimed that **This Establishment Protected By Smith & Wesson.**

And that was just the front of the building. Around the north side, where we'd parked, there were enough burglar bars to repel the walking dead. Square black steel bars covered the whole side of the building—both stories. Curtains on the windows said somebody lived upstairs.

At some point, the original structure had been added on to. A little square extension. Maybe twenty by twenty. **War Room** in big, black, plastic letters over the heavily barred entryway.

"Big on security," Gabe grumbled and slid out of the seat.

"Pawnshops generally are," I said as I pocketed the car keys.

"A better class of people and all that shit."

Gabe pulled open the back door and grabbed a black leather jacket.

"Cold?" I asked.

"Got a feeling this might not be the most PC crowd in America," Gabe said. "No sense in making it any harder for them than necessary."

"You look like Nanook of the North."

"Yeah, but you can't tell I've got tits."

Gabe came around the front of the car. "Let's go."

A muted buzzer began to sound in the rear of the store as I pulled open the door. The place was jammed. Display counters ran around three sides of the room. Six or eight people were bunched here and there doing business.

Mostly guns, it looked like. Guns and military stuff. Medals, uniforms, antique firearms of all sorts. Helmets, decommissioned hand grenades, swords, bayonets. Gabe and I headed down opposite aisles. Poster of George Patton glaring down at us from high on the back wall, like some angry god.

Eight feet in front of me, a guy in a red-and-black jacket leaned over the counter and stage-whispered into a curtained back room, "Bickford around?"

"He's up at the camp," somebody shouted back. Woman's voice.

"Shit," Red Coat muttered. "Who wants to be driving way out there to hell and gone." He opened his mouth to say something else, when he noticed me standing there. He nodded at me and managed a chrome smile before turning back to the counter and whispering something into the empty space.

The curtain suddenly parted, and a woman in a green apron bellied up to the rear of the display case. Stout. Blonde. Familiar. Felt like my heart was gonna beat itself right out of my chest. I turned my back to the counter and pretended to be studying a pair of Civil War cavalry cutlasses.

It was her. The blonde in the car. On that rainy alley off Denny. I stifled the urge to skewer her with one of the swords I was fondling, took several deep breaths, and continued my retail grazing.

"They're out in Conway for the whole weekend," Blondie said. She gave the guy a salacious wink. "Got them a big hootenanny going on," she said with a smirk.

Up at the front counter, looked like a couple of young guys in baggy shorts were trying to pawn an elaborate cuckoo clock. The aproned clerk kept shaking his head and pointing down at the bird.

The clerk looked up and met my gaze. That's when I knew where I'd seen him before. On the CCTV video from the night of the city council shooting. He was the guy closest to the door. My chest tightened. Breathing got harder.

I could feel Blondie's eyes on me as I shuffled past.

"Help you, sir?" she asked.

"Just lookin' around," I said.

Her eyes raked the side of my face. I kept my focus on the merchandise and kept moving. Her gaze never left me as I moved down the aisle.

"Do I know you?" she asked to my back.

I felt like I was balancing on a razor blade, expecting her to shout . . . to call me out . . . waiting for her to recognize me. The tension sent me sliding between display cases into the other aisle, where only the muted negotiations from the counters and the general rustle of humanity came to my ears. "Can't do it, son," I heard somebody say. "Just can't do it."

Gabe was up at the front counter handling what appeared to be an old Ithaca shotgun, like the one my grandfather used to take on his legendary Canadian goose hunts. "Hell of a range," the clerk was saying. "Thing's a damn howitzer. That baby'll knock down satellites."

Fear had faded. And all of a sudden, I was angry as hell, steaming, trying to keep my rage from spilling out all over the floor. Felt to me like I musta had smoke coming out my ears. I'd waited a long time to settle up with the people who'd attacked me. I nearly couldn't control my desire to grab her by the lapels, pull her over the counter, and work her until she told me where to find that son of a bitch who'd taken a knife to my chest and then run my legs over with a car. I could feel the blood rushing in my head. Thick . . . like red syrup.

I stepped up close to a musty-smelling Confederate Civil War uniform. Lots of faded gold braid on the shoulders, ceremonial saber by his side. I closed my eyes and worked at leveling my breath. Pulling the stench of the centuries into one nostril and then forcing it out the other. Kept at it until the roar of outrage quieted in my head and the adrenaline surge ebbed to a trickle.

Gabe must have picked up my vibe. Next thing I knew Gabe had lost the shotgun and was welded to my shoulder. "You okay?"

I inclined my head toward the door and began to move in that direction, Gabe following along in my wake. The outside air slapped me sensible as I stumbled toward the rental car. We got in and buckled up before either of us said another word.

"What's up?" Gabe asked.

"The blonde," I choked out.

"With the apron?"

"Yeah," I whispered. "She's the one who was in the car that was following Martha. She was there when the guy . . ."

"You want me to drive?"

Suddenly my anger had an outlet.

"What in the hell is that supposed to mean?" I shot back.

Turned out, if I didn't want to know, I shouldn't have asked.

"For the second time in two days," Gabe said, "you're lookin' a little soft to me. Never seen you back off like you did when that cop was busting your ass in the hotel room. A year ago, you'd have cleaned his teeth for him and worried about the fallout later."

I wanted to defend myself. Deny everything. Demand a retraction. Do all the dumb stuff people do when they don't want to admit the other guy is right, but I was graced by a sudden spasm of lucidity and instead took a breath, turned my face away, and zippered my lips.

Gabe put a hand on my shoulder. "What now? 'Cause we sure as hell can't stick around here."

As with most points Gabe took the trouble to make, there was more than a grain of truth nestled somewhere inside.

"I don't know," I said. "I need to think about it."

"You notice the guy up front, talkin' to the kids about the clock?"

"Same guy who was standing by the door the night Matthew Hardaway shot Valenzuela at the city council meeting."

"Yep," Gabe said. "Lemme drive."

This time I didn't argue. Instead, I heaved a mental sigh, popped the door, and slid out. As I came around the front of the car, I glanced over at Bickfords Bunker; the door was jacked open by a stout white arm, and Blondie was standing wedged in the doorway, apron and all, hands on her hips, watching Gabe and me change places.

"You sure we ain't met before?" she shouted from the doorway.

I averted my eyes and kept moving. When I sneaked a look her way a moment later, the door was closing, and she'd disappeared from view.

Gabe slid behind the wheel, dropped her into gear, and pulled out on to Evergreen Way heading south. "Let's get the hell out of here," Gabe muttered as we slid across town on Sixteenth, heading for Broadway and the open road.

▪ ▪ ▪

Six blocks later: "We've got company," Gabe announced. I watched those green eyes flicking back and forth between the roadway ahead and the rearview mirror.

I resisted the urge to gawk. "Cops?" I asked.

"I don't think so," Gabe said. "Rusted-out Subaru wagon. Even unmarked cop cars aren't that bigga pieces of shit. He's been with us ever since we left Bickfords Bunker."

We were rolling down the southern end of Broadway, on our way back to Seattle. Whipped and wounded, tails between our legs, headed for I-5 and the friendlier climes to the south.

"What now?" I asked.

"No idea," Gabe said.

Gotta admit, right about then, I was feeling pretty low, like I needed to redeem myself, to take some action that would miraculously reclaim something vital I'd lost . . . something I felt like I couldn't live without.

"What say we find out who it is," I suggested.

Gabe gave me a minor *Are you nuts?* look. "You sure?"

"Get in the right-hand lane."

Gabe complied.

"Just stay on Broadway," I said.

Gabe checked the mirror. "He's comin' along for the ride."

"There's a big cemetery up ahead on the right," I said. "Go in there."

Gabe required no further explanation. We bounced past an empty sales office and started up the hill into the burial ground. The place was well tended. Lots of flags and flowers. These were people who honored their dead. Gabe gave it a little gas, putting a bit more distance between the Subaru and ourselves as we climbed and twisted our way through the tree-shaded boneyard.

At the top of the rise, a traffic circle and a parking area announced the end of the line. From this point on, you were hoofin' it. Gabe braked to a halt, looked around, and then threw the Lexus into reverse and backed the car out of sight behind a wisteria-covered mausoleum. I got out and peeked around the corner.

The wind had freshened a bit, swaying the trees, swirling bits of dirt and leaves in the air. This far up the hill, the freeway was little more than the dull roar of eternity.

We waited. Thousand one . . . thousand two . . . nothing. At about thousand thirty, I began to wonder if whoever was following us had lost heart and turned around, but right at that moment, the Subaru poked its nose over the top of the hill. The driver stopped for a minute, surveying the scene, confused—wondering where we could have gotten to, how he could have missed us—and then he began to creep forward again, turning left around the circle at half a mile an hour.

About halfway around the rotary, when the driver's back was to us, Gabe pulled the Lexus out onto the roadway, blocking the pavement. No way out, assuming of course you weren't willing to run over tombstones in some ill-advised, all-out attempt to avoid a confrontation.

Apparently, the Subaru's driver wasn't feeling quite that desperate. The second he caught sight of our car blocking the way out, the Subaru skidded to a halt. Both of us were standing by its side windows before it stopped rocking on its springs. Gabe stuffed an empty hand inside the jacket and brought it out full. The sight of a .45-caliber automatic pointed at his forehead reduced the driver to jelly. I could hear him hyperventilating right through the closed windows.

I held up a restraining hand. "It's the kid from the newspaper," I said disgustedly.

Gabe stuck the automatic back into the jacket.

Ben Forrester pulled the hand from his throat and used it to crank down the window. He looked up at me with his mouth hanging open. Standing there in the land of the dead, we shared an uncomfortable moment.

"I . . . I was . . . ," Forrester stammered.

Gabe pulled open the passenger door and slid into the seat next to Ben Forrester. "You was what?" Gabe demanded. This was just the kind of white-privilege kid Gabe made it a point not to like. Entitled frat boys brought out the worst in Gabe.

Forrester swallowed hard. "I was just . . ." He swallowed again.

"Make it good," Gabe growled.

"It's my day off," he stuttered out of the blue.

"How nice for you," I threw in.

He dropped his hands onto the steering wheel with a smack.

"Okay," he said. "You got me interested in the Hardaway thing again. I was keeping an eye on Bickfords . . . you know . . . on my own time."

"How'd you find out about Bickfords?" I asked.

"Way back when . . . back before Ron told me to kill the story . . . I talked to a girl Matthew knew . . ."

"Wendy Bohannon," Gabe said.

Surprised, Forrester nodded. "She said Matthew had gotten a job—"

I cut him off. "We know," I said. "We talked to her too."

"So . . . you know . . . I figured I'd spend a little of my own time . . . and maybe see what was going on with the Bickford place . . . And then you two come bopping out the front door, and I figured . . . you know, what the hell . . . maybe you guys were on to something."

"What we were *on* was our way out of town," Gabe said.

"Turns out you were right, Ben," I added. "Nobody in this town wants to talk about what Matthew Hardaway did. All they want is for the story to fade away and for us to get lost."

"Did she tell you how Matthew started to change once he got the job? How he suddenly turned into the angry young man?"

"She told us," Gabe said.

"I figured . . . you know . . . if she was right . . . you know . . . maybe it was worth a little of my time." He shrugged. "As long as Phil doesn't find out."

"You know where Conway is?" I asked.

He nodded. "Up north someplace. Never been up there, though," the kid added.

"Supposed to have a tavern that serves great fried oysters," Gabe threw in.

"You heard of some kind of camp these guys have up there?" I asked the kid.

"A shooting club."

"Shootin' what?" Gabe inquired.

He looked confused. "I don't know," he said. "You know, skeet maybe . . . targets . . . stuff like that."

"You up for a little ride on your day off?" I asked.

Gabe's eyes rolled like a slot machine.

"Where to?" Forrester asked.

"To hell and gone," I said.

Chapter 3

The iconic image of rural America always includes a mongrel dog sleeping, undisturbed, in the middle of Main Street. Here in Conway, the dog had given up and gone home too.

"Where's the rest of it?" Gabe wanted to know.

"Methinks this may be the whole damn thing," I said.

"I hate places like this," Gabe groused. "Everybody got their noses stuck in everybody else's business. Like livin' in a freakin' fish tank."

There was the obligatory feedstore, across the street from an old wooden warehouse, a tired-looking Shell gas station, and of course the Stars and Stripes flying outside the U.S. post office, along with the Conway Tavern of song and story, and down at the end, Maggie's Market with a rusted Coca-Cola sign hanging askew on its weathered shingles. That was it. A little quarter-mile loop off the main road, rolling around one corner before reconnecting with the two-lane blacktop.

"Just a place for the local farmers to get feed and have a beer," Ben said from the back seat. He waved his phone. "Google says that according to the two thousand ten census, ninety-three people live here full-time."

From the look of it, that was about ninety more than needed to keep this place afloat. We'd spent the morning crawling along behind massive tractors pulling even bigger farm equipment, which had added at least an hour to the trip.

I had no idea what they were growing in the black dirt fields we'd driven past, but whatever it was, they were growing a hell of a lot of it. And it was either a fall crop or they had managed a second planting, 'cause the fields were fuzzy with lime-green growth.

A pair of battered pickup trucks leaned against the curb in front of the Albers feedstore. Half a block down the street, a dozen mud-flecked trucks and SUVs decorated the street in front of the tavern. Gabe pulled into the last parking space.

"Shall we?" I said.

"What?" Ben Forrester asked.

"Oysters," I said.

"I hate oysters," he whined. "I mean, who in hell ever opened one of those things, looked inside, and said, 'Wow, that pile of snot looks real good'?"

Gabe grabbed the door handle and hopped down out of the driver's seat. "Well then, kid, push the envelope and order something else."

I turned toward Ben as I stood in the street and stretched my back. "It's like Gabe said. Everybody knows everybody else's business in a little burg like this." I gestured at the tavern. "And this looks like the only watering hole anywhere around here, so whatever's going on in these parts . . . somebody in this place will sure as hell know about it."

The yellow ruffled curtains told me somebody lived upstairs above the tavern. Gabe held the door. I stepped through. The joint was bigger than it looked from the street, and it was jamming too. Not a table to be had, so we wandered down to the far end of the bar and appropriated the last three stools before you were officially in the toilet. The aroma suite, I imagined they called it. Buoys and Gulls, of course.

The bartender was a weathered old woman. Seventy anyway. Tall and wiry, she moved like she was on wheels. Rolling the length of the bar, saying a few words to one of the customers, and then rolling back our way, all without ever making eye contact. Looked like there were four of them handling the crowd. Two big girls waiting tables and somebody in the kitchen cooking. Somebody who spoke Spanish, because that was the language the girls used when they hung tickets and shouted instructions into the delivery window.

It was strictly a John Deere crowd. Lots of coveralls and muddy boots. Several cowboy hats and a couple of sombreros bobbing here and there too. Lots of Hispanics. Maybe half the clientele. Unlike Everett, seemed like everybody was comfortable with everybody else.

Ben kept trying to get the bartender's attention, waving, standing up, clearing his throat like a chainsaw and such and sundry. And, not surprisingly, she made it a point to ignore the shit out of him. "The service in here . . . ," he finally sputtered.

"Calm down, kid," Gabe rumbled. "The more you keep thrashing around, the longer she's gonna make us wait."

Took the barkeep the better part of fifteen minutes to get around to taking our orders. Gabe and I opted for the world-famous oysters. The kid pushed the culinary envelope with the ever-popular bacon cheeseburger. By the time the food arrived, the place had mostly cleared out. Apparently they all went back to whatever they were doing at about the same time every day.

I was dipping my last oyster when the bartender rolled over and asked, "Everything all right?"

"Delicious," I said.

"Glad you liked them. Get 'em fresh every day from just down the road. We been doin' 'em that way for the better part of fifty years now. Hate to think we'd lost our touch."

At the other end of the bar, one of the waitresses was cashing out the last of the lunch crowd. I leaned closer to the old lady and asked, "You know anything about some kind of shooting club up here? Buncha guys from Everett . . . wannabe military types."

She looked at me as if I'd maligned her mama.

"You're kiddin' . . . right?"

"Not that I was aware of," I confessed.

She eyeballed me up and down, like there'd been a pop quiz and I'd just failed miserably. I knew the look all too well. Me and my old man had a lot of practice at it.

"Well . . . ," she said finally. "If you was one of them idiots, you wouldn't be in here chowing down and askin' questions, now would ya?"

"Why not?" I asked.

"'Cause somebody'd kick your ass for sure, that's why."

"Why would they do that?" I inquired.

"'Cause we don't put up with none of that Aryan Nations skinhead crap round here. They come struttin' in here 'bout five years ago, talking 'bout niggers and greasers and Jews and all that racial purity twaddle of theirs." She waved her hand over the room. "You seen the crowd in here, mister. Agriculture isn't just the thing round here. It's the *only* thing. Without the Mexicans, this whole shootin' match wouldn't last a month. These are good, hardworking people. Nobody who comes in here talkin' trash about them is gonna walk out in one piece. I can damn well guarantee ya that." She gave me a gap-toothed grin. "They doan even bother coming into town these days. They bring everything they need with 'em from down south, 'cause ain't nobody round here gonna sell 'em one damn thing."

The door opened. A kid about fifteen came blinking through the door with a small brown dog on a leash.

"Get that damn dog out of here, Rusty. You hear me?" she shouted.

"He's a service dog," the kid protested.

"We gonna be holdin' a service for his ass you doan get him the hell outta here."

He opened his mouth, but she jumped in first. "Not to mention you can't be in here without an adult. You wanna lose me my liquor license?"

The kid turned to leave. The dog, however, was having none of it. He braced his legs, bowed his back, and refused to move, so as the kid dragged Fido stiff legged through the door, the old lady stood behind the bar shaking her head.

I heard a snort of laughter from Gabe. "You know," Gabe began, "I get it that people love their dogs and shit, but the notion that you need to bring them into restaurants and supermarkets just baffles me. I mean . . .

yeah . . . they're cute and cuddly and all, and I never met a human being as true as a dog, but this is an animal whose idea of an aperitif involves the commode and whose preferred snack involves their own ass. Anybody says dogs are a clean animal ain't spent nearly enough time watchin' 'em. Why they gotta be where I'm shopping or eating is a mystery to me."

"Me too," the bartender sighed. "Same thing with these skinhead morons. What it is makes them think they're better than everybody else is one of the great puzzles of our time. If I ever laid eyes on the shallow end of the gene pool, it's those yahoos. It's like all the losers in the Pacific Northwest got together and decided it wasn't their fault that they're unemployed or fifty-seven years old and still baggin' groceries. Couldn't be on them. No way. Gotta be some other explanation. No . . . gotta be because of the niggers and the Jews and the handicapped draggin' us all down. Biggest bunch of nothings I ever saw in my life, all of 'em looking to blame their uselessness on somebody else."

She realized she'd been rambling and took a moment to collect herself before turning to the sink and starting to rinse glasses. "You know, mister . . . I don't know what kinda business you got with those creeps, but if that old saying is right and timing is everything, then you all picked a real good time to show up here. They got some kind of big something or other goin' on this weekend. They been haulin' supplies in here for the past week or so. Bulletheads comin' in from all over the West. Get 'em all riled up to play toy soldiers some more. To cleanse the planet," she said with a salacious wink.

"And where does one find these genetic wonders?" I asked.

"Oh, they ain't hard to find." She pointed west. "You all just drive up to the corner, and instead of turning right to get back on the highway, you just keep going straight. That's Grove Street. That Rodman kid inherited nine hundred acres from his dad. Used to be a federal Job Corps Center. You know . . . they took a bunch of city kids and brought 'em out here and tried to teach 'em a trade. When they finally shut it down, the land and buildings reverted to the tribe. Old man Rodman knew somebody on the tribal council and somehow finagled a ninety-nine-year lease from the tribe. Got a guard gate and a paved road runnin' up the gully there to the other side of the bluffs. Real fussy about who they let in. That's where they run around blowing things up. Ya can't always hear it 'cause of the hill, but once in a while the ground shakes when they set something big off." She shook her head in disgust. "Out-of-town idiots started showin' up here yesterday. Gettin' ready for their big shindig."

A self-satisfied look found its way to her face. "They don't even drive through town when they come out here. They come in the back side. They know better than to expect anything outta Conway. Folks round here wouldn't piss on 'em if they was on fire."

That got me to thinking how the gathering was a mixed blessing. On one hand, there were going to be a lot of strangers around, making it easier for us to get lost in the crowd. On the other, whatever security these guys had put together was going to be on high alert.

I picked up the check and thanked the barkeep for the information, and we were halfway to the car when my phone began to vibrate in my pocket. It was Tim Eagen. I stopped walking. "Hey," I said.

"Got a preliminary report from the army on what's missing from down in Salem, Oregon. Seems they're light a hundred forty assault weapons, thirteen land mines, nine mortars, almost half a ton of plastic explosives . . . And get this: they can't find three rocket launchers."

"And the army just figured this out?"

"No . . . they been investigating for a while. I got the feeling that a whole shitload of stuff was missing and they weren't about to admit it. They're pretty sure it was a guy named Scooter . . . yeah, that's his real name. Scooter Allison, worked there for about three months early last year, but they don't have anything like enough to make a case, so they had to turn him loose. I emailed you his picture. What's up on your end?"

"We're up in Conway. There's some kind of skinhead gathering going on up here this weekend."

"I know," he said. "SPD's got about a dozen of them under lock and key downtown."

"For what?"

He laughed. "For being racist assholes. We always give the hater crowd a little extra attention. So does every other police department I know of. If nothing else, we can keep their ignorant asses off the streets for seventy-two hours or so.

"And that traffic ticket you thought your assailants got on Second Ave.? Dummy registration and driver's license. No such number. No such zone. That's why it took traffic six months to get back to me on it . . . according to them, anyway."

"Figures," I sighed.

Long pause.

I finally said, "I've got an idea."

"God help us all."

■ ■ ■

"We're the Christian Conscience delegation from Banks, Idaho," I announced.

Gabe laughed out loud and said, "Can't for the life of me figure how you've lasted this long, Leo. You're one rat-shit crazy dude, you know that?"

I didn't argue, just tilted my head toward Ben in the back seat.

"Yeah," Gabe said. "That's the rub, isn't it? What to do about Opie here. We sure as hell can't be taking him in there with us."

"What are we gonna do . . . just leave him here?" I asked.

"I could shoot him," Gabe offered.

The kid's eyes went wide.

"Too messy," I said.

"Where's Banks?" Ben segued quickly.

"'Bout forty miles north of Boise," I said.

I knew because Eagen had told me when he called me back an hour or so later. "We had ten of the skinheads in the cooler. Two of whom already bailed out. Everybody else had a warrant of some sort out on them. I had everything we took from the ones we still got brought up from the property room. My office looks like a fucking crime scene," he'd groused. "None of 'em got the same things in their pockets, or in whatever they were driving, so there don't seem to be any sort of universal ID they're all carrying, but when I saw those two guys from East Jesus, Idaho, carrying the same word around in their wallets . . . that got my attention."

"What's the word?" I asked.

"RAHOWA," he said. "The domestic terrorism guys tell me it's short for *racial holy war*."

"They do have an ear for the language, don't they?" Gabe chuckled after I filled them in.

I turned in the seat and made eye contact with Ben Forrester. "Listen to me, Ben," I began. "This is where the rubber meets the road. We go in there and they make us, I don't think there's any doubt about it. We're dead." I paused to let it sink in. "They got nine hundred–some acres to hide our bodies in. They could burn our bodies, and nobody'd ever know. This isn't journalism anymore. This isn't a city council meeting. This is real life and death here. These assholes are probably a bunch of loser wannabes, but all that does is make 'em even more dangerous. With professionals you more or less know what you're going to get. With these guys . . . anything can happen."

He nodded solemnly but didn't speak, so I went on. "This is my personal little crusade I'm on here. Mostly it's between me and me. Got nothing to do with you. You want to wait this out, nobody's going to think less of you. We can drive you somewhere you can Uber yourself home from."

He looked over at Gabe and then back my way. "You guys aren't really writers, are you?"

Gabe laughed again. "Must be why he's a reporter. Kid's got a keen perception of the obvious."

He took half a minute to think it over. "I want to go," he said finally. "But I'm . . . I'm not too proud to admit it . . . but I'm scared."

"That's a good sign," I told him. "'Cause this here is some scary, scary shit."

"You going with him?" he asked Gabe.

"Where he goes, I go," Gabe said. "My boss would be seriously pissed off if anything happened to him."

"What do I have to do?" he asked suddenly.

Gabe's eyes rolled. "Just do what we do, and keep it buttoned," Gabe cautioned. "This here is gonna be a real loose-lips-sink-ships situation. Just keep your eyes open and your mouth shut. Go along with the program . . . no matter what."

The kid nodded but didn't say anything. He sat back hard in the seat and closed his eyes. Looked to me like he was having a serious crisis of confidence.

Gabe reached down to an ankle holster and came up with a little black Beretta.

Gabe handed it over the seat. Ben looked at the weapon as if it were a viper.

"Take it," Gabe said. "Put it in your pocket."

Gingerly, Ben took the gun from Gabe's hand. "I'm not sure I could use this on another person," he said as he stared at the gun.

"Things go to shit, you might want to use it on yourself," Gabe joked.

"You sure you want to do this?" I prodded.

"I'm sure," he said after another moment.

■ ■ ■

I rolled down the window. "Christian Conscience," I said. "Banks, Idaho."

He was wearing a black T-shirt with a picture of a heavy-metal band and the words ANGER WITHIN. He fingered his way through his clipboard for a minute and a half. "And you'd be . . . ?" he asked finally.

I gave him the names I'd gotten from Eagen. Ben was Ezekiel Evers. Gabe was Bobby Jo McCalister, because it had a certain androgynous feel to it, leaving me, by default, to be Forrest Hamner.

"Where's Boyd?" the guy demanded. "Supposed to be four of you."

"We got rousted down in Seattle. Spent the night in the can. Boyd got into it with some nigger in the holding cell. Nigger got a busted face. Boyd got himself some fresh charges added on. 'Fraid ol' Boyd ain't gonna make it."

"Those Seattle assholes arrested a whole bunch of the brothers," the guy with the clipboard said. "Time's a comin'," he chanted. "They about to get what's comin' to 'em."

I figured this was the point where I oughta play my ace, so I said, "RAHOWA's comin'."

The guy looked up at me and grinned. "Your tech session is right after the orientation, over at the auto shop. Bay five."

The pistolero posers standing locked and loaded in front of the car stepped aside. Clipboard waved us in. "Time's a comin'," he said again as we drove by.

I had a pretty good idea of the geography because Ben had managed to download an old schematic of the Job Corps Center onto his phone.

From what we'd gathered from the Internet, the facility had been closed in the late seventies and had sat vacant until about five years ago, when a kid named Bertram Rodman showed up in town claiming his father had a ninety-nine-year lease on the property, which he'd, in turn, then leased to the U.S. Forest Service for the Job Corps Center. A lease that Bertram claimed had now expired. Turned out it was true.

The years had been unkind to the road. Massive tree roots had wormed their way beneath the asphalt. We were bouncing up and down like a clown car as I followed a black Ford F-150 through a funnel of trees out into an open pasture they were using as a parking lot. Guy who looked like a member of ZZ Top was waving me in his direction.

Probably twenty cars and trucks were parked in the clearing. Over in the shade a dozen or so motorcycles were lined up under the trees like shiny missiles.

I parked the car as directed, and we got out. Couple of hundred yards north, smoke was rising above the canopy of trees. The smell of roasting meat drifted to my nose, and all of a sudden, I was salivating like Pavlov's dog.

The woods were wired for surround sound. From what sounded like twenty or thirty speakers mounted in the surrounding forest, the air came alive with a recorded message.

"*The white race is the only pure race. The white race is morally and intellectually superior to the mongrel dogs who have invaded our domain. That purity must be maintained at all costs. The white race is the only unadulterated race, and that purity is being endangered. We are the first soldiers of that war.*"

Clipboard #2 saw me wiping the corners of my mouth. "Grub's over there," he said, jerking a thumb in the direction of the smoke. "Mr. Marshall talks in an hour or so, so if you want to chow down, now's the time." And then he walked off.

By my reckoning, we were somewhere near the middle of the property. Six or eight cinder-block buildings surrounded the central clearing. Guys were scattered around in smaller groups, drinking beer and shooting the breeze.

"Shall we?" I asked.

I heard the unseen speakers hiss to life again. "*The white genocide has begun. These mongrel dogs flow across our borders like the sewage they are. They must be stopped. The only real race is the white race.*"

Trying to keep our profile as low as possible, I started off in the opposite direction of the food. "Let's find the auto shop," I said back over my shoulder.

"You got any idea about what this so-called *tech session* is about?" Gabe asked the back of my head.

"Nope," I said. "Guess we'll just have to show up at the appointed time and see what's happening."

Ben was shaking his phone like a maraca. He looked over at me.

"No bars," he said. "No service."

"Guess we'll have to return to those thrilling days of yesteryear," Gabe quipped.

We spread out over the road and started following the curve around to the left, making a big half circle toward the nearest building. The woods were dark and deep. Everything in sight was awash in pine needles, soft underfoot and vaguely fragrant.

Way back when it was a job training center, it looked like they'd had the inmates fashion rustic wooden road signs, kinda like the ones you see in national parks. Problem was . . . somebody'd quite literally blown them to sawdust.

And I'm not talking a few random holes here and there. I'm talking smithereens; somebody'd touched off enough ordnance to start a war in the Balkans. I was still taking in the scope of the carnage when, in one of those tricks of the mind, I suddenly remembered the first trip I'd ever taken to Europe. How somewhere in . . . I think it was Austria . . . I'd noticed an interesting phenomenon. The road signs were pristine. No holes.

Not a single one. I was someplace way the hell up in the mountains, far enough off the beaten path where you could do just about anything you wanted and nobody was gonna know, and shooting holes in metal signs was simply not considered an artful amusement.

It was memorable to me because that was the first time I'd ever had doubts about the American way of life. I remember standing there on a windswept mountain road wondering about the fact that nearly every road sign in my country was riddled with bullet holes, and I wondered what, if anything, that penchant for puncturing signs said about us as a nation and as a people.

Naturally, I dealt with my doubts in precisely the manner we do with any of the things we don't like to think about, like racism and poverty and death. Little matters such as that. I ran the dilemma through my circuits a couple of times, hit the usual brick walls, and then stuffed it right back under the bed with the rest of the great unanswerable and went on with my life. It's the American way.

Adolf started in again with the recorded messages. "*We must eliminate the race traitors who seek to usurp our rightful place. Those fools who seek to transform the moral order with things like race mixing, affirmative action, and the American Civil Liberties Union. Now is the time to put them in their place. Under our heels.*"

On the south side of the parking clearing, seven buildings were scattered around under the trees. Turned out four of them had long ago been deserted and were well along the path of composting back into the forest floor. We walked over and peered over a collapsed wall into what appeared to have once been a machine shop. Old concrete platforms with big bolts protruding up from the floor to anchor the machines. Somewhere in time, a huge spruce tree had taken root in the middle of the room. Somehow found a home among the cracks and crevices of the shattered concrete floor. A tree grows in Conway.

Looked like some mythological monster, with its thick black branches spreading in all directions, hydra-like, pushing through the roof till it collapsed, oozing out the windows like an octopus trying to escape a cage, limber, alive, and desperate to shake hands with the sun.

Nobody said anything. What we saw spoke for itself. These guys had set up a firing range worthy of an army installation. Spotting stations. Firing stations. Fifteen or twenty silhouette targets down at the far end. And from the look of the craters in an adjoining field, they'd been blowing things up on a fairly regular basis. Big things.

It was the last of the old buildings that got our attention. Sitting at an angle to the others, all the way back where the paved road seemed to end in a cul-de-sac. You could back a truck right up to the doors.

Long cinder-block structure, unlike any of the others, dug halfway into the ground. Stone stairs leading down to a set of new overhead garage doors. I was still wondering why anybody would dump several grand into a set of new garage doors for a derelict building when the roof caught my eye. Brand-new, red-metal roofing, not the old twisted shakes peeling off the others.

Gabe stepped around me, moving along the south wall of the building. About three windows down the side, Gabe stopped, rubbed the dirt-covered windowpanes with a sleeve, and peered inside. I watched as Gabe used the same sleeve technique again, and again, before looking my way and motioning for me to come and have a look.

The forest loudspeakers blatted out a diatribe I didn't quite catch. Something about Jews not being white and how we were being sullied by our forced contact with other races.

I picked my way among the rubble until I was at Gabe's side. Gabe stepped to the side. I bellied up to the window, bent at the waist, and looked inside.

Took a second for my eyes to adjust. U.S. ARMY was clearly stenciled on the mass of boxes filling the room from floor to ceiling.

"Stuff from the armory in Salem," Gabe said.

"Jesus" was the best I could come up with.

On his way over to have a gander, Ben tripped over a rusted-out five-gallon bucket and fell on his face in the underbrush. I bent over and pulled him to his feet.

I watched as he dusted the bark and leaves from his clothes and then squinted in the window. "Holy moly" slipped out. "They've got enough military equipment to start a war," he said after a minute.

Gabe leaned in close to me and whispered, "I'm thinkin' maybe we ought to get the fuck out of here. This ain't what we bargained for."

The sound of voices brought me back to the here and now. Somebody laughed out loud. Half a dozen black-clad storm troopers, awash in weapons, were coming out of the woods. Felt like my lungs left town. Every joint in my body ached.

The one in the middle. The one without a gun. With the curly hair. Felt like I'd been stabbed in the gut. I nearly doubled over. My legs began to shake. Wanted so bad to hug myself but sucked it up and forced myself to keep walking.

I looked back over my shoulder. Gabe read my face, put one hand on the shiny automatic in the jacket pocket and the other between my shoulder blades, urging me forward. Ben was nowhere to be seen.

We passed within six feet of one another. Maybe it was the adrenaline, maybe just plain fear, but I felt light-headed and nauseous as we came abreast of them. My back was on fire. I managed a curt, manly nod. Guttural "Heys" and "Howdys" ricocheted among the trees as we passed shoulder to shoulder. I started to stumble and almost immediately felt Gabe grab me by the shirt and keep me upright and moving forward.

Seemed like I'd walked another mile before Gabe let go of my shirt. I staggered over to the side of the trail and leaned against a tree.

"That was him," I said. "The one with the curly hair and no gun. He's the one who carved me up."

Ben appeared from the bushes on the far side of the path.

"Where the hell you been?" Gabe demanded.

"I was pretending to take a piss," he blubbered. "The guy with the ammo belts across his chest . . ."

"What about him?"

"That's Milton Forbes. He's the city hall security guard who shot and killed Matthew Hardaway. Rest of those guys are from Everett too. I know all of them, and even worse, they all know me. Couple of them work for Bickford at the store."

Gabe snickered. "So much for wondering how somebody got a gun into city hall. Be easy for him. Just smuggle it in and pass it to Matthew on the night of the meeting."

I leaned harder against the tree. Going to Bickfords Bunker had been a serious mistake. What if Blondie or one of the other people from the store showed up here and saw Gabe and me again? What if one of the other guys from Everett recognized Ben?

Gabe shot me a *told you we shouldn't bring this asshole along* look. I'm guessing we were all thinking the same thing, but Ben was the first to blurt it out.

"You suppose that was their plan the whole time?" he asked nobody in particular.

"What plan is that?"

"To take a screwy kid like Matthew Hardaway, indoctrinate him with all this stupid racial hatred stuff, send him to kill Mr. Valenzuela so it'll stir up all kinds of trouble, and then kill Matthew themselves so nothing washes back on them? Almost sounds like the idea was to get Matthew killed, and Valenzuela was just a convenient way to get it done," Ben said.

"That's pretty cold," Gabe threw in.

Off in the distance, somebody let loose with an automatic weapon. Sounded like fifty or sixty rounds. The sharp cracks bounced around the forest and then went silent.

"Maybe we ought to lay low till the party starts, then get out of here while everybody's listening to whatever," Ben said.

"That's not a bad idea," Gabe said and looking my way, added, "Don't know what you got in mind for those assholes who fucked you up, Leo, and you know I'll back your play no matter what, but we start anything in here, and we're not walkin' out alive."

No denying it. Gabe was right. The situation had suddenly become a *live to fight another day* scenario. The questions were no longer of the who and why variety. We knew the answers to those. The question had become what, if anything, we planned on doing about it, and where and when, and it sure as hell wasn't going to be here and now. Much as I hated to admit it, I'd been running on emotion and hadn't really thought this thing all the way through. I'd sort of assumed that we were gonna find a bunch of yahoos shooting clay pigeons up in the woods, pretending to be cowboys. Running into a heavily armed collection of lunatics and haters had never crossed my mind. Silly me.

I checked my watch. "We've got about twenty minutes," I said. "What say we wander over in the direction of the car. See what the gate security looks like once the festivities start."

"We may have to leave the car," Gabe said.

"Enterprise'll have to get over it," I said.

Gabe looked around in a circle. Pointed. "Gate's that way. Maybe half a mile. Let's take the overland route."

Nobody in sight. Seven minutes till the speech. I slithered out of the trees and began to edge my way between vehicles, trying to catch sight of the Lexus. Gabe and Ben followed along in my wake as I slipped from row to row. Took me about three rows to realize that we'd originally come into the clearing from the other direction, which was why nothing looked familiar to me.

"*The Zionist Occupation Government acts in their own interest, not in ours. The Zionist Occupation Government actively seeks to subvert the goal of racial separation and supports the mongrelization of the white race.*"

Before I could internalize this new piece of nonsense, the deep rumble of an engine dragged my attention toward the entrance road.

Big, dusty 4x4 Dodge Ram popped into view. Either black or blue, it was hard to tell under the dust. Two guys, replete with aviator shades and assault rifles, stood in the bed as the truck bounced along. Instinctively, I squatted down. When I checked behind me, Gabe and Ben had followed suit.

We crouched there, mouth breathing and immobile, until the truck faded from hearing.

I peeked up over the hood of a Jeep Cherokee, didn't see anyone, and then slowly stood all the way up. I made eye contact with Gabe. "It's over there," I stage-whispered, pointing in the opposite direction.

The old adage that says timing is everything was never truer than in that moment.

If the three of us had been found crouching between cars, I don't think it would have been possible to explain it away. Even these fuckers weren't that dumb. That probably would have been the end of us, right then and there.

As it was, we were all upright and moving toward our car when the two guys stepped out from behind the white Chevy crew cab. In true Three Stooges fashion, we bumped to a stop.

Same look as most of the others. Bald, beer bellied, and inscribed mostly all over with jailhouse tattoos.

The one with the tattooed throat asked, "You boys lost?"

Normally, I might have taken the question as an offer to help, except both dudes had their weapons pointed directly at us. Kinda changes your perspective a bit.

"Tryin' to find our way to the orientation," I said, trying to sound casual.

"You figure it was gonna be out here in the parking lot?" the other guy wanted to know.

"We figured we might find somebody who could help us if we come over here," Gabe said.

Throat Tattoo walked over and got right up in Gabe's face. "Well . . . what we got here?"

"More than you're lookin' for," Gabe said.

Seemed like everything stood still for a second or two. No breath . . . no breeze. The guy looked Gabe over from head to toe. His frown said he couldn't make up his mind exactly what to make of Gabe. Tension buzzed in the air like wasps.

About the time the air got thick enough to spread on toast, the other guy decided it might be a good idea to let a little air out of the balloon.

"Orientation's over there," he said, looking out over Ben's head to the left of where the barbecue had been. "We'll show you the way," he said and started off.

Throat Tattoo formed a rear guard. I kept flicking my eyes in his direction as we marched along. He kept his finger inside the trigger guard as we trooped past the barbecue area and around the corner. Soon as I cleared the forest, I saw it. Another brand-new, red-metal roof poking up through the trees. Looked like what must have at one time been the Job Corps dining hall.

I was trying to stay calm. The sight of the guy who'd carved me up had my ears buzzing with adrenaline and my body vibrating like a tuning fork. And, as if that weren't bad enough, we were about to go into a room with any number of people who might recognize one of us, at which point we could pretty much count on being dead.

As we approached, the rumble of voices began to fill my ears. Four more Blackshirts manned the door. More clipboards. "Who you?" one of them wanted to know.

"Christian Conscience. Banks, Idaho," I said.

He looked down, flipped a page, and then looked at the three of us. "Supposed to be four of you," he announced.

"Boyd's in the can down in Seattle."

He shook his head. Spit on the ground. "They got all the Fresno boys and one of the Oregon contingents too. Buncha assholes gonna get what's comin' to 'em," he said.

The pair of thugs holding down the door stepped aside. The room was full.

Funny thing too. All the black-shirted skinhead types with guns were lined up around the perimeter of the room, holding up the walls. Everybody who was sitting down in the chairs looked pretty much like us. Probably a few more tattoos and ponytails than your average gathering, but other than that, your basic nine-to-five, working-class crowd.

In the front of the room was a raised platform, kinda like the stage in a high school gymnasium. No microphone or flags or anything. Just a bare platform about four feet above floor level. Probably where they made camp announcements from back in the Job Corps days.

We crossed behind the seating area and found ourselves chairs on the left edge of the assembled multitude about halfway to the stage. When I peeked back at the doorway, Throat Tattoo was still there, glaring at us. Still had his finger inside the trigger guard too.

Gabe leaned over and whispered in my ear. "Seems to be some degree of social stratification in here."

"Yeah, shirts and skins," I whispered back. "Any ideas why?"

Gabe gave a nearly imperceptible shrug. "Maybe they needed people for whatever they're doing here, maybe they needed people who could fit in. Not be noticed by their neighbors as white supremacists. Just regular joes." Gabe waved a hand. "Lot of these guys are gonna attract way too much attention right from the get-go."

Behind us, the doors banged shut. A quick look said the gang must all be here, and whatever was happening was about to start. There were about forty of us there in the nonskinhead section. Another thirty or so tough guys with guns were spread around the room at precise military intervals.

Mr. Throat Tattoo had gathered half a dozen of his brethren into a tight, glowering knot just inside the closed doors. Judging from the number of furtive glances thrown our way, I had a feeling we were the subject of the discussion.

Up in the front of the room, the party—or whatever—was about to begin. My curly-haired assailant was the first guy to walk onstage. I forced myself to breathe deep and concentrate on the other people who were coming out onto the platform. I recognized one of them as the guy who'd been manning the door the night Matthew Hardaway shot Valenzuela. The rest of them I'd never seen before.

A medium-size guy with rimless glasses stepped to the front and started patting himself down, looking for something at large in his pockets.

Ben Forrester leaned forward and shot me a look. "Bickford," he whispered.

The news didn't really register with me. I was, at that moment, transfixed by a pair of onlookers just offstage to the right.

Phil Hardaway was standing just offstage wearing full camo gear. Hands clasped tight behind his back. The brim of his cap nearly obscured his eyes. Ben leaned forward again. I waved him off and leaned closer to Gabe. "Guy in the camo is Matthew's father," I whispered.

"He's got the George Patton stance down," Gabe commented.

I didn't think, under the circumstances, there was much chance he'd recognize me. That's not what had my heart bleating like a car alarm. No . . . it was Blondie standing just off his right shoulder, wearing the same red-satin military jacket she'd been wearing the day she and Curly Hair had changed my life forever.

She'd almost recognized me back at Bickfords Bunker. If she saw me again, the jig was gonna be up, like big-time. I slid lower in the seat, pulled a baseball cap from my coat pocket, and put it on. Wasn't much of a disguise, but it was all I had.

When I looked up again, Bickford had found whatever he was searching for, which apparently was a much-folded piece of paper.

He stepped to the front of the platform and cleared his throat. "Well . . . ," he said. "Ain't no point in preaching to the choir. We all know why we're here. The time for talkin' is over. Time's come to take back that which is rightfully ours. To wash the pollution from our shores."

A stirring of agreement rolled through the crowd. Gabe and I shared a bewildered glance.

Bickford cleared his throat again. "We been putting this together for a long time. Nobody knows that better than you guys," he said to the haired-over section. "Lotta you guys made sacrifices to be here today . . . lot more of you might make an even bigger one before this is over." He looked like he wanted to go on but decided not to. "Now's the time," he finished with.

He looked down at the piece of paper in his hand. "Carlsbad, California," he bawled out over the crowd. Four guys in the front row stood up. The one on the far right, wearing the Dodgers cap, threw a fist in the air and shouted, "Come to Jesus." Another bigger ripple surged through the crowd. From the offstage area a guy in a lovely pair of baby-blue coveralls appeared.

"You boys go along with Dave here. He'll handle your orientation. And God bless ya." We watched as Dave hopped down from the stage and led the "Come to Jesus" quartet out the side door.

It went on like that for another ten minutes. Groups were called out. A new orientation instructor appeared from the woodwork, and then they'd march off toward destinations unknown. ACT for America. American Front. American Vanguard. Fortress of Faith. Repent Amarillo. American Freedom Party.

By my count, thirteen groups in all. As the room began to empty, I started to get a little nervous, thinking that maybe we'd already been found out. Maybe they were going to isolate us and then take us out, but with about only a dozen of us still sitting down, Bickford called out, "Christian Conscience . . . Idaho."

Another guy in designer overalls hopped down to floor level. Gabe, Ben, and I got to our feet. I kept my face pointed away from the front of the room, hoping Blondie wouldn't notice. The orientation guy didn't say a word. Didn't even look at us as he loped by, heading for the side door. We followed along.

The wind had freshened a bit. I could smell Puget Sound on the breeze. The trees swayed back and forth, rustling like ghostly dancers as the wind waltzed among them.

We followed a pine straw path deeper into the forest until we came to a galvanized cattle gate. Overalls produced a shiny new key, ushered us through, and told us to stay put while he went inside.

No new roof for this building. Or anything else. Matter of fact, the whole rear half of the structure had collapsed into a twisted pile of sheet metal and splintered wood. If the thickness of the moss growing on the remains was any indication, I'd guess it had been communing with the sod for several decades.

Funny thing, though . . . somebody'd bothered to run a yellow electrical extension cord all over hill and dale so this bristly ruin could have electric power. Second weirdness was that there was a big flat-screen TV sitting on a metal stand right to the left of the number one weirdness of all. A FedEx truck. Big-ass, purple-and-green FEDEX on the side. Cursive GROUND beneath it. Nice and shiny and new looking, and about as out of place inside a derelict building as a barnacle in a béarnaise sauce.

The *Twin Peaks* theme song started playing in my head, and I suddenly had a hankering for pie. I was still trying to recall the name of the damn song when Gabe bent and whispered in my ear.

"Must've found 'em a Sears special on those pastel overalls."

Overalls was walking our way, so I swallowed the urge to smile.

"You boys are from Idaho," he said.

We reckoned how that was true.

"And you're down one of your number?"

"He's in the can in Seattle," I said.

He nodded gravely. "We can do this without him," he said without hesitation. "How familiar are you with Boise?"

Before anybody else could speak, I blurted out, "Not at all. We keep about as far away from that pestilential hellhole as we can get."

Not only did it have a nice overly pious ring to it, but the way I saw things, it was better to be deemed ignorant than to get caught in a lie somewhere down the line because we'd claimed to know something we didn't.

Overalls smiled as if he'd known it all along and turned to the TV.

"I know you all must be anxious about what exactly your mission is gonna be. If it makes ya feel any better, even the orientation guys like me have been kept in the dark. All I know about the reckoning is this assignment right here." He grinned. "You know what the Hells Angels say: Only way three people can keep a secret is if two of 'em are dead." He paused for the laugh. When he didn't get so much as a titter, he picked up the remote for the TV and started pushing buttons.

The TV screen came to life. Street scene, some midsize city. I was guessing Boise. I'm clever that way. The six-story building in the center of the shot had like a porte cochere sticking way out over the front doors. "This, gentlemen, is your objective. Champion Cable, Inc., 1324 Empire Avenue, Boise, Idaho. Cable and Internet provider for almost eighty percent of the people in the metropolitan Boise area."

He pushed another button; the tape turned faster. For the next minute or two we watched in silence as a succession of delivery vehicles—FedEx, UPS, a plumber's van, a linen-and-uniform service—pulled to a stop in front of the building. More FedEx trucks in several sizes. More UPS. We watched as the drivers found the proper packages and, depending on the size, either carried or wheeled them inside. If I had to average it out, I'd guess they were inside for about five minutes.

"Champion receives between sixteen and forty-five deliveries a day. Nearly half of them from FedEx." He pointed at the truck. "The word *ground* there on the side of the truck indicates that this is a long-distance FedEx delivery, so if any of the local delivery guys see you, they won't expect you to be somebody familiar."

"So what are we delivering?" Gabe asked.

"Retribution," the guy said.

Ben opened his mouth to say something. Gabe put a death grip on his leg and shut him down before a single syllable escaped.

He motioned us forward. We followed him to the rear of the truck, where he pulled open the doors and stepped aside. I walked over to the right-hand door and peered inside. Just what you'd expect. The interior was filled with packages, many of them carrying the FedEx logo. Envelopes and smaller packages up on the shelves, bigger stuff on the floor.

"What's in the boxes?" Ben inquired.

"Four hundred fifty pounds of plastic explosive," the guy said in a tone that made it sound like he was talking about nothing more important than lunch meat.

Instinctively I started to backpedal. Overalls read my mind and grinned.

"Completely harmless until you flip the switch. You could shoot bullets through that stuff and it wouldn't go off. You could get T-boned out on the highway and nothing would happen; but you flip the switch, and you've got six minutes to get as far away as you can get, boys . . . and I mean hotfoot it the hell out of there. This baby'll wipe out the whole damn block. Vaporize the fucker from head to toe. You don't want to be nowhere in the vicinity when this baby touches off."

He started around to the passenger side, or what would have been the passenger side, except the steering wheel was over there, which, when I thought about it, made sense . . . you know . . . so the driver could get out on the curbside.

"Who's gonna drive the truck?" he wanted to know.

I raised my hand. He slid the door open and motioned that I should get in.

Musta been a midget in the seat last. I had to motor the seat all the way back before I could stretch my legs out.

"Look over on your left, on the floor," he said.

I did as I was told, and there it was. A red handle like an old Castle Frankenstein circuit breaker, with a metal band over it that you'd have to take off before throwing the switch. No way was anybody going to kick it into the "On" position by mistake.

"This here's a pretty simple operation, boys," the guy said to all of us.

Took twenty minutes for him to spit it out. The longer he talked, the straighter our spines got. These yodels had this thing planned out. They'd been working on it for months. They'd Google Earthed the whole damn thing too, so we'd have firsthand visual experience with the street scenario. Sort of a terrorist PowerPoint presentation.

The plan went like this: About seven thirty tonight, with Gabe and me in the FedEx truck and Ben following in the rent-a-car, we were to leave the compound and start driving toward Boise on a predetermined route. One stop in Oregon for gas and sustenance. Bogus credit card provided. Just over five hundred miles. Which ought to put us in the vicinity of Boise at four or five in the morning, at which point we were to drive to 1363 Stafford Street, a tumbledown garage in the south part of the city. We were to unlock the garage with a brass key we'd also been provided, and then drive both vehicles inside and lock the door. He told us the building had once housed a trucking company, so there were half a dozen sleeping cubicles behind the office area where tired truck drivers used to get a little shut-eye and that we should feel free to avail ourselves of the accommodations, so's we'd be all bright-eyed and bushy-tailed for the next morning's festivities. Like it was the first day of school we were planning for or something.

Listening to this guy was like watching a bad horror movie, where the suspense builds and builds until the heroine makes that fateful decision to look in the basement, carrying a single wavering candle, while wearing thirteen-inch heels and a worried look.

The only thing we were tasked with until the next day was wiping down the rent-a-Lexus for prints and then power washing the inside and outside of the vehicle with a mixture of bleach and hydrogen peroxide designed to effectively eliminate biological evidence. Tools provided. No assembly required.

At eleven fifteen the following morning, the real fun would start. All three of us were to put on our FedEx uniforms and hats, get into the FedEx truck, drive down to Champion Cable, and park the truck under the porte cochere. Once parked, Ben and Gabe, carrying our civilian clothes in a shopping bag, were to let themselves out the rear doors, which they would then lock. One standing on each side of the truck, like outriggers, while I locked the truck doors, and then finally, when I was certain we had everything together, I was supposed to throw the big red switch, and walk away. After that, the instructions were the same as they had been for the trip from Conway. Anybody stops you, anybody gets in the way . . . kill 'em. If, anywhere along the way, it looks like there's no way out, throw the switch. Get the hell away from the truck. Maybe get a few first responders that way. If you can't put serious distance between yourselves and the truck . . . well then . . . He grinned again.

"It won't hurt a bit," he promised.

Provided we got to the point of walking away from the FedEx truck, the key concept became six minutes. We had six minutes to put as many street corners between us and that delivery truck as possible. A car would be waiting for us in the middle of the 400 block of Sawtooth Avenue. West side of the street. Keys in the ignition. Get in. Go east or south. Get the hell out of there. Change out of the FedEx uniforms on the fly. Find a place to hole up for the night. Split up next morning. Disappear into the ozone. Stay way under the radar until the whole thing's over, about this time next week. Await further orders.

We went over it four times, playacted the whole thing out, until he was satisfied we had it down. "Well, boys," he said as he turned off the TV. "Back here ready to go at nineteen thirty hours. Get whatever personal stuff you need for the trip and bring it with you. Won't be no coming back here again. By the time . . ."

Then he stopped talking and brought a finger up to press his earpiece deeper into his ear. Didn't move a muscle for a minute and a half.

Just stood there listening to his earpiece, looking over at us occasionally, nodding his head.

"You all stay right here," he said. "I'll be back in a few minutes."

He left us standing there with our jaws on our shirtfronts, watching as he and his blue overalls traipsed off through the trees and disappeared from view.

Nobody said a word.

When I looked over at Ben, he was the color of day-old oatmeal.

"What are we going to do?" he finally asked in a low voice.

"I'll tell you what we're not gonna do," I whispered. "We're not going to drive this rig to Boise, park it in front of a local cable TV company, and blow the hell out of downtown Boise. That ain't gonna happen."

"Four hundred–some pounds of *plastique*." Gabe made a dubious face. "This fucker . . . that time of day . . . this thing could kill thousands of people, man . . . thousands."

"If Tim's info is right, that's only half the plastic explosive missing from the armory," I said.

"So there's at least one more bomb truck."

"And there's fourteen or so other teams headed God knows where to do God knows what," Ben threw in. "We gotta do something," he said. "We can't let this happen."

"Try your phone," I said to Ben. He gave it a go. Shook his head.

"No service. Nothing."

The white race are God's chosen people. Our innate qualities separate us from all other races and make us superior. RAHOWA is upon us.

I looked over at Gabe, who was doing the same thing. "No bars at all," Gabe said.

"Then we gotta get the hell out of here and tell somebody what's going on," I said.

"It'd be real helpful if we could get ahold of that list Bickford had in his pocket. It'd go a long way to putting a stop to this whole shit storm."

"And then what?" Gabe demanded. "We off Bickford and whoever's there and in the way. Suppose everything goes right and we get ahold of the list . . . what then?"

"We jump in the Lexus and run," Ben said.

Gabe's head was already shaking. "Running the Clint Eastwood gauntlet in the Lexus ain't gonna float, kid. That's swiss cheese time right there. Too many idiots walking around here with full autos. They could put a thousand rounds into whatever we were driving before we ever got out the damn gate." Gabe waved the possibility away. "We gonna have to put our tails between our legs and sneak the fuck outta here on foot."

"What about the FedEx truck?" Ben asked.

"What about it?"

"Maybe they'd be less inclined to shoot at us if they thought the thing might blow up and take them with it."

"And then what?" Gabe scoffed. "We outrun 'em in a delivery truck? Some kinda *Mad Max* road scene, with them chasing us in pickups and Harleys?"

"This whole thing feels like a bad movie," Ben muttered.

"That's what makes these assholes so scary," I said. "They talk about blowing thousands of people to dust . . . reducing city buildings to rubble . . . they talk about it like it's nothing. Just the price of returning them to their rightful place in the universe. Like it's a movie or something. Like somehow it just needs to be done, so things can return to their normal order."

"Because God is on their side," Ben muttered.

I walked over to the corner of the building and peeked around. .Overalls had found himself some friends: the curly-haired cutter, Blondie, Phil Hardaway, and a half dozen guys with assault rifles. They were about a hundred yards away, moving through the trees at a dogtrot.

I pulled my head back in. "We been made," I said. I pointed in the opposite direction. "That way," I hissed.

Gabe was off and running. Ben stayed put, as usual, wanting to ask a question. I limped by him as I headed for the cover of the trees.

When I took a quick peek back in his direction, he'd closed his mouth and was tottering along behind me.

I had no idea what, if anything, was on this back part of the property and at that point didn't much care. We needed to be someplace else. Right now.

A hundred fifty yards into the bush, Gabe took cover behind an enormous cedar tree. The chrome automatic was out, pointed straight up. Ben and I fell in behind the tree, breathing heavy. I pulled out the Smith & Wesson, checked the load, and then patted myself down for the box of ammo I'd brought along.

I squatted and then duckwalked around the forest floor until I found a line of sight through the tangle of branches and bushes and leaves. They were moving in for the kill. Slowly working their way around all four sides of the building, guns at the ready, using hand signals to move people around. I looked over at Ben and pointed deeper into the woods. "Let's go," I mouthed.

No stragglers this time. Single file, me in front, we picked our way through the dense undergrowth. The sound of shouts and curses spurring us along, making it clear they knew we were gone and weren't real happy about it.

Somebody decided to vent his frustration by spraying the surrounding forest with gunfire. Then another one joined in, and then a third.

As we crouched in the underbrush, the air was suddenly alive with bullets. Ticking this, tearing that, thudding into trees, ricocheting off rocks. Sounded like we were inside a beehive. Instinctively, we all got down and crawled on our bellies, found the nearest big tree, and got behind it. The storm of lead continued to shred the shrubbery like a giant Weed Eater. Over on my right, a sapling scrub oak took a high-velocity round about three feet up from the ground. Slowly it began to lean toward the missing chunk, bending double until its leaves came to rest on the pine straw.

Shouting suddenly rose above the gunfire. Somebody blew a whistle. The onslaught petered to silence. Tense seconds passed before we began to hear the sound of people thrashing through the undergrowth in our direction.

No strategy session required. We crept backward, stayin' low, tryin' to make as little noise as possible. The vegetation was jungle thick; the going was slow. No telling what was in front of us, the only comfort being that whatever was out there couldn't be any worse than what was behind us now.

Ben took a tumble over a root, went down hard, lost his pistol. Gabe yarded him up by the collar, reunited him with his weapon, and then plunged off through the thicket.

The forest speakers began assuring us that the holocaust was a Jewish conspiracy designed to make whites strangers in their own homeland.

And then, midsentence, the electronic voice crackled to static, and the speakers began to fill the forest with a screeching electronic alarm signal. *Security Alert, security alert.* Every ten seconds or so. Ten bleats and then another *Security Alert* echoed among the trees.

We kept moving. Inching our way through the tangle. Toward what . . . we had no idea. Just toward something else. Somewhere else. *Security Alert. Screech, screech, screech* . . . crawl . . . keep moving . . . head down . . . keep moving. *Security Alert.*

That's when I heard the rumble of an engine. Not far either. I silently cursed.

There obviously was a road not far ahead, in front of us. They were coming at us from both directions now.

I pointed off to the left and then began to veer that way. Up and running now. Not worrying about making noise, just trying to be anywhere other than where we were. Gabe's bad ankle was beginning to give out. Limping now, laboring. Ben ran smack into a giant spiderweb and was trying to wipe it from his face when the first Blackshirt showed up unannounced.

The guy must have been a faster runner than his friends. He was holding his weapon vertically, so's he could fit between the trees when he popped into view and slid to a stop six feet in front of me. I was in the process of bringing the Smith & Wesson to bear when Gabe shot him just below the right eye. The impact blew him completely off his feet and spay-painted major portions of his cranium all over the rough gray bark of a thick Douglas fir tree. I sucked in some air and watched as the bone and gray matter began to slide down the side of the tree.

Gabe grinned my way. "Ain't hide-and-seek no more. It's *on* now, baby," Gabe yelled. I took off running, gun waving like a conductor's baton as I loped through the forest. All around me, I could hear people breaking trail through the dense underbrush. Curses, orders, the sound of breaking branches. A shot rang out.

Somebody screamed, "Hold your fire, goddamn it. Hold your fire."

I stopped, stood still, and listened for a minute. I could hear an engine running. The tick tick tick of a loose valve. I put my head down and drove through the nearest bush, with Gabe and Ben hard on my heels.

I could see light ahead. Sky. I took off running, dodging left and right around trees and rocks like a halfback.

Security alert. Security alert. Screech, screech, screech.

I burst from the bushes. Damn near ran into the front of a blue Chevy pickup standing there with both doors wide open and the engine running. Seemed likely the truck's owners had jumped out and gone off into the wilds looking for us.

Funny how fast a situation can change. In the space of ten minutes, the idea of making a run for it, of driving through a hail of gunfire to get out of here, had gone from a dumb-shit idea to what now appeared to be the best chance we had.

I crawled up into the driver's seat. Gabe limped over to the passenger side and got in. I yelled out the window to Ben, "Get in the back. Stay low."

Ben must have been a high jumper somewhere in his younger days. At a full gallop, he hoisted a leg high in the air and flopped into the bed of the truck with a resounding thud, rocking the Chevy on its springs.

Before I could stomp the accelerator, a volley of lead came roiling out of the darkness, gouging jagged holes in the front of truck. The radiator began to belch steam. I threw it in reverse and put her all the way down. The truck jumped backward like a scalded cat. I swept the wheel back and forth, trying to create a zigzag pattern, making us harder to hit. We went swerving backward across the small meadow, throwing a thick rooster tail of dust and debris out in front of the truck, kinda like an inadvertent earthen smoke screen.

A round shattered the windshield, blew off half of Gabe's headrest, sending Gabe scrambling for the floor, filling the air with airborne bits of padding. I jammed the truck into drive and floored it back the other way, fishtailing across the grass toward the woods, just as our pursuers were stumbling out of the thicket and into view.

I veered hard left, nearly putting the truck up on two wheels. In the back, Ben was bouncing up and down like a Ping-Pong ball, airborne at every big bump, pinballing around as centrifugal force shoved him from one side of the bed to the other.

Another round shattered the back window, taking out the rearview mirror on its way by, sending a spray of shattered mirror shards into my face.

I was trying to drive with one hand and wipe the glass from my face with the other, so I didn't see the other truck until half a second before it T-boned us.

The impact tore my hands from the wheel. Next thing I knew Gabe was on top of me. I could feel the truck losing its battle with gravity. We rolled once . . . and then again. Everything inside came loose, filling the cab with more snow-globe debris.

My body had reached its limit. My back was nearly immobilized with pain. My legs ached liked bad teeth. At that point it would have been easier to list what didn't hurt.

Funny how the mind works too. The thing I remember most vividly was a single petrified french fry, musta been at large under one of the seats for years . . . I remember it floating by my face in the seconds before the Chevy came to a rest on its roof and how bad I wanted to snatch it from the air and eat it.

Gabe managed to get one foot on the steering column, trying to relieve me of most of the extra weight. I heard a voice say, "Gonna have to rock it back onto the wheels, if'n we're gonna get 'em outta there."

"Fuck that shit," another voice said. "I say we off 'em right here and now."

"Brass wants 'em alive," the first voice said. "Needs to know what they know."

Somebody snickered. "That fucker over there . . . he ain't tellin' nobody nothin' no more. Not ever."

Gabe groaned. "The kid."

It took them about five tries to roll the truck back onto its wheels. After that, things got a bit hazy. I recall somebody with a skull ring on his middle finger reaching in the partially collapsed window frame and cutting my seat belt with a sheath knife. Then a multitude of hands squeezing me out through the narrow opening in the broken glass. By the time they got all of me hauled out, I'd already seen Ben. And wished I hadn't.

I knew right away he was dead. Something changes in that instant when the spark of life leaves a person. A person suddenly becomes little more than a rented vehicle, a bag of bones having little or nothing to do with the person you knew in life.

He lay in a twisted heap, about fifty feet from where I was being held up by the elbows. Somewhere along the line, during one of the rolls, something had very nearly torn his head off. I stifled a gag reflex and looked away and knew, in that instant, that the image of him lying there in the dust would be etched on my optic nerves for the rest of my days.

On the other side of the truck, they'd manhandled Gabe out of the cab. I shrugged off the guys on my elbows and started for Gabe in the instant before a rifle butt tenderized the side of my head and separated me from my remaining consciousness.

■ ■ ■

At first I thought I was blindfolded. Took me a while to realize that my eyes were okay and that the room was deep-space dark. Right after that spasm of lucidity, something about the way the air caresses a naked body told me I was also naked.

"Hey," I said to the darkness.

"What?" Gabe said from some distance away.

"You naked?" I asked.

"Yeah . . . I think so."

"Can you move?"

"Not much."

I curled my fingers up toward my wrists and discovered the plastic zip ties that were holding me to the chair. I silently cursed. Only way to get out of a properly attached zip tie was to chew off your hand like a friggin' coyote.

"Can you move the chair?" Gabe asked.

The best I could manage was to lift the front legs off the ground by getting up on my toes. Then I added scrunching my ass forward while holding the front legs off the floor. The chair moved about two inches forward and then dropped back down.

"A bit," I said.

"Let's see if we can't get next to each other," Gabe said.

Twenty minutes of grunting, groaning, and sliding got us knees to knees. My eyes had partially adjusted to the lack of light. I could just make out Gabe's sweaty silhouette about three feet in front of me. That's when the lights snapped on and somebody began to throw latches and levers on the door.

I cracked my eyes several times, getting them used to the light. We were in a shipping container. Gabe and I and two old-fashioned wooden chairs. That was it. That and the overwhelming smell of dampness and mold. Half of Gabe's face was a giant purple bruise. One eye was completely closed. A trickle of dried blood ran from the hairline until it disappeared into the ear canal.

The door on the left groaned open. Then the other one. A blast of cool air washed over my naked body like an avalanche. I shuddered twice and then looked up.

They'd brought out the taxi squad for this one. The whole gang was here. Didn't recognize the first guy through the door, but all the rest of them were familiar faces.

Bickford, Blondie, Curly Hair, Phil Hardaway, our orientation guy, and a pair of glowering Blackshirts.

Blondie stepped right up in my face. She bent down and put her face in mine. I could smell her breath mints.

"I'm tellin' ya . . . that's him," she said. She straightened up and pointed at my face. "Same guy Scooter carved up. Him and that . . . that freak over there, they come in the store earlier today. Grew all that faggot hair since Scooter cut him, but that's him for sure."

Curly-haired Scooter dropped to one knee in front of me and squinted at my chest.

"Oughta be some scars here," he said. "I don't see shit," he declared.

"Maybe he got it fixed," Bickford said from over by the door. "Phil, what about you? You've seen him before."

Hardaway walked over and stood about six feet in front of me. He was silent for a few seconds. "Not sure," he said finally. "It was a long time ago. He's about the same height, maybe." He grabbed me by the chin and pulled my head up. "Not sure," he said finally and walked back out of view.

"I was given to understand you'd met the guy," the new voice whined.

"Long time ago."

"Is this or is this not the fellow your father-in-law tried to hire to look into that boy's death?"

"I took care of that," Hardaway protested. "I gave that nosy old asshole what he had coming. What does it matter if this is the guy?"

He thought it over. "Well . . . you know, you're probably right. It doesn't really matter, now does it?" the new guy said. I might not have recognized him, but I recognized the voice. It was the guy running his mouth over the loudspeakers. The one spouting the white supremacy shit. Gabe knew it too. I could tell.

"Apparently these people are not who they claimed to be. That's sufficient to assume they are not part of our glorious cause."

Somebody cocked a weapon. The snick of a metal slide sent me squirming in the seat. Felt like something with hot breath was breathing down my neck.

The Voice held up a restraining hand. "No," he said. "First we must ascertain what they know and to who else they might have told what they know." He looked to his left. "Mr. Allison," he said. "If I recall correctly, you have a particular talent for extracting information from the unwilling."

Curly Hair leered. "Sorta a hobby of mine. Got me a little 'truth kit' back in my car."

"Go get it," the Voice said. "Then we'll begin the interrogation."

The Voice pinched his nose and made a prissy little face. "Interested parties can wait outside until you return. It stinks in here."

Everybody headed for the door. Scooter stayed for dessert. He walked over and stood between Gabe and me. Looked my way. "Gonna cut your cock off, boy," he said, then pointed at Gabe. "Gonna cut off whatever the fuck that freak's got down there too. Then I'm gonna make you eat both of them."

He stood there for a moment, letting the horror sink in, before letting himself out the door, leaving us sitting there staring at one another in the darkness.

Nothing needed to be said. We'd fucked up royally. Severely underestimating the enemy had been stupid, and we were about to pay the price. My frustration boiled over. I began to struggle. To pull on my bonds for all I was worth. Grunting and sweating, trying to break a zip tie I knew perfectly well was unbreakable.

When I had to stop to catch my breath, I watched as Gabe turned purple trying to break loose. When Gabe ran out of gas and stopped struggling, I started trying again. The force broke the skin. Blood was rolling down over my fingers when I heard a sharp crack and felt something give.

My first thought was that I'd broken my wrist, but I've broken quite a few bones in my time and knew this didn't hurt enough for a broken bone, so I gave it another go, this time twisting my wrist on the wooden arm of the chair as I tried to pop the zip tie.

The arm came apart with a crack. I stopped and sat still. Waiting for the doors to open. Nothing happened. My brain was screaming at me, "The chair . . . the chair . . . the weak point's the fucking chair."

I shifted my weight and then threw myself sideways, sending the chair toppling over onto the remaining arm. The force broke the arm loose from the chair bottom.

I slid the zip tie down and pushed it over the end of the arm support. With both hands loose, I channeled my suppressed anger and quite literally tore the remains of the chair to pieces.

I started for Gabe, had a better idea, and picked up one of my chair's arm supports from the floor. I stuck the skinny milled end in between Gabe's right wrist and the arm of the chair. "This is gonna hurt," I whispered.

Gabe nodded and smiled. I began to twist the piece of chair wood. One time around and Gabe was breathing like a locomotive, huge bulging veins rising from the wide forehead.

Took everything I had left to turn it another complete revolution. Gabe was groaning now. Eyes rolled all the way back, teeth starting to gnash together, when the tie snapped. The chair tipped over on its own. Without shoes it hurt like hell, but I stomped Gabe's chair to kindling.

A moment later we were standing side by side, shattered chair arms dangling from wrists, ankles festooned with splintered chair legs. We looked like a pair of giant naked wind chimes. Gabe winked and gave me a bloody-toothed smile.

The bolts and latches on the door began to snap and slide. Gabe and I painted ourselves to the front wall on either side of the doors. The door on my side swung slowly open. First thing over the threshold was the business end of an assault rifle. I grabbed it in both hands and twisted with all my might. I heard his trigger finger snap like a Popsicle stick as I wrenched the weapon from his grip. The door started to close.

I lowered my shoulder and tried to run right through the metal door. I felt the impact drive whoever was on the other side to the ground.

I came out of the container with the assault rifle spewing rounds like a garden hose, not much caring who was still out there, just wanting them dead. As far as I was concerned, anybody whose idea of a good time included watching that Scooter asshole work somebody over with his "truth kit"—anybody like that, the planet could do without.

Turned out only four of them had stuck around for the show. Pity was that none of them was the little guy on the loudspeakers. Scooter wasn't back with his torture bag yet, and Phil Hardaway had somehow disappeared into the ozone.

Bickford, Blondie, Throat Tattoo—whose gun I'd appropriated—and our very own orientation guy, baby-blue overalls and all, lay strewn around the forest floor like broken flowers. They'd all taken multiple rounds and had hated their last. Throat Tattoo was the only one still moving. He slow-motion spasmed on the ground like a dog running in his dreams. Gabe hustled over, pulled Bickford's sidearm from his belt holster, and shot Tattoo right between the eyes. The squirming stopped. The forest got quiet. I stood up and looked around. Nothing. You could hear leaves falling to the ground.

I got down on one knee and started to go through Bickford's pockets, looking for the list of which groups were going where to do what, when out of the blue, I remembered I was stark naked. Real game changer that.

Suddenly the fact that we were surrounded, out in the middle of nowhere, with a bunch of heavily armed maniacs bent on murdering us didn't matter nearly as much as finding a way to cover my ass. Go figure.

I undid Bickford's belt, rolling him back and forth on the ground as I wiggled his trousers down his rubbery legs and over his engineer boots, finally swinging them loose into the air.

He was way smaller boned than I was; it was a tight fit, but I got them on. I was doing the same thing with his stinky camo jacket when I noticed Gabe standing there.

I looked over. "The blue overalls are about your size," I said.

The suggestion got me a big, bloody-toothed grin. "Why the hell not," Gabe said and started that way.

I got to my feet and stuck my hand into the right-hand pants pocket and found a cell phone. I button pushed my way to recent calls. Mostly the Everett area code. Looked like business mostly. Except for half a dozen or so calls to and fro with somebody named Thomas Henry Mitchell, who I was betting was the guy on the loudspeakers.

The phone began to buzz. I pushed a button and brought it to my ear.

"Bickford," the voice bleated. "It's Scooter. What in hell is going on down there? What's all the shooting?"

I didn't say anything. I wanted to tell him I was coming for him, that he better never close those nasty little pig eyes of his again, 'cause I was gonna be somewhere out there in the darkness waiting for him. But I bit my tongue instead.

"Bickford . . . you there . . . what's . . . Bickford!"

He broke the connection. I looked Gabe's way.

"A vision of loveliness," I said as I watched Gabe borrowing orientation guy's shirt and then letting out the overall's suspenders.

"We got four stiffs lying here," Gabe said. "One more ain't much gonna matter."

I got the message and started going through the rest of Bickford's pockets. I found what I was looking for in the back pocket of the pants. Unfolded it. Yep, there it was. I refolded the list and returned it to where I'd found it.

I shuffled over and searched Throat Tattoo. Poor bastard looked like he had three eyes. Like I figured, I found two extra magazines for the assault rifle in his backpack. A good thug never goes out without being properly prepared.

Gabe, who was doing the same thing to the others, had come up with three more handguns from the Cadaver City residents and had stashed them in the various overall pockets, usually intended for tools. I particularly admired the black revolver dangling from the loop which generally housed a hammer. Nice touch there.

Gabe looked my way. "Not to belabor the obvious, but we better get the fuck out of here."

I nodded. "I hate leavin' Ben's body here with these assholes," I said.

"Yeah . . . I know whatcha mean." Gabe shrugged. "You got any ideas, I'm listening, but the way I see it, tryin' to get him outta here is strictly a suicide mission."

"I'm not ready to go yet," I said.

"Me neither."

"Let's roll."

■ ■ ■

Even from beneath the thick canopy of trees, the slanting remnants of late-afternoon sun made it easy to tell which way was west. Instead of following the dying of the light, we headed back the other way. Due east. Toward the miles and miles of farms we'd passed on the way in. That was the plan at least.

The Job Corps's old road system was big-time serpentine. Seemed like it must have had more to do with keeping the inmates busy than it did with creating a viable infrastructure, so we kept coming across sudden sections of roadway that didn't seem to lead anywhere but required that we scuttle silently across them whenever we came upon another loop. On several occasions we had to throw ourselves to the ground and cower in the bushes when trucks full of Blackshirts thundered by. What mostly kept us from being spotted was that these were the kind of guys who like their truck exhausts throaty and muscular. You know, a manly exhaust throb you could hear coming from quite a distance.

By the time the sun disappeared altogether, we'd made so many veers and zigs and zags, crossing roads and forest clearings and avoiding passing vehicles, we were pretty much traveling blind. Any real sense of direction had disappeared with the light.

Gabe and I were sitting on a fallen fir tree, catching our collective breaths and trying to figure out which way was up. Gabe pulled a cell phone from a jacket pocket and held it tight to the baby-blue overalls so's the light wouldn't give our position away. Checking for cell service. A disgusted shake of the head told me all I needed to know.

"No service," Gabe announced.

I got up and started walking in the general direction we'd been going before. You know things have pretty much gone to shit when falling in a ditch is the best thing that happens to you all damn day. The brush had thinned and tall grass was now underfoot. One second I was picking my way through the chest-high prairie grass, and the next I was hurtling downward like a Holstein cow in an elevator shaft.

The landing was surprisingly soft. Wet and muddy, with enough collected debris in the bottom to cushion the fall. When I looked up, Gabe was standing at the edge of the forest looking out over my head, with the biggest grin I'd ever seen on that face. I stood up and looked in that direction.

The road. The beloved road. I had to stifle a cheer. Gabe slid down the side of the ditch, then boosted me up the other side. I set the assault rifle on the pavement, lay down, and put out both hands. Gabe grabbed ahold, and half a heavy-breathing minute later, we were panting, side by side, facedown on the two-lane blacktop.

Took us a minute to glue ourselves back together before we struggled to our feet. I hung the assault rifle back around my neck and looked around. We'd made it to the road all right, but the question immediately became, where on the road? Which way was civilization? We were too beat up to go marching off in the wrong direction again.

Gabe pointed. "See the glow," Gabe said.

Fuzzy in the onshore fog, but I saw it. A dull, muted glow coloring the underside of the clouds.

"That's gotta be Conway," Gabe said.

"Nothin' else out here."

We started off in that direction. Half a mile later, the moon broke through the cloud cover for a minute or so. Long enough for me to get a glimpse of our shadows following us down the road. All we were missing was a fife and drum.

Mercifully, only one car used that desolate stretch of road in the forty minutes or so we were staggering along the shoulder. We saw the lights coming from a long way out and repaired back into the ditch. Took us three tries to get out. We decided we'd either have to tough the next one out or spend the night in the ditch.

We still hadn't sorted it out when something ahead in the darkness pulled my eye in that direction. A few more steps and a streetlight peeped out from the foliage. Yet a few more steps and a road sign showed its face. Green and white in the half light. **CONWAY.** Underneath, **POPULATION 73.** Musta been an old sign.

"I was our Aryan brothers and I was lookin' for us, I'd have people waitin' for us in town. Lots of 'em," Gabe offered.

"Let's go in down the far end," I said. "Real low profile. Maybe come in behind the post office."

So we did just that. Walked an extra mile or so, then cut back into the trees and looped around behind Main Street until we were peeping out of the trees about forty yards behind the 76 station.

Not one truckful of Blackshirts, but two. Four guys to a truck. Two in the cab, two in the truck bed. One stationed at each end of town. Lights off. Every once in a while somebody inside the trucks would sweep the area with the truck's spotlight. Looked like a prison break was going on.

No way were we going any farther. No way could we stay where we were either. About the time it got light out we were gonna be a whole lot easier to find.

I heard a radio crackle. And then another. The two trucks were jawing back and forth. The nearest truck's taillights flashed and then went out. In the half light, it took me a minute to see that one of them was moving. Trouble was, it was hard to tell which truck was moving. It was like having the car next to you in traffic start to creep forward, and you stomp on your brakes because you think you're rolling backward. Took a couple of seconds of staring to be sure. The nearest truck was rolling down the street toward their friends at the far end of town. The two guys standing in the bed had turned around and were looking out over the cab.

"Now," I said as I pushed myself to my feet. Gabe was breathing down my neck as we skulked across Main Street in the darkness, hoping like hell that driving without headlights in nearly complete darkness would keep the guys in the truck sufficiently occupied so's they wouldn't notice us creeping around behind them.

We made it. Plastering ourselves against the weathered side of the old warehouse, hotfooting it toward the darkness at the back of the building. Once we turned the corner, we kept slide stepping along the back wall, picking our way carefully through the maze of century-old farm equipment and agrowaste littering the uneven ground.

By the time we reached the far end, I'd added three divots to my shins. I ventured a quick look between buildings. Wavering brake lights told me the nearest truck was backing down Main Street to take up its former position.

We darted across the space and flattened ourselves across the back of the tavern. Forty feet in front of me were three concrete steps leading up to a doorway. The light fixture above the steps had been ripped from its moorings and now hung disconsolately by its wiring.

I stayed low as I duckwalked over to the steps. I was on the second step, working up the nerve to knock on the door, when two things happened at once. First, the door opened. Second and most worrisome, somebody stuck a double-barreled shotgun into my face so hard it sent me back on my haunches, which in turn sent me skidding the rest of the way down the stairs on my ass.

I was still at the mouth-breathing stage of things when a voice said, "Oh, it's you."

Actually . . . it was her. The old woman from behind the Conway Tavern. Except that, since we'd chatted earlier in the day, she'd either been in a serious car wreck, or somebody'd worked her over pretty good. Her lower lip was just about split in two. Her left eye was sporting one of the most colorful shiners in Christendom, and to top things off, she had what appeared to be about ten stitches' worth of cut below her other eye.

She lowered the shotgun. "Where's the boy?" she wanted to know.

Gabe and I exchanged glances, but neither of us said anything.

"Aw . . . don't tell me . . . goddamn it."

So we didn't.

She pointed the shotgun at the ceiling and motioned us inside. Seldom has a flight of stairs seemed so steep. Felt like were chugging up one step at a time for about twenty minutes. The upstairs apartment had been trashed. Tables thrown over on their sides. Lamps in pieces on the floor. Pictures askew on the walls.

"They come up here a couple of hours ago," the old woman said. "Started slapping me around, looking for you guys."

I opened my mouth to apologize, but she waved me off.

"Don't," she said. "Wasn't your doing. They're just hateful people."

We stood in silence for a moment.

"They'll be back," she said. "Bunch of 'em are outside in the street."

I told her we knew about the guys outside in the trucks. "Your phone work?" I asked.

She shook her head. "Did till they ripped it outta the wall. Cell service is so damn spotty out here, most everybody got them a landline."

I pulled Bickford's phone from his pants pocket. No bars. "Shit" slipped out.

"We gotta get out of here," Gabe said.

"Your car still in there?" she asked.

"'Fraid so," I said. "Anybody but you live in town at night?" I asked.

"Nope," she said right away. "Just me."

"Where's the nearest phone?"

She didn't have to think about it. "Potter's Junction. It's about nine miles back toward Stanwood. Everything works back there. They got their own microwave tower."

"We need to get there. Right now," I said. "Those Aryan morons are planning terrorist attacks. We've gotta keep that from happening. Lotta people gonna die if we don't."

"I got an old truck," she offered.

"You're coming with us," Gabe rumbled.

"Me? Oh no. I couldn't." She looked around the room, like she was seeing it for the first time. "This place is my life. My Charlie . . . he would never . . . no . . . I couldn't . . ."

"You can walk, or I can carry you, but either way, you're coming with us," Gabe said in a low voice. Something about when Gabe uses that voice seems to get people's attention. Like life or death may be involved somehow.

The old woman's shoulders slumped. After a few seconds of staring at the floor, she gave us a barely discernible nod, walked over to the biggest kitchen drawer, and took out a thick ring of keys. She underhanded them my way. I pocketed them, then picked up her shotgun and handed it to Gabe.

"You got more shells someplace?" Gabe asked.

She opened a closet to the right of the stairs and produced a full box of shotgun slugs. Punkin balls, as we used to call them when I was a kid. Put holes in things the size of a pocket watch. Didn't have that much range, but if one of 'em hit you, whatever it hit was blown to mist and gone forever.

"You know . . . ," the old woman began. "There's a storage shed around back of the post office. All the state agencies used it for emergency equipment . . . you know, since we're so damn far out of the way. And since I'm the only one out here twenty-four seven, they give me a key, in case of disaster or something like that."

Gabe was beyond impatient. "So?"

"So . . . last time I looked in the shed there was a couple sets of those things the troopers throw out in the road to bust up your tires if'n you won't stop when they tell ya to pull over. Just hangin' there on the wall big as life."

"Spike strips?" Gabe and I said in unison.

"Unless the staties moved 'em in the last coupla months."

"How old's your truck?" Gabe asked.

She stuck out her chin. "Eighty-nine," she said. "My Charlie wouldn't drive nothin' but Fords. Said Chevys were pieces of crap."

Gabe looked over at me. "We ain't gonna outrun those big old Dodge Rams in an eighty-nine Ford."

■ ■ ■

We had to wait about forty minutes before the nearest truck rolled to the other end of the street to chat with their brethren again, at which point Gabe and I got both spike strips spread across Main Street as far apart as we could get 'em, so if the second truck saw something wrong with their buddies, they'd be inclined to swerve around and would run into the second strip in the darkness at the edge of town. That was the plan anyway.

I was driving. The old woman, whose name turned out to be Betty, was strapped into the passenger seat. Gabe, the assault rifle, and the extra clips were in the back of the truck, prepared for a rearguard action. The Ford had tall wooden gates on both sides and a nice thick tailgate to shield Gabe as much as possible.

"You ready, Betty?"

She pulled the old-fashioned lap belt tighter. "Ready as I'm gonna be," she said.

Been a while since I'd driven a stick shift, but it was kinda like riding a bicycle—once you learn, you never forget.

I popped the clutch, wound up first gear until we bounced out onto the road, then jammed the transmission into second and began roaring up Main Street in a cloud of smoke and gravel.

Behind us, both of the trucks were suddenly ablaze with lights and staging frantic K-turns in the middle of Main Street. Muzzle flashes lit the night. Smoking tires began to scream. I slammed the transmission into third and tried to push the pedal through the floor. We fishtailed wildly as we swung out onto the main road and went roaring off into the darkness.

In the rearview mirror, I caught sight of the first truck hitting the spike strip. The front tires exploded, and huge chunks of steel-belted radial went flying off in all directions, like a murder of frightened crows rising together from the ground.

The second truck swerved around the first. The boys in the back began firing out over the cab. Gabe ducked behind the tailgate. Slugs thumped into us from behind. Betty unbelted herself and hit the floor. Sometimes you get lucky. About five seconds after Betty hit the floor mats, a slug came ripping through the back window and buried itself in the dash, right about where she'd been sitting. Would have taken her head clean off if she'd still been sitting there.

I checked the mirror. They were gaining on us . . . fast. Must have missed the spikes somehow. More thuds rained on the truck. Gabe let loose a burst from the truck bed. I checked the road ahead and then the rearview. They'd dropped back out of range. Only one guy was still standing in the back of the truck.

I forced my vision forward and started doing my Parnelli Jones impression.

I pushed harder with my foot, but not much happened. Eighty-five miles an hour was all the old truck had in her. I leaned out over the steering wheel, as if shifting my weight would help us go faster. The windshield disappeared into a thousand pebbles of safety glass, some of which landed in my lap and some of which got blown out onto the hood of the truck.

I scrunched down in the seat and kept driving. Felt like a cannon was trained on the back of my neck. Gabe let go with another blast. Our pursuers dropped back out of range again, firing blindly out the truck window as they swerved back and forth, trying to make it harder for Gabe to keep them in the sights.

We covered another six or seven miles. Gabe kept up a successful rearguard action. Betty crawled up from the floor and looked out the former back window of her truck. I heard her laugh and checked the mirror to see what could possibly be funny about a moment such as this.

That's when I first saw the sparks. The spike strip had indeed gotten one of the Ram's front tires; they were running on the rim, and the rim didn't like it one bit. We were half a mile in front of them, driving at eighty-five, with most of the windows blown out, and I could still hear the scream of steel on asphalt and see the fountain of bright-orange sparks rocketing high into the night air, causing the truck to veer back and forth erratically as the driver fought to maintain control.

"They're pullin' over," Betty announced.

I was in the process of breaking out a smile when she added, "There's somebody else . . . way back there," she announced. She read my mind. "Gotta be more of them Aryan idiots. Don't nobody drive out here this time of night."

She was right. Dead-straight road. Dead-flat country, and way the hell back there, five miles anyway, a pair of halogen headlights was racing in our direction.

She leaned my way and checked the gauges. "She's gettin' hot," she announced.

Yup. Engine temperature was three-quarters of the way up. Through the former windshield I could smell hot engine oil. Real hot. Burning.

"How much farther?" I asked her.

"Three, four miles," she said through tight lips.

It was like going to the dentist. You just sit there and bear it. They were gaining on us, no doubt about it. Next time I caught sight of the temperature gauge, it was one little notch from being pegged.

Then, with a shudder, the old Ford started to slow. I could feel it in my feet. Something in the engine had given way. Something like the head gasket maybe. What had been a roar now sounded a bit like a fart.

Betty pointed forward. "There it is," she said. "Potter's Junction. See the glow?"

I pumped hard on the gas pedal. Nothing. Then three exhaust explosions shattered the night. I took the Ford out of gear, turned off the engine, and let her coast. I checked the speedometer. Seventy and going down. Sixty-five and then sixty.

I threw my eyes back onto the road. I could make out a big, yellow Shell gasoline sign up ahead of us. Steam was pouring from the truck's engine compartment. Unconsciously, I started scrunching forward in the driver's seat again. Fifty . . . forty-five.

I pulled my eyes up. We were almost there. I could see the two bays of gas pumps now. And the garage. I jerked the wheel hard to the right. Hit the gravel driveway at a stunning thirty miles an hour and slid to a stop.

"Where's the phone?" I yelled as I groped for the door handle.

"Percy keeps it under the counter in the office," Betty said as she slid out of the seat. I was hot on her heels as she headed for the office door. Gabe was already out of the truck bed, standing behind the engine block with the assault weapon at the ready.

"How far back are they?" I shouted at Gabe as I followed Betty.

"Three, four miles," Gabe threw back my way.

Betty was rattling the door for all she was worth, but the lock was holding its own. Stayed that way until I put a size 13 through the glass.

I used my elbow to break out most of the jagged glass in the door frame and then ducked inside. The phone was where she'd said it would be.

Old-fashioned rotary phone, but the sucker worked. I dialed one of the few numbers I knew by heart. Three rings. "Yeah."

"Tim, it's Leo."

"Fuck, Leo . . . you know what time it is?"

"Can you record this call?" I shouted into the mouthpiece.

"Sure."

"Do it. Right now."

One of the longest minutes of my life passed before he spoke again.

"Yeah, so I'm recording."

I gave him the *Reader's Digest* version and then pulled Bickford's list from his pants pocket and began to read out loud. Name of group, members' names, where they were from, where they were assigned to. All of it. Tim had enough presence of mind not to interrupt. The longer I talked, the less annoyed he became.

The flash of headlights outside stopped my recitation after about eight groups. I ducked down behind the counter and kept shouting into the phone. "This is the real shit, Tim," I shouted. "These fuckers are crazy."

I watched in astonishment as a food truck squealed to a stop. A food truck! **Tacos Supremo** was painted on the side. Fresh tortillas handmade daily.

"Gotta go," I said as the food truck's serving window began to roll upward. Except it wasn't tacos they were peddling, it was bullet holes. They'd mounted a .60-caliber machine gun on the service counter.

I screamed at Betty, "Get in here." She didn't need to be invited twice.

I dropped the phone, grabbed Betty by the arm, and sprinted into the garage about five seconds before they let loose with the machine gun, and Potter's Junction more or less ceased to exist.

I don't expect there have been many occasions in human history when falling in a grease pit could be considered good news, but this was definitely one of them.

By the time Betty and I hit the slimy concrete floor, the building above us was beginning to come apart. The shelling stopped for a moment. I heard Gabe let loose with a volley and almost immediately heard someone groan. The next burst of machine gun fire was directed at the truck. From six feet down in the pit I could hear the enormous rounds peeling the sheet metal off the truck.

That's when I realized I was still holding Betty's shotgun in my hands.

"Stay here," I told her as I crept up the concrete steps. Half the door frame had collapsed. The back wall of the garage was waving in the night air and appeared to be about ready to join the doorway on the floor. I crawled under what was left of the door frame, got down on one knee, and peeked out at the Taco Terrorists.

The guy behind the machine gun was reloading. Gabe was down. Not dead down, but crawling-around-in-pain down, holding a lower leg.

I raised the shotgun to my shoulder, put the bead on the guy's face, and pulled the trigger. The slug hit him flush in the lower jaw, reducing the bottom half of his face to red mist. The force of the huge lead slug propelled him all the way to the other side of the taqueria. I winced when I heard him hit the opposite wall.

I started to crawl back into the grease pit, but suddenly everything went dead quiet. I kept moving, thinking there hadda be another guy inside the taco truck, waiting for one of us to stick our head up.

But no. Only the silence persisted. Louder and louder until Gabe's voice broke the tension.

"Leo," Gabe yelled. "You okay?"

"Yeah," I shouted. "You?"

"Took a little shrapnel in the leg."

"Cops are on the way."

"We got these two," Gabe said. "Don't see nobody else comin' down the road neither."

I stood up. As far as my focus could focus, nothing was coming our way. No lights. No nothing.

I reloaded the shotgun and began to inch toward the taco truck. I couldn't even bear to look at the guy I'd hit with the punkin ball. I've got a strong stomach, spent twenty some-odd years dating a woman who cut dead bodies apart for a living, but there's a limit to everything, and the pile of pulp lying there on the floor was way past my limit. Gabe had stitched the other guy twice in the chest. The bug-eyed expression on his bloodless face said he couldn't believe it had happened. I was guessing that Taco Tuesday was officially over for the week.

By the time I got over to Gabe, Betty was already there. Gabe had a piece of sheet metal about as big as a tongue depressor sticking out of the left calf.

"Part of the fender," Gabe snarled.

The old Ford was quite literally shot to pieces. No glass left anywhere. Most of the hood gone. Three tires shot out. Had so many jagged holes in it, the old girl looked carbonated. The look on Betty's face told me the truck meant more to her than simply a way to get from place to place. Some tender connection to her late husband, I guessed.

"Sorry about the truck," I said.

"Just stuff," she said grimly as she daubed at Gabe's wound. "They's lots of trucks."

"They're gonna be lookin' for the Taco Brothers here," Gabe said through gritted teeth.

"Yeah, I know," I said.

"You get the info to Eagen?"

"Yeah," I said. "Tim's on it. Cavalry will be on the way by now."

"Never been so glad to hear the cops were coming before," Gabe joked.

"You think maybe we ought to try prying this thing outta here?" Betty asked, pointing at the decorative shard of metal protruding from Gabe's leg.

"Within a half an hour, this place is going to be crawling with aid cars and every kind of cop there is. I think we ought to let the pros do it."

Looked to me like Gabe was definitely in favor of the idea.

I reached down and picked up the assault rifle.

"Got about half a clip left," Gabe said.

I tried to hand the shotgun to Gabe.

"Take it with you," Gabe said. "Probably best neither of us is heeled when the cops get here. Give 'em something to figure out on their own."

I started for the taco truck.

"Where ya goin'?" Betty asked as I slid into the driver's seat.

"Soon as they find out we got away, those skinhead bastards are gonna hotfoot it out of that camp. They'll try to send as many teams as they can out to kill people. I'm gonna see if I can't slow those fuckers down a bit," I said.

"You wouldn't be goin' lookin' for old Curly Hair, would you?" Gabe asked.

"Only if I'm right up in his face," I said. "I get a chance at him, it's gonna be up close and personal. He's gonna know it was me."

■ ■ ■

You forget how many stars there are when you live in the city. You gotta get away from all the man-made lights before the twinkling carpet stretched out above you blinks into view. I suppose mental health professionals would say I was in denial as I raced down that country road. But, the way I saw it, I was simply enjoying the view.

I was about five miles out from Conway when the radio crackled. Scared the hell out of me. I hadn't noticed the handheld mic clipped to the dashboard.

"You get 'em?" a voice crackled. "Trace . . . you boys get 'em?"

I grabbed the mic and pushed the "Send" button. I worked up a little phlegm. "It's done," I gargled into the mic. "On my way back. Be there in five minutes." At which point I turned the radio off.

Never got a chance to go back to admiring the stars. The lights of Conway came into view, spilling a dull yellow glow over the roadway about a half a mile in front of me.

I slowed and made the turn into town. Nothing. No trucks, not a soul in sight.

I gave the taco truck some more gas and went rolling through town, aimed at the compound's driveway directly in front of me. I was trying to remember exactly how far the gate was from the main road, when a movement in the corner of my eye brought my foot down on the brakes.

The kid from the tavern. The one with the dog. I skidded to a halt. Set the E brake and got out of the truck. The kid was trying to back away from me, but the dog didn't want to go. "Rusty, isn't it?"

He stopped backpedaling. "Who are you?" he wanted to know.

"From the tavern earlier today. I was talking with Betty . . . remember . . . when you tried to bring the dog inside."

"He's a service dog," the kid insisted.

"Well, I've got a service you and him can do."

"It's a her," he corrected.

"Okay . . . her."

"What kinda service is that?"

"There's gonna be all kinda cops and firemen and other guys about to show up here. You gotta tell them not to go into the compound. That the place is wired with all sorts of explosives. Can you do that?" I pressed.

"Really?"

"Say it."

"Stay outta there 'cause they might get blown up," the kid said.

"That's it," I said. "They'll probably give you and your dog a medal. He'll . . . She'll be the most famous service dog in the country."

"Really?" the kid yelled at my back as I sprinted for the taco truck. "Really? . . . a medal . . . oooowee."

I hopped up into the seat, shoved the truck into drive, and went boiling up the compound's private road. I picked up the automatic from the floor and stuck it out the window in case I had to shoot my way in, but the gate was unmanned.

They'd chosen a good place for the security gate. Squeezed in among an enormous copse of old-growth timber. You were either leaving through the narrow aperture where the gate stood, or you weren't leaving at all. I skidded the taco truck to a stop on the pine straw. Backed as far as I could in one direction, gained an inch or two, reversed again and I had it wedged so tight between two stout sugar pines—less than a foot from either one of them—that the only way anybody was getting in or out was on foot.

I gathered up the weapons. Set the brake, locked it up, and threw the keys into the gloom. I hung the assault rifle around my neck, grabbed the shotgun, and loaded it. Four loud booms and the tires were blown to pieces.

I helicoptered the shotgun out into the woods, emptied my pockets of shotgun shells, and started jogging into the compound. That's when I heard the voices. Lots of them. Everybody talking at once. Sounded like it was coming from the clearing where the cars had been parked.

I got the hell off the road and crept soundlessly through the grove of cedar trees that surrounded the parking lot. The voices got louder. I peeped out from between a couple of scrub oaks. The gang was all there. The Voice was standing on something, talking through a handheld bullhorn. Phil Hardaway was just off his right shoulder, in his George Patton stance. "We have unconfirmed reports that those two spies have been dealt with," the Voice said. "Once we get confirmation, we will commence operations on a greatly accelerated schedule. All events will begin today."

That was all I needed to hear. I backed out of the foliage and started running, only to skid to a stop less than a hundred yards down the trail.

Whatever I'd eaten last rose up into my throat. Ben. They'd hung him up by the feet from a tree. I pulled Bickford's sheath knife from his coat and walked over and started sawing the yellow plastic rope until I could lift him down and carry him across my shoulder. No way was I letting anybody send him home to his parents in Bloomington like this. No fucking way.

I could hear engines roaring now, the sound of churning tires. My legs were getting to be like spaghetti. I was beginning to wobble as I walked, so when I caught sight of the ruined garage where the FedEx truck had been, I staggered in that direction.

I peeked in the window of the truck. Keys still in the ignition. I walked around the back of the truck, pulled open one of the doors, and laid Ben on the floor beside four hundred or so pounds of plastic explosive.

As I came around the passenger side, which really was the driver's side, a silhouette appeared in the mouth of the garage.

"What?" was the only word he managed before I stitched him up like a quilt.

I launched myself into the driver's seat and turned the key. The engine turned over but didn't start. Tried again. Nothing. Third time was the charm. The truck sputtered for a second or two and then roared to life.

I could hear shouts, angry voices coming my way. Lots of them. I dropped the truck into low gear and came bouncing out into the night. Instead of following the path that had been cleared from the front of the collapsed building up to the paved road, I plowed straight ahead. Smashing through the undergrowth, swerving around trees as I bounced across. I heard gunfire. Felt the bullets smashing into the back doors of the truck as it plunged through the woods.

And there it was. Hadn't moved a muscle. The long, low bunker where they'd stored all the ordnance they'd stolen from the armory. I'd say I drove through the back wall, but truth was, the FedEx truck was just too damn big to fit. Damn near tore the roof off the thing. We ended up half in and half out of the building.

I reached down next to my seat and tried to undo the metal band holding the red trigger handle to the floor. My hands were shaking. I couldn't get the strap undone. I sat back in the seat and tried to get a grip on myself. That's when I had my first lucid thought in several months. What if? What if Christian Conscience from Banks, Idaho, was never intended to survive their mission? What if there was no six minutes to get the hell out of the vicinity? What if I pulled the red handle and the fucking thing went off like a roman candle? No muss, no fuss, no questions, no witnesses. Clean as hell.

I gave it ten seconds of serious thought and decided I didn't give a shit. Way I saw it, either way they wouldn't be using their arsenal to kill people.

Took me two more tries to remove the metal band. I heard a crackle of electricity run through the truck. Closed my eyes and steeled myself for oblivion. Nothing happened.

My thoughts scattered like windblown leaves, until a single syllable was all that was left inside my head. *Run*. Neon red. Blinking somewhere in my mind's eye.

I had the keys in my hand as I stepped through the back of the truck and let myself out the back doors. Locked them, precisely as I'd been instructed, and heaved the keys off into the darkness. Then . . . I ran.

Wasn't sure which direction I was running, but at that point it didn't matter a whit. All I wanted was distance between me and that truck. Then I had a thought and pulled up short. If I could draw my pursuers here, they might suffer the same fate they'd planned for the first responders. Seemed fitting to me.

I stepped up onto a semirotten stump and emptied the assault rifle in their general direction. Shouts, orders, curses rang from the forest. I dropped the rifle, picked up the shotgun, and sent a couple of slugs surging through the shrubbery. I hopped to the ground and took off running again, legs churning, arms pumping.

Behind me I could hear bullets slamming into the FedEx truck and the sound of lead bees buzzing through the vegetation around me.

It was slow going. The voices behind me sounded closer. Since the alternative was an agonizing death, I kept plowing farther into the thicket, finally falling into a deep brush-encrusted gully. An eight-foot depression in the natural topography that, in the final offing, saved my life.

I'd scrambled to my feet, checked for broken bones, and was about to climb out the far side when FedEx made its final delivery.

Nothing in my previous experience had prepared me for the initial burst of explosives. It was as if the universe suddenly sucked back all its air, leaving the world still and silent. And then . . . a white flash and a high-voltage crack.

And then . . . *BOOOOOM.*

The forest lit up like Safeco Field. Even eight feet below ground level, the concussive force of the explosion tore the air from my lungs, then picked me up and slammed me into the far bank. A plume of fire rose hundreds of feet into the sky. And then another smaller explosion and then another. It went on and on for what seemed like an hour.

My nose was bleeding, entire trees came raining down, dirt, rocks . . . what looked like a human leg . . . all of it blown to bits and showering back to the now-flaming earth. I covered my head with my arms and waited for it to be over.

That's when I realized that my left arm felt hot. Not because I'd broken it when I'd fallen, but because my fucking sleeve was on fire. I beat it out with my bare hand, caught my quavering breath, and clawed my way out of the gully.

The forest was mostly gone. What wasn't shredded or vaporized was on fire. Coupla hundred yards on all sides of the truck, nothing but a flaming desert remained. Massive trees had been shattered like balsa wood. Blown to splinters along with everything else. Looked like *The War of the Worlds*. I heard a groan. And then what sounded like a death rattle. Then more airborne debris sinking back to the shattered ground.

Wasn't till it stopped raining forest that the crackling sound of burning wood reached my ears. I know I should have run the other way. Run until my legs gave out and then run some more, but I couldn't do it.

I was drawn like a lemming back toward that flaming wasteland I'd created. The earth beneath my boots felt loose and granulated like sugar. The surrounding air was alive with floating embers. My lungs hated it, trying to cough it out as fast as I pulled it in, but I kept forcing myself forward until I was back where I reckoned the FedEx truck had been sitting. A smoking fifty-foot hole in the ground was all that remained. The ordnance bunker I'd crashed the truck into had disappeared from the face of the earth.

I gave Ben Forrester a two-fingered salute and looked around. The carnage was mind bending. It was like walking into a slaughterhouse. Bodies and parts of bodies littered the ground like discarded children's toys.

Forty yards in front of me, a big Douglas fir, maybe six or eight feet around, had been blown to oblivion. A body was impaled on the splintered stump. One leg pointing in each direction like he was running a race. Looked like he'd been blown up into the forest canopy and come down on top of what was left of the tree. The face was so twisted in agony as to be unrecognizable, but I knew the curly hair.

I stood there for quite some time. At first I was angry. I'd wanted to kill him myself. Make sure he knew it was me, come back from the grave for vengeance. But the longer I stood there, the more I realized another part of me didn't like the sound of that at all. Something inside me didn't want me to be a guy with that much malice in his heart, so I stepped over a chunk of burning bark and walked away.

Off in the direction of the gate, I could hear the roar of engines and a chorus of angry, frightened voices. The survivors were trying to get out. Farther out, the sky was alive with pulsing lights. Red, blue, white, red, blue, white. I sat down on the blackened earth and looked around. Without wishing it so, I began to cry.

Chapter 4

"You'll have to excuse me, Special Agent Cummings, but I don't see how going over these same questions for about the thirty-fifth time is going to accomplish anything."

"I'll decide when enough is enough," he snapped in that pinched little voice of his.

He snatched an iPad from the metal table and pushed a couple of keys.

"Am I under arrest?" I asked for about the fifth time that morning.

"I've told you before, Mr. Waterman, you're being held as a material witness," his partner, Jennings, said.

They were slick; I'll say that for them. Good suits, good educations, and a really fervent desire to get to the bottom of whatever had happened up there in the woods.

I was being polite because the FBI wasn't bound by the legal constraints that local and state cops faced. Most important, they weren't required to either charge you or release you within seventy-two hours. These guys could hang on to you until you grew moss on your north side. Nor were they required to let you make a phone call, so I was being as nice as I could be under the circumstances . . . those circumstances being that I wasn't telling them anything they wanted to hear.

Rumor had it that the blast had separated me from all memory. Don't even remember how or why I got there. Never even heard of Conway, Washington. That was my story, at least. Bare bones. Nothing to conflict with anything else. All nice and neat and dumb. They'd made only one interrogation mistake so far, but it was a big one. Early on, Special Agent Cummings had tried to scare me by telling me that I was gonna take the rap alone because Gabriella was in another room coughing up the whole story.

Since the chances of Gabe telling them one goddamn thing were about equal to my chance of winning the Powerball lottery, I knew right away they didn't have shit to go on and were trying to screw something out of me as a last resort.

I mean, it just made sense. Yeah, I was found on the premises, but anything resembling forensic evidence had surely been blown to hell and gone. I wasn't even wearing my own clothes when they found me, and since I was the only one who knew what had actually happened, as long as I kept my trap closed, sooner or later they'd have to let me go.

What *I* really wanted to know was to what degree they'd managed to stop the terrorist attacks. They just kept telling me it was an open investigation and they couldn't discuss it with me. What *they* really wanted to know was who had set off the explosion, so they could fix the blame rather than the problem. It's the American way.

Cummings started to read from the iPad. "As of this moment, we have sixteen confirmed dead. Another eleven hospitalized, three of whom are not expected to live, and the smoking remains of an explosion that was heard sixty miles away, and you mean to tell me that you don't recall a single thing about it."

"Really?" I said. "Sixty miles? Must have been a hell of a boom."

It went on and on. Same shit, different day. I'd spent the first two days in a federal medical facility somewhere in Alderwood, then had been passed hand to hand from the local cops to the Washington state troopers, and finally on to the Bureau, who'd spirited me off to the downtown federal building, where they'd been busting my balls for the better part of two days now.

The door to the room eased open. A uniformed Washington state trooper, Smokey Bear hat and all, leaned in and whispered something in Special Agent Cummings's ear. Cummings set his jaw hard enough to press license plates. I could feel his frustration boiling from across the table. I swallowed a grin and waited for cartoon steam to come out of his ears.

He got to his feet, snapped the iPad shut, and put it under his arm.

"Your attorney, Mr. Diaz, has obtained an injunction . . . ," he began.

Which in itself was interesting, since I had no idea who this Diaz guy was, never heard of him in my life, but it told me what was going on outside. It told me they'd let Gabe make the obligatory one phone call, and of course, Gabe had called Joey Ortega, at which point Joey had loosed a battalion of lawyers onto the system. It also explained why they'd shunted me from place to place trying to keep me under wraps. Cops are like that. They just hate losing to the robbers.

Diaz entered the room at full volume. He was stocky, with a head of salt-and-pepper hair thick enough to require a hay rake and a brown mole the size of a quarter on his left cheek. Tasseled shoes. Good suit. The lawyer Daggett in the flesh.

"You think I'm going to meet with my client in a fucking interrogation room?" he bellowed. "I need a clean room. No recording of any kind. I'm putting you on notice. I am exercising my statutory right to confer privately with my client. And I mean privately. Is that understood?"

"It's an interview room," Cummings insisted.

"It's an abridgment of my client's constitutional rights is what it is." He raised a stiff finger in the air and shook it. "And there will be no more interagency transfers of my client without prior notification. As his attorney, I have a constitutional right to be advised of his whereabouts at all times—in advance. Is that understood?"

They kicked it back and forth for another five minutes. Diaz did most of the kicking. The Bureau Boys just tried to keep their knees together.

When the echoes faded, I ended up in the private office of Federal Judge Harvey Brighton, down on the first floor, with a couple of staties standing guard across the hall from the door.

Diaz sat down across from me.

"Joey?" I asked.

"Of course," he said. "Are they keeping you over in the jail?" he asked.

"Nope," I said. "There's like a private suite up on the top floor of the courthouse. I'm guessing they use it to house federal witnesses. They lock me in there at night. Beats the shit out of Casa Vomit down the hill. Hell, they feed me decent Italian food from TULIO so there's nothing to bitch about there."

Diaz agreed. "Gabriella sends regards," he said as he got to his feet. "You'll be out of here in an hour," he promised. "But I think I'm gonna stick around till it happens. I wouldn't put it past these bastards to move you before the paperwork goes through. So I'm sticking around." He leaned close to my ear. "Mr. Ortega wishes me to inform you that someone he calls Tim wishes to have an urgent word with you. The message is one thirty P.M. today. The mud."

He started for the door, turned around, and asked me in a low voice, "You got somewhere you can go for a while? This is all over the news. CNN's going apeshit over it. This skinhead thing even upstaged national politics for a couple of days. Gone international it has."

"I'm going home," I said.

"Mr. Ortega suggests—"

I cut him off with a raised hand. "I haven't been home in a long time," I said.

▪ ▪ ▪

I tipped the Lyft driver twenty bucks and squeezed out of the Prius. I stood in the mouth of my driveway and watched him make a lazy U-turn and then buzz away down the hill. I took a couple of deep breaths before I turned around and looked at the house I'd lived in, on and off, for most of my life. My old man's house. He'd built it when I was five. Tudor. Huge. Glowering. A million small, dark, locked rooms. I'd moved out at twenty and stayed gone until a year after his death, when I'd moved back in and staged major renovations. Fewer rooms, bigger open spaces. All new lighting. Five more windows than the original design. It was still a bruiser of a house, but at least it was light instead of dark and open instead of closed.

After he'd been put in the ground and his legal eagles had cleared up his financial affairs, I'd seriously considered bulldozing it to the ground and building something of my own choosing, but something in me knew it wasn't about the house. It was about my father and me. All Freudian and such. About our relationship, or lack thereof, and how I'd never managed to make what he considered to be the *smart* decision in my life. As far as he was concerned anyway. Not in anything. Ever.

I stretched way up, reached over the gate, and pushed the button. The gate began to grind across the asphalt. Soon as the opening got big enough I slipped inside.

The place was immaculate. Somebody'd taken care of everything. The shrubs had been trimmed. The leaves had been raked. The driveway power washed. Looked like I'd never left, but it sure as hell didn't feel that way to me. I felt like a gypsy in the palace as I tiptoed toward my front door.

Which was unlocked. And that was a good thing too, because I didn't have anything. No keys, no wallet, no remotes for the garage and the gate . . . no nothing. I was just here. Neither Leo nor Leon. Just here.

Back at the federal courthouse, I'd been getting my personal effects, which were actually the late Mr. Bickford's effects, from the property room, when the lawyer Diaz appeared at my elbow and handed me a fat white envelope. I peeked inside. Looked like a grand or so in cash. Small bills.

"Traveling money," he whispered in my ear.

I had made the Lyft driver stop at Fredrick's Big and Tall on Fifth Avenue so's I could finally get out of the late Mr. Bickford's clothes. What I really wanted was an hour-and-a-half shower, but clean clothes were somewhere in the vicinity of the next best thing.

The kitchen light was on. I followed the glow up the flagstone floor and pulled open my junk drawer. I blew out a huge sigh of relief. It was still there, right where I'd left it all. My wallet, my key ring, the fistful of plastic cards that said my name was Leo Waterman. Back before Leon Marks ever existed. Before what now seemed like the greater portion of my life.

I sat down at the kitchen table and fingered through it all. More than once. And then, for no logical reason, I felt a deep need to have it all back on my person, so I stuffed the pockets of my new store-bought clothes with every single thing that said my name was Leo Waterman. You know . . . just in case. What if I was killed on the highway?

▪ ▪ ▪

Tim Eagen and I had a long-standing place down in south Seattle where we'd meet when he didn't want to be seen in public with me . . . which was pretty much all the time. Apparently, the secret to a clandestine meeting spot was to choose someplace out of the way, where nobody in their right mind would want to go of their own volition.

The Lower Duwamish Waterway was just such a locale. Used to be a river. Used to not be the color of ethylene glycol antifreeze and smell like something's ass either. That was back when you might have been able to take a quick dip without having the chemicals in the water flay the skin from your body. Those thrilling days of yesteryear.

Tim was waiting for me. Leaning against a tall pile of worn-out tires somebody'd kindly left along the banks of the waterway. We had a funny relationship, Tim and I. For reasons I don't fully understand, twenty-five years of courting the same woman had, rather than alienating us from one another, somehow drawn us closer together. Go figure.

He hugged me hard. "Good to see you, man."

"Did they stop all of 'em?" I asked.

"All but two," Tim said with a resigned shrug. "Coupla guys from Riverside, California, shot up a day care center. Eleven dead, before they blew their own brains out. Also what we think was four guys in a panel truck blew a twenty-foot hole in the freeway down by Roseburg, Oregon. The general consensus is that the bomb went off by mistake. Some sort of technical problem. Killed the couple driving next to them on the interstate. The Bureau's got another bunch of them in custody but isn't naming names . . . 'cause you know, as usual, the Bureau cooperates with nobody, and everybody's expected to cooperate with them. Most everybody else on the list is missing and presumed vaporized."

"They find a guy name Thomas Henry Mitchell?" I asked. "He seemed to be somewhere pretty high up in the Aryan food chain."

Tim almost laughed. Shook his head. "No way of telling," he said. "They're gonna be doing forensic work for months," he growled. "Tryin' to figure out which foot belongs to which body, which ear to which head. Finding out who the DNA profiles belong to. They're figuring the DNA testing alone is gonna cost about four million bucks. Already applied for a federal grant."

"Art Fowler didn't kill himself."

"No?"

"Phil Hardaway killed Art because he wouldn't keep his mouth shut about his grandson. Kept asking questions. Tried to hire me. They'd been planning this thing for a long time and weren't about to let one nosy old man get in their way."

"How could somebody set up his own son like that?" Eagen asked.

"I think Martha had it right. I think Phil couldn't stand the fact that his son was damaged in some way. Felt like Matthew's very existence diminished him, so he sacrificed him to the glorious cause."

A pair of blue-and-yellow Pacific tugboats putted past us, sending a carcinogenic wake lapping up onto the shore. I stepped higher on the bank, not wanting any of that water to touch my shoes. Didn't fancy a double amputation being part of my future.

I went through the whole thing with him. Told him everything I knew. Every detail I could remember. Took the better part of twenty minutes.

"Jesus," he said when I'd finished.

"I went in there thinking we were gonna find a bunch of losers playing cowboy out in the sticks. I had no idea what we were getting ourselves into," I admitted.

I could tell from his manner that he was holding something back.

"What?" I said.

He sighed. "Last few days . . . while the Bureau was keeping you on ice, I took some sick days. Went down and decorated my sister's couch in Federal Way for a few days. Staying out of the office, so's the Feds wouldn't be able to find me. Claimed like the whole thing had so upset my tender psyche that I needed to take it easy." He rolled his eyes. "That's what I told the captain anyway . . . 'cause . . . you know . . . once the panic calms down, which is right about now, somebody's sure as hell gonna want to know where I got that info from." He shrugged. "Sooner or later here, I'm gonna have to come up with something. I can't be claiming I found it under my pillow. The tooth fairy narrative ain't gonna float here, Leo. This is big-time shit."

"Tell 'em it was a guy named Ben Forrester who broke the case. Called up and gave you the list." I spelled it for him.

"And who the fuck might that be?"

I told him. About a minute in, he pulled out his cop pad and took some notes.

"And where's this cub reporter of yours now? I haven't seen his name on any of the lists, and we're gonna need to get our stories straighter than a stiff dick."

"He didn't make it," I said.

"You're sure? 'Cause I can't have—"

I waved him off. "I'm sure. Ben Forrester's remains were on top of four hundred fifty pounds of plastic explosive when it went off."

He eyed me hard. "You have this on good authority, I suppose."

"The best," I assured him.

Brief stare down. A bit of silence. A slight nod of the head.

"Probably get him a Pulitzer."

"Undoubtedly," I said.

"Probably gonna get me a captain's office too."

"A real good bet."

"Keeps your name out of it too."

"Just the way I likes it."

More silence.

"You saved a lot of lives, asshole," he said after a minute.

"Shoulda never taken that kid in there," I said.

"Adults make their own choices."

"I feel like he's dead because of *my* choices," I said.

"Life is not without its inherent risks."

Couldn't argue with that, but there was still something unsaid. I could tell.

I tried to break the logjam with small talk. "House looked great when I got back," I said out of the blue.

Tim laughed out loud. "It was that shit-faced crew of yours from the Zoo," he said. "They did everything. They were fucking dervishes. It was like they were preparing for the Second Coming of Christ or something." He threw an amused hand in the air. "Lawn mowers, hedge clippers, yard rakes . . . all that shit. Never thought I'd see those dead-beats get so organized."

"Rebecca?"

The second it was out of my mouth, I knew I'd pinned the tail on the donkey.

He shuffled his feet and studied the mud beneath his shoes.

"Yeah . . . I've been . . . you know . . . giving her a call now and then . . . but I can tell she's just not interested . . . it ain't gonna work out . . ." He looked up from the mud. "Just so you understand," he said.

I knew what I was going to say because I'd practiced it in my head a bunch of times in case the subject came up, which I knew it was gonna.

"What I understand is that love is hard to find, and that if you find it, you better hang on, because it's even harder to keep."

"Yeah," was all he said.

■ ■ ■

It wasn't like I made a conscious decision to become a demihermit, but somehow the days just seemed to get away from me while I was puttering around the house, lookin' in this, lookin' in that. Just seemed to happen. For the best part of a week, I ordered out for everything. AmazonFresh and Bite Squad wore out a couple of sets of tires hauling things up the hill to me.

I tried to get real organized. Ready to sneak back in the side door of my life. But funny thing was . . . six days of the void, and I didn't feel any more at home than I had when I'd first walked back in the door. Something had changed. Something intrinsic. I could feel it, but I couldn't put a name to it, or find the dark burrow where it was holed up.

Most of what Tim and I had figured would happen had already come to pass. Ben Forrester's parents in Bloomington had been notified of his heroism. By the time they learned of his sacrifice, he was well on his way to becoming a national hero. You couldn't turn on the tube without seeing his youthful visage smiling back at you. I thought it interesting that the folks at the *Sound Sentinel*, the same people who'd pulled him off the Matthew Hardaway case after less than a week, jumped right on board the Forrester express. Yes, they'd assigned Ben to the story. Yes, they'd always known he'd been bound for glory. Knew it all the time.

When I saw his shattered parents on CNN, I had to content myself with the thought that their grief, however painful, would not outlast the story of the ultimate sacrifice their son had made and what a hero he'd become.

Tim was honored with a medal ceremony on the courthouse steps and invited to take the captain's exam. Seemed a little more like things were under control. That's when I decided that it was time to get myself sheared like a sheep. I was thinking that maybe if I looked more like the self I remembered, then I might feel more like that too, so I toddled down to Rudy's Barbershop in Belltown and had myself decluttered. By the time the stylist got through with me there was enough hair on the floor to stuff a queen-size pillow top, and I looked remarkably like the guy I used to be. A little more gaunt, maybe a little older, but definitely familiar.

I stepped out onto Pine Street, pulled my arms above my head, stretched and looked around while I made those stretching noises we all make. There must have been thirty construction cranes in sight. The building boom was making the city of my youth feel tight, as if little by little, the new concrete canyons were closing in on us like the jaws of a vise.

I found a miracle parking space on Eastlake, down by Starbucks and the taco joint, locked the car, and started up the street toward the Eastlake Zoo.

The boys followed a highly irregular regular schedule. Their days started with a few eye-opener beers in bed—just to get the circuits humming, you understand. Anything more than four tallboys was considered problem drinking. Once they were up and about, they would further restore themselves with a couple of what they called phlegm cutters—you know, just to clean the pipes. Thus suitably fueled, they'd segue into a couple of more serious cocktails, designed to firm both the chin and the resolve, prior to actually venturing into the great outdoors.

Right around noon, they'd extrude themselves out onto the sidewalk in front of whatever flop they were using at the time, from whence they'd trek to the Eastlake Zoo, single file, like penguins on the march. There, as their somewhat skewed social contract demanded, a couple of more cocktails at the Eastlake Zoo's bar provided a civilized prelude to a sumptuous lunch of beef jerky, peanuts, pigs' feet, and pickled eggs. All very paleo, you know.

For afternoon sippage, beer was the nectar of choice, while they sat around and shot the shit, played snooker, and generally made nuisances of themselves, which was semiokay with management because the folding-money crowd was rather light in the afternoons. By the time evening rolled around they were generally fully squashed, running out of day money, and beginning to annoy the zoo's more hygienic clientele, at which point they'd stumble, blinking, out into the early evening and weave their way back home, where, of course, they'd drown the remains of the day with an appropriate nightcap of two. Cue the sleep apnea.

I threw a twenty on the bar on my way by. The day bartender was a kid named Malcolm. We had a deal. He could collect his tip up front soon as I came in the door. All he had to do was turn down the fucking death metal he played at ear-shattering volume so he didn't have to listen to the boys. There's no robbery to a fair exchange.

I made it all the way to the far end of the bar, where the room makes a hard right turn, before anybody noticed my arrival. Large Marge was lining up a bank shot on the snooker table when she caught me in the corner of her eye, straightened up, and rolled the cue stick out onto the table.

"Leo," she whooped.

I'd like to think my dazzling personality and rapier-like wit were the cause for such delirium, but truth be told, the fact that I generally bought several rounds of drinks whenever I showed up had to be considered a major player in the gaiety.

They rushed me like a lynch mob. Sweeping me from the floor in a maelstrom of arms and legs and shouts and sloppy kisses. They squeezed me like the Charmin and pounded my back like a bongo. My name floated on the beer-scented air.

Soon as I could get my feet back among the peanut shells, I signaled Malcolm for a round on me. The crowd went wild.

They were all there: George and Harold and Ralph. Red Lopez and Large Marge, Nearly Normal Norman towering over the crowd like a construction crane. Tiny something or other, who was about the size of a two-bedroom craftsman in Ballard. Heavy Duty Judy was welded to my left arm, drooling in my ear. Little Joey was dancing some strange little hopping dance under the mezzanine. People I'd known all my life and others I'd picked up along the way. The party was on. I felt as good as I had in a long time.

By the time I managed to appropriate a seat, the assembled multitude were on to their second round, and gaiety had morphed into bleary-eyed bliss. About the time they started line dancing around the snooker table, I paid for another round and eased out the front door.

▪ ▪ ▪

It was two weeks later. Nothing much had changed. I was still feeling like a stranger in a strange land. Seemed like my life had holes drilled in it. Like I couldn't remember how I used to fill my time before all of this had happened. Rebecca . . . yeah, sure . . . I could feel the empty space. Interestingly, in addition to the sense of loss, I also felt a certain sense of release, but it was more than that. I was sitting in the kitchen drinking coffee, ruminating on that very matter, when the gate buzzer rattled my brain.

The speaker crackled. "Leo, it's Tim. Open up."

I walked to the front of the house, pushed the gate button, opened the front door, and watched a black city car roll up to the front steps. Tim Eagen got out. No driver, meant he didn't want witnesses to whatever he'd brought to my door.

"You take the captain's exam yet?" I asked as he came inside.

"Studying my ass off," he said. "Lotta shit's changed since the last time I went over that stuff. Week or two maybe."

We wandered into the kitchen. I poured us each a cup of coffee.

"To what do I owe the honor of a celebrity visit?"

"You're the one's about to *become* a celebrity," he answered.

"How so?"

"The FBI's releasing its report on the white supremacist investigation at five P.M. on Friday on CNN. They're naming you as a person of interest."

"You're sure?"

"My newfound status gets me a look at everything ahead of time. Yeah, I'm sure."

"Why would they do that?"

"Because they're pissed, man. They don't like losing. They really didn't like the army of attorneys Joey Ortega sicced on them, so they're gonna put as much pressure on you as they can, see if they can't get you to change your story." He shrugged. "Means they don't have shit too," he added. "Your girlfriend Gabriella and the old lady from the tavern claimed they didn't know shit from shoe polish. According to them, they were out for a little spin when they were suddenly attacked by a taco truck. Other than that, they claimed not to know anything."

I didn't speak for a while.

"So . . . who were these guys climbing over my wall?" I asked finally.

"We're thinking it was guys from Everett. Phil Hardaway finds out his father-in-law Art has been to see you and decides they need to put out your lights too."

I opened my mouth, but he cut me off. "And it's worse than that now, Leo," he said. "Counterterrorism is picking up a lot of online Aryan chatter to the effect that this thing's gone national. It's not just a bunch of paranoid yahoos up in Everett jumping the gun anymore. Whoever's at the top of that Aryan-idiot food chain wants your big ass dead. They're calling you a race traitor and a nigger lover. They want to make an example of you. Offering fifty grand for anybody who puts you under the sod."

"Only fifty?"

"This isn't funny, man."

"Nothing about hate is funny."

"Don't you get it, man? The Bureau's using you for bait, Leo. Hoping that if they embarrass those Aryan assholes, they'll do something stupid like killing your ass. Hoping they can catch 'em in the act. Maybe turn somebody, get something that way. As far as they're concerned, no matter what happens, they got nothing to lose."

"Hardly a sustainable future for me."

"No shit," Eagen said. "I saw some of the printed material those guys had. They're out of their goddamn minds. Ya can't stop a killer who doesn't care whether he gets out alive or not." He cut the air with the side of his hand. "Not possible. Best case scenario, you both die. They're nutcases."

"Actually, Tim, they're a lot like Matthew Hardaway," I said. "They're searching for a community, a sense of purpose, anything that makes them feel like they're part of something. You give them a chance to blame their problems on somebody else, and they will. It's basic human nature, and worse yet, from there it's just a short step to 'it's the government,' or 'it's the Jews,' or anybody other than them."

"Caribbean vacation time, Leo. Go down there and soak up some sun with Carl and the reggae twins. Maybe something'll break on this end."

"Can't live like that." I shook my head. "Just can't."

"Then you better have your friend Joey send Cinderella and a few friends over to keep an eye on you. Like twenty-four seven."

"Can't live like that either," I said.

"I knew you'd say that."

It's true. I'm predictably pigheaded.

"What are you gonna do?" he asked.

"Think about it."

"I'll beef up the local street patrol as much as I can get away with, but that's about all I can do."

"Oh . . . man . . . you don't need to . . ."

"Shut up."

■ ■ ■

And it's not like I didn't take precautions. I had my security company come out and go over everything. The gates, the motion detectors, the lights. A day and a half later the system was deemed state of the art.

I loaded every weapon in the house and stashed them in places where they might be of use. Even the little derringer my old man used to carry in his watch pocket. I checked the locks on the doors and windows more times than I'm willing to admit.

Strangest of all, I kept returning to the office safe, where I'd stashed all that money I'd made down in Arizona, selling off a couple of pieces of property owned by one of my old man's shadow companies—money I'd have gratefully paid the tax on, except that I'd then have to explain to the IRS where the money came from, which would surely open up yet another chapter in my old man's illicit financial history. Maybe even give the city cause to sue me for the return of the money yet again. I couldn't bring myself to do that.

It was like some part of me wanted to grab that money and just start my life over, but another part wasn't willing to say it out loud. Instead I took it out of the safe several times and fondled it unmercifully. Even rubbed one bundle of cash on my cheek a couple of times. Don't ask me to explain it.

My basic plan was to lie low, be safe, and hope that this crap would blow over. These days, nothing stays at the top of the news cycle for long. As a society, we have the attention span of a sparrow. It's short-attention-span theater. That's what I was telling myself anyway.

By the time Friday rolled around, AmazonFresh had delivered me enough supplies to feed an armored division, and I was doing my best to see it didn't go to waste. I'd also gotten a delivery from the liquor store down in the village and was pretty much prepared for another round of unwanted notoriety.

I'd decided not to watch the CNN broadcast. The way I saw things, watching wouldn't serve any purpose other than to raise my blood pressure, so I was binge-watching *Goliath* when the gate buzzer sounded. I paused Billy Bob, shambled out to the front door, and peeped out.

They must have had a Shirley Jacksonish lottery to see which one of them was gonna push the gate button. The kid looked like he was scared to death. Best as I could see through the trees, there were at least four mobile satellite units parked outside my gate.

I turned the volume on the gate speaker up to "Enter Sandman" volume and used my best Jack Webb voice: "This is private property. Any unauthorized entry is illegal and will immediately be reported to the police and to your employer. I have no statement to make at this time." Click. Then I turned on the yard lights. They lit the neighborhood up like a ball game. After a while, my neighbors would get pissed and come out to see what was going on, at which point they'd start giving the news crews a raft of shit and calling their attorneys. The wrath of the well-heeled would immediately descend upon their bosses, who would begin to feel the heat, and after a while, they'd go bye-bye.

Took a while, though. I'd been through a media siege several times before but never anything quite as insistent as this one. They stayed out there for over a week. Day and night. I did the same thing but on the inside of the fence.

So, a few days after the last satellite truck disappeared, and dazed and confused Leo Waterman was no longer the story du jour, I walked out to the north wall and boosted myself to the top, where I could survey the street. The street was devoid of assholes, so I moseyed back to the garage, fired up the car, and let myself out the gate.

It felt like when I was a kid and I'd been home from school for a few days—you know, out with the flu or something—how the world suddenly seems shiny and bright when you've been away from it for a while. Felt a lot like when you got let out of jail.

Mostly I just ran errands and cursed at the traffic. I took it around several blocks and backed into a couple of parking lots, making sure I didn't have anybody on my tail. Stopped for lunch at the Two Bells Bar & Grill, inhaled a cheeseburger while I caught up on old times with the owner, Jeff Lee.

It's a well-known fact that Seattle Parking Enforcement Officers regularly eat their young. I was halfway back to my car when I spotted one of the accursed ones working her way down Fourth Avenue handing out parking tickets like party favors.

I broke into a dogtrot. Once they started pushing buttons, you were out a hundred fifty-four bucks, no matter what, so I gave it all I had.

I skidded to a stop beside my car, hopped into the seat, and started her up. When I looked to my right, she was standing there, electronic ticket book in hand, gazing disgustedly at me through the window. I buzzed the window down.

"You're four feet onto the red curb," she said.

I make it a point not to argue with cops unless I'm already under arrest, at which point all bets are off. So I opened the driver's door and stepped back into the street to check my parking job. Maybe I hadn't been paying attention.

But no. The car wasn't hanging over the no-parking zone. I turned my head to protest and found myself staring down the barrel of a revolver. Instinctively, I dove for the ground. In the process, I collided with the open driver's door, slamming it into the murderous meter maid, sending her staggering backward into one of the sidewalk tree wells, where she went down on her ass.

Without rising, she two-handed a round my way. The window became a thousand individual pieces and waterfalled down into the street.

I scrambled around the back of the car. Peeked around the corner. Lovely Rita was on her feet and coming my way. I hustled up the passenger side, slid around to the front just in time to see her coming around the rear. She snapped off another round. I kept shuffling to my left. Doing the best I could to keep the engine block between us.

One thing was for sure—if we played this game of ring-around-the-Chevy for long enough, she was eventually gonna get a clean shot at me. That's why I was so damn glad to hear alarmed voices bouncing off the buildings. Problem was, my assailant didn't seem to give a shit. She was still coming.

I slid left until I bumped into the back of the open door. I pirouetted around the door. She was up at the front, sliding between cars now. I reached into the car and pulled the shift lever down into first gear. The Chevy lurched forward, pinning her between cars. In a spasm of pain and agony, she put two more rounds through the windshield before the pain became too much to bear. I watched her eyes roll back in her head and then heard the pistol slip from her grasp and hit the pavement.

▪ ▪ ▪

"They must have followed me," I said. "I've had no established routine for a while now. I don't go to see Jeff all that often, so it's not like they could have had the place staked out waiting for me to show up every few months.."

"That means they've got a whole crew someplace around here," Tim said.

I'd told my story twice. The cops took notes both times. Half a dozen other witnesses attested to the fact that things had transpired pretty much the way I'd said they had. Plus they had the perp in custody, so the whole thing took less than an hour.

Tim was smirking. "Glad you're all right, man." He snickered. "Though, I'll tell you, Leo, I wouldn't have minded watching her chase you round and round the car."

"How's she doing?" I asked.

"She'll live," Tim said. "Mashed sternum. Bunch of broken ribs. Collapsed lung."

"She say anything?" I asked.

"Not a peep. Her prints say her name is Violetta Standish from Norman, Oklahoma. She got three arrests on her sheet. One for hate crime assault. Two for simple assault. She did nine months. At the time of her last arrest, she was homeless."

"My old man used to say you should never do business with anybody who has less to lose than you do."

"Something called the Spiritual Awakening Alliance is standing by to post bond after her preliminary hearing on Thursday. Regardless of the amount, I'm told." Tim treated me to his most baleful stare. "Well?"

"Well what?"

"What are you gonna do? You can't just sit up there in that big house and wait for them to try again."

"What else is there? Let 'em drive me out of my own home? Run away somewhere and pretend they can't find me?" I spread my hands in resignation.

"Caribbean vacation," Tim suggested again. "Give this thing a few months to settle down. God knows you can afford it. By that time, you'll have a nice tan, and these assholes will be back to purifying the white race, and they'll eventually forget you ever existed."

When I didn't say anything, Tim went on, "These kind of hummers aren't like they used to be, Leo. This is secret-agent racism now. That's how come all the guys they had scheduled for terrorist raids looked like regular folk and not skinheads. At work, they nod and smile at diversity training sessions and say all the right things. They get themselves promoted into positions of power where they can bring other racists on board and keep nonwhites from getting in. Wasn't long ago, you told me this crap, I'da thought you'd slipped a cog. Woulda sounded like a bad joke. Not anymore, man. Not anymore."

"I'll think about it," I said.

He jabbed me in the chest with his finger. "Vacation."

■ ■ ■

The bullet holes in the windshield whistled as I drove. Sounded like "Clair de lune." On my way home, I either reinvented the concept of clandestine or expanded the perimeters of paranoia—maybe both.

Took me an hour to cover the five miles back to my house. I used every dodge I'd ever heard of to make sure I wasn't being followed. Under the circumstances, I'd probably have felt better if I had spotted somebody on my tail. At least that way I could have done something stupid.

By the time I rolled into my garage and locked everything in sight, I'd made up my mind. I couldn't spend the rest of my days backing into alleys and driving to the bottom of parking garages and waiting to see who showed up behind me. Tim had a point about how the alt-right were hidden among us now. Brought to mind an old B movie starring the wrestler Rowdy Roddy Piper, where the United States had been secretly invaded by lizard aliens, but you could see their lizardry only while wearing a special pair of x-ray sunglasses. If I stayed around here, that was what my life was gonna look like. I was gonna spend my days trying to figure out who was a lizard and who wasn't. With getting it wrong pretty much guaranteed to be fatal.

I knew there'd be days when I'd hate myself for turning tail and running, but at least I'd still be around to have regrets. So I started making phone calls. Arranging this, arranging that. Hired a security company to keep an eye on the house while I was gone. Called my landscaper and told him where to send the bill. Everything else got paid automatically.

By the time the sun went down, I had my affairs in order and was ready to pack.

I rummaged through the upstairs closets until I found my old duffel bag, the one I'd dragged all over Europe thirty years ago.

I piled the rest of the three hundred Gs from the safe into a perfect cube, but there were two bundles too many, so I stuffed the extras in my pants pockets. The money cube I wrapped in butcher paper and duct-taped it all around. First thing in the bag. Then the clothes, then the shoes and underwear and socks. Finally my toothbrush, razor, and such. My little Smith & Wesson auto felt heavy and warm in my coat pocket.

I'd decided that figuring out where I wanted to hide out long term was gonna take serious thought, and since I think better when a gun isn't pointed at the back of my head, my plan was to hitchhike my ass out of here first thing in the morning, soon as the rush hour was over, then take a few days in some roach motel to plan my retreat in a sober and thoughtful manner. Like my life depended on it, which it did.

I had enough cash to not leave a paper trail, and easy access to whatever else I needed, so I felt pretty confident I could get short-term lost without requiring anybody's help this time.

By midnight I was ready to go. Whatever could be done had been done. I only had one loose end and couldn't make up my mind whether or not to pull it. I sat on the edge of the bed staring down at my cell phone. Reached for it a couple of times but pulled my hand back.

At one point, I put the phone on the nightstand, turned off the light, and got under the covers. Lasted about two minutes. Light on, quick speed dial.

She picked up on the fourth ring. "Hey," I said.

"Hey," Rebecca responded. "Kinda late, don't you think?"

"I'm taking a little trip in the morning," I said. "Won't be around for a while."

"I saw the footage of the meter maid on TV."

"I seem to have gotten in a bit over my head this time."

"What else is new?"

"I've exceeded even my own high fuck-up standards."

"And that's saying something."

Long pause.

"Sorry things ended like they did," I said.

"It was inevitable. You and I aren't on the same life path."

"We used to be."

"No we didn't," she said. "We only pretended to be."

I couldn't think of anything to say, so we lapsed into silence again.

Finally, Rebecca broke the ice. "You saved my life, Leo," she said. "You saved my career . . . you've been my best friend since the fifth grade . . . Don't think I don't appreciate that . . . I do. But . . ." For a moment she seemed at a loss for words, then she found some.

"I see enough pain and suffering every day at work; it makes me want to keep it out of my personal life. You, on the other hand, seem to revel in it."

"It's a gift," I joked.

More silence. Thicker and heavier this time.

"Be careful, Leo. Be well."

"You need any help . . . I'm sure Tim would be happy—"

She cut me off. "Stop matchmaking," she said.

"He's a good man."

"I have absolutely zero physical attraction to Tim Eagen. Never have. Never will. Besides which, he's a cop, and if there's a warehouse for toxic masculinity, police departments are it. Pushing other people around is why the vast majority of them join the force in the first place." She made a rude noise with her lips.

"Tim's not like that," I said.

"Doesn't matter. My mother was right. Remember. She married one . . . No cops."

Dead air.

Finally, I cleared my throat and said, "Okay . . . I guess this is it for a while . . ."

"Goodbye, Leo, and good luck. See if you can't keep yourself from getting killed."

She broke the connection.

I flipped my phone onto the bed and watched as it bounced a few times. I'd been down this road before. More than once. We were approaching the intersection of self-doubt and human frailty, a four-way stop somewhere out in the desert, where the oncoming lanes were always filled with skeletons you recognized.

I read a book once where the author said that psychopaths very often believe that everybody else on the planet believes the way they do but are just scared to say it out loud. A rather queer notion that has been rattling around in my head ever since.

Because . . . you see . . . I just don't have a "we" inside myself. I think in "I," not "we." Don't get me wrong; I'm just like everybody else. I want to love and be loved, but I'm not willing to mortgage the rancho to get it. Probably explains why I never got married. I'm just not a "we" person. Never seemed to me that what I stood to lose was worth the risk.

Like everybody else in high school, I read all the dewy-eyed Romantic poets wasting away over a lost love or for the even dewier Annabel Lee at the bottom of the sea, and you know . . . it never seemed real to me. It always seemed overblown. Like a bunch of stuff people made up so's they'd seem more sensitive. Seemed so over-the-top that I could only take it as a metaphor for something else, except I didn't know what.

That's where the psychopaths come back into it. Somewhere along the way it crossed my mind that maybe *I* was just weird that way. When you looked around the planet, it sure seemed like coupling up was the natural order of things, and I began to wonder if maybe I wasn't one of those empty shells who thought everybody secretly thought like they did. Could be, I supposed, but that's just how I am.

The lights went out. I held my breath and waited for the generator to kick on. Nothing happened. I walked into the kitchen and looked out at the backyard. Everything in the neighborhood was out.

I pulled out the Smith & Wesson as I walked to the front of the house. Hairs on the back of my neck were beginning to vibrate. Much as I'd have liked to pretend this was just a normal power outage, something in me knew better.

I jogged back to the bedroom and called 911 . . . *men with guns* . . . then pulled my granddad's 12-gauge goose gun out of the closet and headed back to the front, figuring if I could stay alive for the next five minutes or so, the cops would be showing up.

I found myself a tight little corner up at the front of the house, stone on three sides. And then peeped out the nearest window. I could see my new neighbor's house across the street. No lights there either. I duckwalked across the room and peeked out in the other direction. The Morrisons' lights were out too.

Outside, nothing was moving. I called 911 again. *"Yes sir, officers responding."* As I huddled against the wall, it occurred to me for the first time that the power outage might be just that and that I was so paranoid I'd turned it into a murder attempt.

Where are those damn cops? my brain was screaming.

That's when I heard the first shots. *Rat ta ta ta tat*, from somewhere over in the direction of the Morrisons' house.

Ten seconds later, the truck hit the front gate. Some kind of big black Ram coming as fast as you could be going and still make a ninety-degree turn. The gate bent, but the pillars held. The truck engine screamed like a panther as it tried to shoulder its way through the steel bars. The driver kept it pegged. The engine started to smoke. The truck began to bounce on its tires in the moment before the engine blew up with a bright-yellow flash, bending the hood into a crouch. Flames spewed from under the hood like a fire-breathing dragon. I caught a flash of movement out in the orchard.

I heard shots again. This time from the other direction. The truck doors bounced open. I saw the bottom half of two men getting out and sprinting for the street as more shots rang out.

Then it hit me: *They're not letting anybody get up to the top of the hill.* The cavalry wouldn't be arriving anytime soon. I was on my own. Worst of all, I'd underestimated these haters yet again, as if some suicidal part of me could simply not deal with the fact that these hate-fueled maniacs were sufficiently skilled to pull off something of this magnitude. This wasn't a murder attempt—this was a military operation.

I got to my feet, sprinted for the front door, and twisted the handle, pulling the huge wooden door inward and hitting the deck. When my eyes stopped bouncing, I got to see the very moment when he touched the thing off. This loud whoosh. Then the sparks coming out the back of the tube. I watched in slack-jawed horror as some kind of handheld missile screamed across the yard directly at my forehead, screeching and dripping sparks as it closed the distance.

I tried to press myself through the floor. It was all I had time to do. The missile flew down the hallway at a slight angle, hit the front left corner of the kitchen door, and tore the back half of the house off. I blinked my eyes in disbelief. I was looking at the garage. Everything between the garage and me was gone or on fire or both.

I began to crawl along the floor. The bedroom ceiling had partially collapsed. I crawled in, pulled my duffel bag from the bed, and then backed out. Inching backward was harder than it looked. I had to stop at one point and beat out a fire on one of my pant legs. I pushed the bag over the stone floor with one hand and Granddad's shotgun with the other. Two-thirds of the way up the hall, I looked up just in time to see a guy in an orange jumpsuit with an assault weapon hanging around his neck.

I pushed myself into the sitting position, lined up the bead on the middle of him, and pulled both triggers. Blew him all the way into the parlor. Blew the assault rifle in half and me over on my back.

I struggled to my feet and looked into my mother's favorite room. The place where I'd met with Art Fowler what seemed like years ago. The drapes were eight-foot candles. Her favorite brocaded couches looked like flaming funeral biers. Orange Jumpsuit had a hole in the middle of his chest the size of a soccer ball. I threw the shotgun at him and crawled toward the back of the house.

The smoke had nearly reached floor level. Looked like the whole joint, top to bottom, was fully engaged in flames.

Why they felt they needed to fire another rocket was beyond my comprehension. The second one hit somewhere up on the front of the house and took the rest of the place with it. The force of the explosion blew me out into the backyard. I landed on my ass in the grass and began to move backward in that position.

The section of roof over the dining room went down in a whoosh. Bright-yellow flames rose sixty feet into the sky, leaving a trail of floating embers to mark their way. Black on black, the rising smoke was even darker than the sky. I crawled to my feet. Stood wobbling in the yard. The heat on my face forced me to turn away.

Above the crackle and roar of the burning house, I could hear the wail of sirens and uneven splatters of gunfire. I ran past the garage and slid my back along its south wall, until I came to the five-foot chain-link fence that stood on top of the retaining wall.

Behind the fence and the wall was nothing. A forty-foot drop to the rear of our property. My old man had built it that way. Nobody was sneaking up behind him. Right from the beginning, they'd let the bluff grow over with blackberry bushes. I used to crawl down and pick the berries as a kid.

Tonight, however, I climbed to the top of the fence and stood on top of the chain links for a moment, wobbling back and forth, holding on to the garage roof with my free hand. I looked back over my shoulder at the world's biggest bonfire, then put my roof hand on the gun in my pocket, clutched my duffel bag hard to my chest, and jumped.

■ ■ ■

They watched as the big yellow front loader went bobbing out through the front gate. The house had collapsed in upon itself. The SFD had front-loaded and backhoed all the debris from the stone foundation, gone through it piece by piece, and then put it all back where it had come from.

The SFD lieutenant crossed the driveway. "It'll have hot spots for a week or so," he said. He waved a hand at the pile of smoking rubble that had once been a house. "Not that there's much of anything left to burn, but the neighbors have volunteered to keep an eye on it for us. Anything flares up, they'll give us a call."

Tim Eagen nodded. It had taken the SPD cops forty-five minutes to fight their way past the skinhead roadblocks. By the time it was safe for the fire department to begin operations, there wasn't anything they could do except keep the neighbors at bay and watch the place reduce itself to a pile of glowing ash.

They stood and watched as the lieutenant hopped up into the passenger side of the fire truck and started off down the driveway.

Tim threw a glance over at Ibrahim, Rebecca's longtime assistant. Ibrahim zipped up the black body bag and began to wheel the gurney toward the medical examiner's van, which stood where the garage once did.

"That's the only body they found," Tim said.

Rebecca nodded. "You sound like you're disappointed," she said bitterly.

"Mighta been better if it was Leo."

She looked at him as if he'd lost his mind.

Eagen held up a hand. "Not like that," he said. "I meant it might be better . . ."

"Better what?"

"Might be better if Leo was listed among the dead."

Ibrahim folded the gurney into the back of the van, closed the doors, and double-timed it their way.

"You gonna be able to get a positive ID on that one?" Tim asked.

"Probably not," she said. "He's Crispy Crittered."

Eagen didn't say anything. He stood there staring at her.

Rebecca threw her eyes over at the van. "That's not Leo," she said. "Believe me, I know Leo. Leo could carry that guy around like a purse."

Eagen bobbed his thick eyebrows up and down. "It's Leo if you say it is. As I understand it, you're pretty much the final authority on the dead in these parts."

Ibrahim suddenly piped up. "Missy . . . ," he said. "We gotta do it for him. He save my family. He save your life. You gotta do it for him. Nobody gonna know but us."

Tim nodded. “Generally I don’t believe people keep secrets worth a shit . . . but I don’t see anybody here spilling the beans. Do you?”

Stony silence.

When the quiet got too much for him, Eagen threw his final two cents into the pot. “These guys ain’t gonna stop, you know, Becky. As long as they think Leo’s alive, they’re gonna keep trying to kill him.”

Nobody said anything for quite a while, until Rebecca looked over at Ibrahim.

“Put him in the old cooler,” she said.

She meant the old part of the autopsy facility that they used these days only when they started to overflow in the shiny new one. “You remember how to turn it on? Number twenty-five,” she said. “The big drawer, way down at the end. No paperwork.”

They watched Ibrahim hot-foot it over to the van, get in, and drive off.

“And if Leo shows up later?” Eagen asked.

“We’ll burn that bridge when we come to it,” Rebecca said.

▪ ▪ ▪

The big eighteen-wheeler hissed and spat like a locomotive as it eased over onto the shoulder. Gravel cracked and popped under the tires as it steamed to a complete stop.

The hitchhiker slid along the rumbling, quivering side of the truck. The passenger door popped open. The driver leaned over the passenger seat and peered down at the hitchhiker. He had a big gap-toothed grin plastered onto his unshaven face.

“Boy . . . you doan mind me saying . . . you look like hell.” He chuckled. “Look like you tried to stuff a house cat in a plastic bag.”

The hitchhiker didn’t speak. The driver pointed at the man’s bloody hands. “Look like you been in a fight too.” He pointed again. “What’s that there . . . sticking in your knuckle there?”

The hitchhiker looked down. "Looks like a tooth," he said.

"Yeah it does. Who's it belong to?"

"Last guy picked me up."

The driver laughed. "Ain't much of an advertisement for givin' you a lift, now is it?"

"Guess not."

The driver watched as the man took hold of the tooth and yanked it free of his hand. He dropped it on the roadside and looked up.

"He said he was going to L.A.," the hitchhiker said.

"Said?"

"Turned out what he wanted was a blow job."

"I'm guessing he didn't get one," the driver cackled.

"Another case of truck-stop love gone bad," the hitchhiker said.

"Lotta perverts out here on the road. Folks get lonely."

"Gonna get even lonelier till he finds himself some new teeth."

"Well then, pilgrim, climb on in. I got a schedule to keep."

The hitchhiker reached up, grabbed the chrome handle, and boosted himself onto the step. "Where ya headed?" he asked as he settled into the seat.

"Bakersfield," the driver said.

"Garden spot of the Western world," the hitchhiker said.

"Ain't it ever." The driver grinned.

ABOUT THE AUTHOR

G.M. Ford is the author of ten other novels in the Leo Waterman series: *Who in Hell Is Wanda Fuca?*, *Cast in Stone*, *The Bum's Rush*, *Slow Burn*, *Last Ditch*, *The Deader the Better*, *Thicker Than Water*, *Chump Change*, *Salvation Lake*, and *Family Values*. He has also penned the Frank Corso mystery series and the stand-alone thrillers *Threshold* and *Nameless Night*. Ford has been nominated for the Shamus, Anthony, and Lefty Awards, among others. He lives and writes in Ocean Beach, California.